"What Are You Talking About?"

she asked. "How could you expect to know me very well after only three days? Be sensible, Adam."

His face darkened. "Don't patronize me."

"I wasn't!"

"You let me make a fool of myself," he grated. "You let me charge ahead and propose to you like an idiot. I suppose it amused you. Well, I don't enjoy feeling like a fool."

The angry, silent duel their eyes fought ended abruptly as his lips met hers.

LAURA HARDY

is a top-selling romance author who now brings her talents to Silhouette's Special Editions. She has been happily married for many years and lives with her husband and five children on Britain's lovely Isle of Man.

Dear Reader:

During the last year, many of you have written to Silhouette telling us what you like best about Silhouette Romances and, more recently, about Silhouette Special Editions. You've also told us what else you'd like to read from Silhouette. With your comments and suggestions in mind, we've developed SILHOUETTE DESIRE.

SILHOUETTE DESIREs will be on sale this June, and each month we'll bring you four new DESIREs written by some of your favorite authors—Stephanie James, Diana Palmer, Rita Clay, Suzanne Simms and many more.

SILHOUETTE DESIREs may not be for everyone, but they are for those readers who want a more sensual, provocative romance. The heroines are slightly older—women who are actively involved in their careers and the world around them. If you want to experience all the excitement, passion and joy of falling in love, then SILHOUETTE DESIRE is for you.

I'd appreciate any thoughts you'd like to share with us on new SILHOUETTE DESIRE, and I invite you to write to us at the address below:

Karen Solem
Editor-in-Chief
Silhouette Books
P.O. Box 769
New York, N.Y. 10019

LAURA HARDY
Tears and Red Roses

Silhouette Special Edition
Published by Silhouette Books New York
America's Publisher of Contemporary Romance

Other Silhouette Books by Laura Hardy

Burning Memories
Playing with Fire
Dream Master

SILHOUETTE BOOKS, a Simon & Schuster Division of
GULF & WESTERN CORPORATION
1230 Avenue of the Americas, New York, N.Y. 10020

ISBN: 0-671-53525-0

First Silhouette Books printing June, 1982

10 9 8 7 6 5 4 3 2 1

Map by Tony Ferrara

Tears and
Red Roses

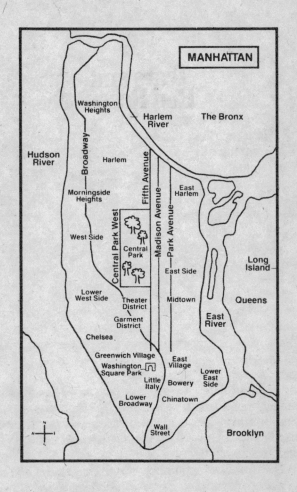

Chapter One

The telephone rang, shattering her concentration, and Carly gave a little sigh as she stretched out a hand to pick it up. "Yes? Carly Newton speaking."

"What time did you say you were seeing Shaw?" Curt asked without bothering to identify himself; not that he needed to, since there could not be two men in the world who talked at the speed of light while somehow making sure that every syllable rang as clear as a bell.

Making a face at the opposite wall, Carly said, "He'll be here at eleven."

"Having lunch with him?"

"Yes," Carly agreed and distinctly heard Curt tapping his fingers on the side of his own telephone, a little mannerism which always indicated irritation in him. He had a habit of drumming his fingers on desks or chairs, as though it helped him to relax his tension in some physical way.

"I would have liked to see him myself but I have appointments all day until four." There was a little pause during which Carly waited patiently for whatever decision was coming, then Curt said abruptly, "Oh, well, forget it."

The phone dropped with a resounding clatter and she grimaced, replacing her own receiver more slowly. Curt normally brought telephone conversations to an abrupt end, but then, he did most things suddenly, surprising everyone around him. Curt Dorsden was an unpredictable man, his mind rapid and hard, who thought twice as fast, just as he talked twice as fast, as any other man Carly had ever met. The deep, gravelly tones of his voice might have led anyone to expect a giant of a man, towering above those around him, and in that he surprised, too, because Curt was only just over five foot four and rather slightly built. Carly had decided that Curt's height was the root of his drive towards success. He was compensating for his lack of inches every time he took on a boardroom battle and won. Some of the staff called him Little Napoleon, but never in his hearing—Curt had almost no sense of humor where his own dignity was concerned. He wouldn't have minded being called Napoleon, but the qualifying "little" could not be applied safely to Curt Dorsden in his presence.

Carly looked back at the half-read manuscript lying on her desk, but the brief talk with Curt had snapped the thread of her interest in it. She was feeling tired, although it was only half past ten in the morning. She had only had four hours sleep the previous night, having been in Boston for a sales conference for the past three days. She had had to catch a dawn flight back to New York in order to keep her appointment with Roddy Shaw, and her mind felt a little like scrambled Morse Code, the messages entering her brain having become somehow dislocated en route. It was no condition to be in when you were having a lengthy tussle with a tough literary agent over a book you wanted very much but did not want to pay the sky to acquire. It would have been useful to have Curt there in one way—he would not have let Roddy Shaw get away with a thing. On the other hand, she decided, if Curt had appeared on the scene it would undoubtedly have given Roddy the idea that his client's book was worth even more than he hoped.

Pushing back her chair she wandered idly over to the window. Sometimes she felt that she spent most of her life in offices, and it helped to check that the sky was still up there, making a blue umbrella over the New York skyline.

She gazed up, sighing, a half-smile on her mouth, as she watched the motion of the cloudless summer sky. A holiday, she thought—that is what I need—realizing that she had not had any time off for months.

Glancing down into the canyoned street some fifteen stories below, she watched the hurrying crowds moving in patterned paths like ants in a narrow maze. Suddenly a pair of figures halted on the sidewalk, turning to face each other. Carly could not see their faces, but even from this height she could sense the confiding tenderness between them as their bodies briefly entwined. They were both wearing blue jeans, the girl instantly recognizable by her long burnished plait of hair and the curve her body described as it clung to the boy kissing her. They parted and walked on, hands swinging linked between them, and Carly turned away, aware of a strange ache inside her, a loneliness that had not begun when she watched the young lovers, but that had been growing inside her for months.

The telephone rang again and she turned back to answer it almost with relief. She did not want to think too deeply about how she felt.

"Mr. Shaw is at reception," she was told, and she asked for him to be brought along to her office. When the door opened to reveal him he was not alone, however, and Carly looked in some surprise at the tall, dark-haired girl with him.

"Oh, hi, Louise, did you want me?"

Louise was smiling, her hazel eyes very bright, but the smile was directed more at Roddy Shaw than at Carly and her glance across the office was merely automatic.

"No, I was just passing the time of day with Roddy." She turned to smile at him and, surprised, Carly caught the half-veiled intimacy between them. She had had no idea that her friend knew Roddy Shaw other than as a polite business acquaintance, but there was no mistaking the way they were looking at each other. "See you," Louise said in a soft voice, and Roddy gave her a nod as she turned away, her slim body swaying as she walked back down the corridor. Louise had a perfectly proportioned figure, legs long and beautifully shaped, waist and hips slim, breasts round and high. If she had not been one of the most skilled copy editors in New York she could easily have been a top-ranking model, and, as Carly often teased her, could have earned a great deal more money, but Louise had a quick, intelligent mind, and she preferred to work in publishing.

Roddy Shaw closed the door and came across the office toward Carly, a little smile hovering around his mouth. In his own way, he was a male counterpart of Louise, a very tall, extremely good-looking man, slim and lithe, with ash-blond hair and almost too beautiful features that looked as if they had been sculpted, the chiseled perfection of nose, cheekbone and jaw flawless. Every time Carly saw him she marveled at his looks and at the fact that she neither liked nor trusted him. There was something hidden beneath that elegant surface, a self-willed petulance that showed now and then in the way his mouth turned down at the corners when he was crossed, or in the way his blue eyes could look sulky.

"Hallo, how are you?" he asked, throwing a smile toward her with the cool self-confidence of a man who usually has his way with women.

"Fine, how are you?" Carly smiled back, offering her hand. He took it, held it for just a fraction of a second too long, gazing into her eyes as though trying to hypnotize her. Carly gazed back calmly, still smiling. Roddy Shaw wasn't hypnotizing *her*—and if he had come along today thinking he was going to wring out of her every concession he was demanding, he could think again.

"You look very lovely today, but then you always do. You just don't look old enough to be a high-powered publishing executive. Is it a secret, or are you going to admit you're only twenty-two?"

"No comment," Carly said, gesturing to the chair opposite her. "Please sit down, Roddy; can I offer you some coffee?"

"I'd love some."

She buzzed her secretary and said, "Could we have some coffee, Sue-Ann?" Looking across the desk at Roddy Shaw she asked, "Cream and sugar?"

His thin brows defined a perfect curve. "Neither, thank you."

"Black, please, Sue-Ann," Carly said.

"Black for both?" her secretary inquired.

"Yes, please." Carly leaned back in her chair and considered Roddy Shaw carefully, like someone preparing for battle. The negotiations had been dragging out for what seemed like years, but the book he was handling had made a strong impression on her, and she had a hunch that it might become a best seller. She wanted that book badly but she was tired of talking to Roddy Shaw, going round in circles until she was mentally dizzy. He was a difficult, tricky man to deal with, for all the charming smiles he was bestowing around this office today.

"Are we going to settle this thing today, Roddy?" she asked, taking the direct path in the hope of cutting a few corners.

"I hope so," he assured her.

"So do I." Her sigh was heartfelt.

"There is just clause five to be considered," Roddy murmured, and Carly looked up sharply.

"We discussed that endlessly last time."

"There was a point I wanted to bring up." Roddy flicked over a little pile of papers and pushed one across the desk toward her. The door opened behind him and Sue-Ann came into the room, carefully balancing a tray bearing two cups. As she handed Roddy his coffee, Carly was annoyed at the wide-eyed look Sue-Ann gave him with it. She sipped her own coffee, conscious of her head banging with pain. She wished fervently that she could go home and sleep for twenty-four hours.

An hour later, they had covered more ground than she had dared to hope for in the beginning, and with a breathless sense of excitement she realized that she was at last within an inch of finalizing the deal. There was a brief silence, and then she looked at Roddy with a pleading little smile. "Are we agreed, then?"

He surveyed her without answering, and she suddenly guessed that he enjoyed the battle more than the victory; he was in no hurry to close their negotiations. Some people were like that—they were prepared to ruin their chances of a deal by delaying too long and haggling too much.

Roddy grimaced, then nodded. "I suppose we are," he admitted flatly.

Carly felt herself sag slightly, the tight tension of the past hour snapping inside her now that it was all over. She smiled. "I'm very happy to have the book on our list; it fascinated me the first time I read it and I think it's going to make quite an impression." She paused, leaning back with both hands on her desk, her blue eyes thoughtful. "What's he like? The author."

"You've read the book," Roddy said dryly.

"A book doesn't always tell you much about an author."

"This one does—it's autobiographical."

Carly was amazed. "Really? I had no idea. You mean, he did all those things? The bullfighting and working in a casino and reporting that war?"

"Yes." Roddy had praised the book to the skies, but he had been uninformative about the author until now, and Carly got the impression he still felt reluctant to talk too much about Adam Blake.

"He must be quite a guy," she said.

"Yes, I suppose so." Roddy paused, shrugging his elegantly clad shoulders. He was English and always looked as if he bought his clothes in Savile Row, which perhaps he did—Carly would not have been surprised to find out her guess was quite correct. When she had first heard of Roddy Shaw she had naively imagined that the fact that she herself was English might make it easier for her to talk to him, but she had reckoned without Roddy's egotism. He liked himself too much to care what anybody else thought, and the fact that they were both English made no shred of difference in his determination to get his own way.

"Is Adam Blake his real name or is it a pseudonym?" she asked, and Roddy nodded.

"His real name."

She started scribbling on a pad, asking as she did so, "Will he be available for publicity?"

"I doubt it, but I'll ask."

"What's he doing now? Is he writing full time?"

"Farming," Roddy said, and she looked up again, startled.

"Farming?" Having been told that the action-packed book she had just bought was autobiographical she could not imagine the author of it settling down to the quiet life of a farmer. If the book was true, he had led a hell-raising, globe-trotting life ever since he was in his teens.

"Where does he live?"

"England, at the moment." Roddy glanced at his watch. "Good heavens, it is almost half past twelve."

Carly put down her pen. "Shall we go to lunch now? I booked a table for one o'clock."

"Fine." Roddy stood up, pushing his sheaf of papers into his large tan leather briefcase and zipping it up.

Excusing herself, Carly went to the washroom and found Louise attending to her makeup in front of one of the mirrors, her face absorbed as she outlined her lips in warm red lip gloss. Her eyes flickered to meet Carly's in the mirror.

"Hi, how did it go with Roddy?"

"I've bought the book; it's all sewn up." Carly was

feeling more excited as each minute passed. She smiled, her blue eyes very bright. "I love that book, Louise; I really love it. I was sick of talking terms and hanging on hoping Roddy Shaw wasn't selling the book to someone else behind my back." That thought had occurred to her more than once during the long drawn-out negotiations.

"He wouldn't do that," Louise said, her face softening, and Carly heard the possessive note in her voice with faint anxiety. She liked Louise and she did not want to see her running into trouble with a man like Roddy Shaw, but she knew that there was no point in saying anything to her. No woman wants to hear home truths about her man, even from a close friend. Louise was going to have to work out what Roddy Shaw was like without any help, however much Carly would have loved to give her a few hints.

Carly began brushing her sleek blonde hair into the usual shining bell surrounding her face, the ends curving in to her throat. Her mind moved from the subject of Roddy Shaw to that of his author. What sort of man was he? She hoped that Roddy could persuade Adam Blake to come to New York to do the launch, because if he was even a pale shadow of the hero of his book, he must be fascinating.

"What are you smiling at?" Louise asked, staring at her.

Carly laughed. "Adam Blake."

"Who?"

"Roddy Shaw's author—I think I'm talking myself into falling in love with him, and he will probably turn out to be some old guy in his dotage with a bald head and a paunch."

Louise grinned. "You're not that desperate, are you?"

"Not quite." Carly paused, remembering the young lovers kissing on the sidewalk earlier that morning and her own sinking sensation of envy and loneliness. She stared at her reflection without really seeing it, her face changing. "Are you ever lonely, Louise?"

Staring, the other girl said, "Sure, who isn't?"

"Sometimes . . ." Carly began the sentence without thinking and stopped short at the first word, her mouth twisting. No, she could not confide in Louise, even if she was absolutely sure what it was she wanted to confide. The strange feeling she had was like some tender bruise on her skin, a faint indefinable shadow that betrayed pain when it was touched. The trouble was, she did not have the courage to face up to what was disturbing her because she had the strong suspicion it had deeper roots than she cared to believe.

"Sometimes what?" Louise probed.

"Nothing." Carly scrutinized herself in the mirror and decided she looked fine, certainly presentable enough for Roddy Shaw. Lunch with him was going to be no pleasure trip. She tucked her cream silk blouse more firmly into the waistband of her skirt, flicked a stray blonde hair off the collar of her jacket and turned toward the door.

"Lunching with Roddy?" Louise asked, and she nodded.

"See you." As she opened the door to leave she caught the look Louise threw after her and read the envy in it. Louise would have been more than welcome to take her place at the lunch date, but Carly didn't bother to assure her of that.

Over lunch, Roddy asked her casually how she had got into a New York publishing house and she explained that she had met Curt Dorsden when he was visiting London eighteen months ago. Carly had gone into publishing straight from college. She had started on the very bottom rung, but with some good luck and a lot of hard work she had soon begun to find her way up the ladder.

"And Dorsden took a fancy to you, did he?" Roddy asked with a cynical little smile.

Carly bristled. If he knew Curt he would never suggest such a thing. Where Curt Dorsden was concerned business was business, and she had never heard of him turning his attention to any woman but his own very beautiful wife.

"Not the way you mean," she said carefully.

"No?" Roddy ran his insolent stare over her from her blonde head down over her slender shoulders.

"Curt's married," Carly said and got another cynical smile.

"So?"

"So his wife is one of the loveliest women in New York," Carly said tightly. "And they are very happy together."

"Quite the little romantic, aren't we?" sneered Roddy, and she felt color creep up under her skin.

"That's right, I'm very romantic," Carly informed him. "And old-fashioned with it—I believe in marriage bells and happy ever after." She fixed him with a cold stare. "Any objections?"

Roddy shrugged. "If you want to live in some kind of wonderland, be my guest."

"You don't believe in marriage?" She looked at him

17

expressionlessly, remembering the brightness of Louise's eyes when she'd smiled at him. Her instincts were obviously right—Roddy was not going to give Louise much besides heartache.

"I believe it exists, as an institution."

"But not for you?"

He gave her one of his smiles. "Is this leading up to some kind of proposal?"

Carly drew back, her face freezing. "No, sir," she said, not adding the rest of that which sprang into her head. She wouldn't have Roddy Shaw at any price. Only someone either very young and innocent or someone willing to shut her eyes to his faults, like Louise, would be interested in him. It was no surprise to Carly to meet a man with his attitude; she had learned to recognize the types of men she met in her world long ago. Some were married men with a streak of restless interest in having an extramarital fling; some were men who had not married but were so used to living alone that they couldn't bring themselves to adapt to any other way of life; and some were men who showed a definite interest in her until they discovered that she earned more than they did and had a high-powered job with a lot of status attached to it. Men of this type tended to vanish as soon as they discovered her credentials—their egos just refused to accept the sort of competition they thought she was likely to give them. Carly found it infuriating that these were usually the men she was attracted to; it seemed so unfair of fate to arrange for her to fall for men who weren't prepared to accept her as she was.

She was quite relieved to say goodbye to Roddy Shaw and get back to the office. But as she was walking down the corridor she ran into Curt, who snapped his fingers at her. "Come into my office in ten minutes; I want to talk to you."

"Yes, Curt," she said, because that was what everybody said to Curt. There had probably never been a day when anyone said, "No, Curt." Even his wife joined in the chorus, at least in public, but she seemed to thrive on marriage to one of the most dynamic men in New York. Curt and Sylvia had three children and a lovely home just outside the city. Sylvia wore fabulous clothes and looked like a film star, but her smile was genuine and impulsive, and she looked at her electrifying husband with an adoring mixture of amusement and pride. Carly always got the feeling Curt surprised Sylvia as much as he did everyone else—whenever she saw them together she had the feeling Sylvia could hardly believe her luck in being his wife, and Carly envied her that shining happiness.

She did not envy her Curt, however—he was too razor-sharp for Carly and she had the definite impression he was never going to slow down. He moved like lightning and always would, which she assumed must be very tiring to live with. Carly envied Sylvia simply and solely because if ever she had seen a contented woman, Sylvia was the one, and she seemed to have discovered the secret of a happy life. Carly marveled that anyone could be radiant because she was married to Curt Dorsden, but she could see that Sylvia was living on a golden cloud.

Going into her office, Carly had a brief conversation on the telephone, signed some letters she had dictated earlier that morning, glanced at her watch, and hurriedly fled to join Curt, who demanded punctuality and accepted no excuses.

He questioned her brusquely about the deal she had

made with Roddy, made a face over the money involved, but seemed quite pleased that they had acquired the book.

"I would like to get Adam Blake over here for some publicity," she told him. "He sounds the type we could make very interesting."

"Get him, then."

"Roddy Shaw doesn't seem to think he will come."

"Roddy Shaw will have to persuade him, then, won't he?" Curt looked at his watch, a signal that her interview was over. "Sylvia asked me to invite you to dinner," he added as she rose from her chair.

"Oh," she said, looking startled. "Thank you, I'd love to come."

"Next week? Wednesday?"

She nodded. "Thank you." She did not bother to check her diary because she knew that any date she had made would have to be canceled in favor of Curt's invitation. He and Sylvia were not in the habit of entertaining their staff, but when a rare invitation did arrive, you went, if you had any sense.

Curt smiled suddenly, giving her a fleeting glimpse of whatever it was that made Sylvia think the sun shone out of him. "We'll both look forward to seeing you."

She left the office at seven o'clock that evening, and went home to the apartment she shared with Louise. She had expected to find her friend there, but there was no sign of her. Carly got herself a very light supper, watched TV for half an hour, went to bed and read a manuscript that sent her rapidly to sleep.

She woke up as daylight struggled into the bedroom, and she yawned, feeling reluctant to get up, very much the way she had felt for the first few weeks after she had arrived in New York. She had gone around then in a state of dazed confusion, like some shell-shocked victim of a battle, unable to take in the mind-blowing rush and fever of the city streets. New Yorkers moved so fast, thought so fast, talked so fast. Their voices baffled her at first, as they did so many English people who arrived expecting to find everyone they met totally comprehensible, only to discover with amazement that even in New York itself accents could vary from district to district and that the name "English" was a loose description that could cover any way of talking at all.

Carly had walked around the city, listening to the permanent roar of the traffic between the concrete walls of the canyons they called avenues, to sirens wailing as police cars sped past, to cops blowing whistles on traffic duty and horns blaring in protest as some yellow taxi cab tried to inch its way ahead of a snarl of other cars. She had never thought she would get used to life in New York, but one morning she had woken up and heard the sound of the city below the apartment windows and found herself smiling and thinking, "Hello, New York," as though the city was an old friend she was happy to meet again.

She had been here over a year now, and each day began with that familiar sound, a background music that she had come to love and that set the mood for the whole day. New York made Carly feel more alive than any place she had ever known, and although she often felt a nostalgic yearning for the quiet English countryside in which she had grown up, she had long ago realized that she felt at home here and would hate to leave.

She had been very lucky to get the chance to share this apartment. Louise had originally shared it with a girl from Kentucky who had gotten homesick and moved out just before Carly joined the firm. Even during her first week in New York Carly had discovered that an apartment was like gold dust, and she had jumped at Louise's offer. The apartment was five floors up from the street, had tiny boxlike rooms with paper-thin walls, plumbing that did not always work adequately and windows that rattled in the wind. On hot summer days it was like living in a sauna; on cold winter nights it was like a wind tunnel. But it was an apartment, and, as Carly had written to her worried mother back in England, it had atmosphere. She did not feel she should describe it too closely—she had the shrewd idea her mother might not be reassured to know that the "atmosphere" included an eccentric jazz musician who played his saxophone whenever he was feeling blue, whatever the time of night; an old lady who had hundreds of birds in an aviary on the rooftop, and a local deli that attracted some very noisy clients in the early hours of the morning, which often woke Carly and Louise up groaning as they turned over with pillows over their heads to shut out the sound of loud voices.

Carly loved the apartment, she loved the district, she loved the color and life of New York, and she loved her job. She was ambitious and intelligent, and she wanted to climb even higher in her career because publishing fascinated her; she adored books and respected writers. Looked at from the outside her world appeared marvelous, a glamorous one for any girl, filled with hectic working days, a busy social life centered on her job, and many friends.

Carly should have been totally happy but she had recently begun to realize that she was twenty-eight and that the ominous age of thirty was looming on the horizon for her. She had had a number of relationships with men over the past few years—none of them had been world-shattering and unforgettable. She had been on the point of falling seriously in love twice, but each time it had all ended suddenly. She was tired of brief affairs and a few inconclusive dates that led up a blind alley. She was tired of coming home alone after parties, but she was also tired of meaningless lovemaking with men she did not love enough to take seriously.

She was aching for something she did not have, but she wasn't even sure what she wanted, only that she had never found it yet. She knew certain things for sure, though! She wanted to feel someone there when she reached out in the dark night, to have someone to tell jokes to and argue with, to feel the world stop spinning on its axis when that someone kissed her, to cook meals and buy surprise presents for someone. She wanted a love affair as real as the sidewalks under her feet and as dazzling as the fireworks on the Fourth of July.

"I want the moon," she said aloud. "I *am* crazy." Sliding out of bed, she went into the hall and tapped on Louise's door and heard her groan.

"We're going to be late," Carly sang out as she fled into the bathroom, and Louise groaned again.

As they drank their coffee before they rushed to get the bus, Carly asked, "Where were you last night? You came in late, didn't you?"

"Don't start checking up on me, sweetie," Louise muttered, putting down her cup and getting up. "I get that stuff from my mother."

"Sorry," Carly said to her back as she walked away.

"Apology accepted." Louise gave her a wry grin. "I was late and I've got a rotten headache so walk on eggshells, will you?"

Had she been with Roddy Shaw? Carly wondered as they made their way to work in the rush hour traffic. Any possibility of comment had been ruled out when Louise snapped at her for daring to show an interest, but Carly couldn't help feeling worried and rather puzzled—it was always a surprise when a friend fell head over heels for a man she wouldn't look twice at.

They separated in the great office block that housed their firm. Carly tore into the pile of manuscripts she found waiting for her, constantly interrupted by the phone or by one of her junior editors asking for advice. The art director came into the office balancing a pile of new covers, his spectacles pushed up into his thick graying hair and a satisfied smile on his face. Carly paused to have a few moments' chat with him, then went back to her manuscripts after a glance at her watch. Sometimes she felt she was in a race against the clock and the clock was winning.

The door burst open and she looked up, startled, to hear Sue-Ann crossly saying, "You can't go in there! Please wait. . . ."

A man filled the doorway, his black head turning to face Carly as he detached himself from Sue-Ann's detaining hand. He did not do it violently or aggressively, removing himself from her in one smooth movement that brought him a step further into the room, which immediately seemed to shrink, as though his presence was too dominating even for inanimate objects. Carly had grown used to working with autocratic men in the year she had spent in New York. Male chauvinism was all around her, from Curt Dorsden downward through the various echelons of the firm. This man, however, easily six feet tall and very broad-shouldered, appraising her briefly yet sharply with cool gray eyes, seemed to breathe an air of male domination.

Swallowing in faint alarm, Carly asked, "Yes? Can I help you?" and was almost tempted to laugh at the nervous note in her own voice.

"He refused to give his name," protested Sue-Ann, hovering in the doorway and giving her an apologetic look.

"Okay, Sue-Ann, I'll deal with it," Carly said, more calmly than she felt, and her secretary withdrew slowly and reluctantly.

"I'm Carly Newton, the editor-in-chief." Carly smiled politely at the intruder, offering her hand with a strange feeling of alarm as though half-expecting him to bite.

"Then I'm in the right place," he said, nodding and ignoring her hand, which she allowed to fall back onto her desk after a moment.

"May I ask who you are?" She smiled, a faint teasing light in her eyes; she was hoping to charm him into relaxing the looming aggression of his attitude, but he merely stared hard at her, his gray eyes narrowing.

"You are the editor who has been negotiating with Roddy Shaw this week?" he demanded.

Carly said, "Yes, I am," in surprise. Was he one of Roddy's colleagues or a rival publisher from England? She had never seen him before but she did not get the feeling his visit was one of courtesy.

"Do you know he's married?"

Carly smiled faintly—she did not much care whether

Roddy was married or not—but as it happened she had once asked Roddy if he was, and Roddy had shaken his head decisively.

"No, he isn't married," Carly said, and the stranger leaned toward her with an angry frown pulling his black brows together.

"I tell you, he is—I should know, he's my brother-in-law."

"Oh," Carly said, her mouth rounding. Roddy had lied, had he? Well, that didn't surprise her, but she couldn't imagine why this man should be eyeing her so accusingly, a harsh light in his eyes.

"But I suppose the fact that he *is* a married man doesn't mean a thing to you?" he grated, and warm color rose in her face.

"Why should it?" She was too shaken by the way he was looking at her to be thinking very clearly, and she stammered as she answered him.

"Why?" He stopped after that one explosive word, pushing his hands into his pockets and rocking backward and forward on the balls of his feet, his expression furious. "His wife has two small children to look after—if she found out what that husband of hers had been up to over here she would be stricken. Roddy isn't much of a man, but my sister loves him, to her cost, and even if you have no conscience about having an affair with a married man . . ."

"What?" Carly was on her feet before he had halted the flow of fast, angry words and was moving around the desk, as tense as he was now, quivering with outrage. "You're crazy! What on earth makes you think I've been having an affair with Roddy Shaw? *Roddy Shaw?*" She was speechless for a moment, staring at him, her face very flushed and her blue eyes blindingly bright with rage. "I wouldn't touch him with a barge-pole."

Her voice carried conviction and her insulted expression carried even more. The dark-haired man stared down at her, still frowning, before he said slowly, "You haven't been dating him?"

"I have not!"

"Not last night?"

"Last night I went home and had an early night after a pretty hectic day," she answered without thinking, but, a second later, as she finished speaking, the memory of Louise came back to her. Oh, no, she thought, I knew Roddy Shaw meant trouble, and her eyes lowered to hide the troubled look in them from the penetrating gaze of the stranger. She did not want to betray Louise or bring the wrath of this man down on her friend's unguarded head. She was certain Louise had had no more idea than she had that Roddy was married.

There was a little silence and she looked up to find the dark man watching her. Carly had had enough time to pull herself together. She met his stare head-on, her own gaze direct and calm. Her blue eyes had the lucid clarity of the summer sky; a mild gentleness usually smiled in their depths, but today her face conveyed a firm insistence that she was telling the truth, her mood tightening her muscles, streamlining the fine modeling of her features, firming her curved pink mouth into a determined line.

There was another brief pause, then the gray eyes lit with a smile whose charm made Carly blink, the alteration in his powerful face taking her by surprise.

"I apologize," he said in a deep, warm voice. "I should have known Roddy wouldn't tell me the truth."

"He told you that he and I . . ." Carly was staggered.

"Roddy doesn't deal in straight statements—he hints; he's a past master at suggesting ideas to people. He talked about you and I must have leaped to the wrong conclusion." His hand came up, held out to her as a wry smile entered his face. "I'm Adam Blake."

Carly automatically put her hand into the firm grasp of his fingers, but she was reeling under a second shock, somehow even greater than the first. So this was Adam Blake? Good heavens, she thought dazedly, he'll sell the book merely by smiling like that. She imagined the impact he could have on television or in the newspapers and wanted to shout with delirious excitement. He was a walking dream and he was *her* author! Flashes of images from the book went through her mind—the passage describing his venture into bull-fighting, where he had risked his life once for the sheer danger and then become angry at the mindless slaughter of a brave animal and refused to kill the bull, running the gauntlet of a furious, contemptuous crowd. He was staring at her, as though amused by her wide-eyed silence.

"You wrote *Red is a Dangerous Color?*" she queried, half-expecting him to be joking.

He nodded. "And you've bought it," he said, smiling at her. His features were lean and tanned, faint laughter lines radiating from his eyes and mouth. "I hope it's going to be a success for you," he added, and she breathed, "Oh, so do I," with heartfelt enthusiasm. "But I'm sure it will be—it's a gift." She halted because she could not say what was in her mind—that Adam Blake himself was a gift to any publicity department. She had never seen any author so breathtakingly good-looking, and imagining him in a toreador's costume made her wonder if they might possibly persuade him to be photographed. . . . She broke off that thought, realizing as she met his amused eyes that it was highly unlikely that he would even listen to such an idea.

"I'm delighted to meet you," she hurriedly told him.

"Thank you, it's mutual," he said, letting his eyes flick quickly and admiringly over her before they came back to her face. Carly laughed, her eyes very bright. She was finding it hard to believe he was real. The denim suit he wore was by no means as expensive-looking as the sort of immaculate tailoring Roddy Shaw always chose, but Adam Blake wore it with panache, a casual self-confidence that seemed not conscious of itself, as though he felt no need to thrust his ego at those he met.

"Won't you sit down?" she asked, gesturing to a chair.

He looked at his watch. "I'm afraid I can't stay any longer, Miss Newton; I have an appointment at one o'clock for lunch and I have to get from here to Greenwich Village."

"What a pity," she said frankly. "I was hoping to persuade you to have lunch with me; I loved your book so much, I've been dying to meet you." Her job gave her the opportunity to be completely honest about that, anyway, she thought.

"Some other time, Miss Newton," he said, as if he meant it.

"Carly," she said. "We use first names around here."

He laughed. "That's good news."

Her color deepened. "I'll walk you to the elevator," she said, moving to the door. As she opened it the phone rang. Hesitating, she decided to ignore it, but

Sue-Ann caught her eye across the outer office and mouthed "Mr. Dorsden" at her. Sighing, Carly said, "I'm sorry, will you excuse me? I have to take that call."

"Never mind, I'll be in touch," Adam Blake said, his brow lifting teasingly, and Carly looked away, biting her inner lip. She was being too blatantly obvious, she warned herself. He was laughing at her, but as he turned away he lightly brushed one finger down her cheek, making her skin burn with reaction as he touched it, then he was gone, and, tingling with shock, Carly answered her phone.

Curt snapped, "What kept you?"

You would be amazed, she thought, but aloud she said, "I'm sorry, I was out of the office."

"I want you to get a move on with the Ramsden contract," Curt said, changing the subject with the remorseless attention to the matter at hand which made him such a formidable businessman.

"Yes," Carly said obediently.

"Get it to me by Friday."

"Yes, Curt."

He was gone even as she said it, and she smiled to herself as she put down the phone. She felt oddly lightheaded and in no mood to settle back into reading manuscripts. Perching on the side of her desk she swung her legs like a child, humming tunelessly to herself and lost in thought.

"Hallo," Roddy Shaw said from the door, and Carly's smile vanished from her face.

"Hallo," she said icily. "I was wanting a word with you—what do you mean by giving your brother-in-law the idea that I was having an affair with you?"

Roddy looked furtively over his shoulder and came

into the room, closing the door. "How do you know . . . ?"

"He came here to talk to me about it. I've never been so humiliated or angry in my life! How dare you. . . ."

"I didn't want to drag Louise's name into it," Roddy said quickly.

"That still doesn't explain why you felt free to drag mine in!"

"I didn't tell him we were having an affair," Roddy protested. "I said I'd been seeing a lot of you, that's all. He arrived yesterday evening and I was out until two in the morning—he wanted to know where and I was a little drunk, I suppose, and I said the first thing that came into my head."

Carly glared at him. "Well, you can tell him the truth next time you see him."

"The truth?" he repeated, as though the word was meaningless to him. "About Louise?" he added, and Carly gave a low, angry sigh.

"I don't see the need to mention any names—just tell Adam Blake you weren't with me."

He eyed her insolently. "You're beautiful when you're angry," he said in deliberate, needling mockery.

Carly made no effort to hide her dislike now. "Would you mind leaving? I'm very busy."

She caught the glitter of his eyes at her cold tone. Roddy Shaw did not like being dismissed with contempt. It pierced his thick skin. He turned to go, then swung round and grabbed her shoulders, his fingers digging into her. She wriggled furiously as she realized he was going to try to kiss her. One hand caught her hair, hurting as he dragged it back, tilting her face helplessly. The hot intrusion of his kiss made her go stiff with bitter affront.

She wrenched herself away at the exact second that the door opened. Both Roddy Shaw and Carly turned to face the new arrival and Carly's heart sank as she met Adam Blake's gray eyes. The smile was dying out of them as he stared at her, taking in the intimate way Roddy had been holding her, their close proximity, the faint smudging of Carly's pink lipstick. Ice formed in the gray eyes. Adam stepped forward into the room and slammed the door behind him with his foot.

"Now maybe I can have the truth," he said through tight lips.

Chapter Two

$\mathcal{R}$oddy Shaw backed up a step or two, a revealing action that told Carly as clearly as words that he was scared of his brother-in-law, something that did not surprise her. Adam Blake was also frightening to her—he would alarm anyone with that angry frown, those contemptuous, cold gray eyes.

Blustering, Roddy said, "What are you talking about? I don't know what you mean."

Adam's mouth twisted savagely. "I think you do. Well, come on, I've heard one very convincing fairy tale today—I might as well hear another." Carly flinched at the sideways flick of his dark lashes, feeling for a moment like a little girl under his hostile glance before she started to get annoyed. Who did he think he was, talking like that?

"Look, Mr. Blake," she began, and halted as he turned his gaze full on her. She swallowed what felt like a huge lump, her throat closing up in shock. Why was he so tall? His anger had made him appear to grow; he seemed to loom over her like some dark menacing shape, the power of his long, lean body vibrating with temper.

"Yes?" he demanded.

Carly couldn't get out a syllable. Say something, she urged herself mentally. Don't just stand there gazing at him like a convicted criminal, you idiot. She knew from the cold stare that her silence was condemning her further, but her nerves were jumping and her mind could not summon up the words of excuse, of explanation, that she wanted to give.

"Well?" he asked, one dark brow rising sarcastically. "Lost for words? I'm not surprised. After the incredible performance you put on for me a little while ago, I'm not at all shocked that you feel slightly uncomfortable now. You had me totally convinced, do you know that? I swallowed every lying sentence. You should be on the stage, Miss Newton. You act the outraged innocent to perfection."

That stung her into speech. "I wasn't acting!"

"No?" He smiled, but it was not a pleasant smile; there was dry satire in it, and Carly felt herself stiffen, her hands clenching at her sides.

"I told you the honest truth!"

"You don't know when you're beaten, do you?" he mocked. "Drop the pretenses now, Miss Newton. You're wasting your time going on with the act."

Her face was so hot she wanted to put her hands to it; she wanted to hide from the dismissive stare of those eyes, but Carly had more backbone than to do anything of the kind. She drew herself up to her full five foot five, her chin lifting in defiance, and opened her mouth to tell him precisely what she thought of someone who jumped to conclusions without giving her a chance to explain. Before she could get out a word, however, the door opened again and Louise came into the office, saying as she walked in, "Have you seen Roddy, Carly?"

Roddy moved once, jerking a step toward her. Louise, unaware of the atmosphere in the room, smiled in lighthearted surprise at him. "Oh, you're here; I've been waiting for you in my office. I thought we were having lunch? I'm ravenous; are you coming?"

Adam Blake looked from her to Roddy and back again. Louise gave him a polite smile, walking over to run her hand through Roddy's arm in an intimate little movement. "Coming?" she asked, and Roddy gave his brother-in-law a nervous look before hurrying out of the room with Louise keeping step with him. As the door closed behind them Carly and Adam Blake heard Louise say, "Darling, do you have to go back to London next week?"

Adam Blake's face was expressionless; she could not read his mind from the blank mask. There was a silence while Carly wondered just how much of the truth he had now guessed and how much she should say to him.

"Who was that?" he asked, making her jump at the harshness of his tone.

"Our chief copy editor, Louise."

He searched her face, frowning. "I'm only a poor baffled man, but I don't understand what's going on here—which of you is dating him, for heaven's sake?"

"Not me!" Carly said with force.

"Then what was going on when I walked in here? Don't tell me he hadn't just kissed you—I saw enough to be sure he had, and your faces would have made me suspicious even if I hadn't seen you almost in each other's arms. You were the picture of guilt, Miss Newton."

"Not guilt—horror," she said, faint humor in her face. "You don't understand."

"Enlighten me, then." He walked over to the desk and leaned against it, his arms folded, making her feel like a schoolgirl in the headmaster's study.

Carly hesitated, sighing, then said, "I told you the truth—I dislike your brother-in-law."

"Join the club," Adam Blake said tersely.

She laughed. "I did rather get the impression you weren't overly enthusiastic about him."

"I can't imagine what my sister sees in him," he confessed.

"Neither can I." Carly brushed a wandering strand of blonde hair back from her cheek, sighing. "I realize it must have looked damning when you walked in to find us together, but I certainly did not invite him to kiss me. In fact, I had just torn a strip off him for lying to you about me and he was so mad he grabbed me and tried to kiss me. If you had come in one minute later you would have seen me slap his face so hard he would have gone spinning across the room."

Adam Blake's face relaxed in sudden amusement, his laughter making Carly smile. "Remind me never to kiss you against your will," he mocked, and she found herself blushing.

"I'll do that," she said, looking away to hide the rapid beating of her heart at the idea he had just planted in her mind—but then, ideas like that had been coming to her ever since she set eyes on him, and maybe even before that. Reading his book she had been fascinated by his mind, by the force of the personality that colored his entire narrative. Writing was like a pane of clear glass; it revealed everything about the mind of the writer, opening a window into his head, and Carly had been dying to meet the writer of that book from the minute she had begun to read it.

"I hope this isn't going to become a habit," Adam

said, and she looked back at him in bewilderment, her blue eyes opening wide.

"You hope what isn't going to become a habit?"

"My having to apologize to you—that's twice in one morning. I don't generally leap to conclusions about people."

"It must have looked pretty clear-cut," she said, smiling. "I can understand why you thought what you did." Her smile went and she sighed. "I'm going to have to break it to Louise later—she has no idea he's married."

Adam frowned. "How involved is she? How long has it been going on?"

"I've no idea—she hasn't discussed it with me; Louise tends to keep her own counsel. She isn't the type of girl to make confidences, and she resents advice."

"Well, she's certainly going to need some now." His face had become grim. "I feel like breaking Roddy's neck. Ever since they were married I've had the feeling he was cheating on my sister, but Jenny's such a fool about him; she always has been, from the day she first met him. She would never listen to advice, either." He shrugged, his mouth twisting. "Roddy Shaw seems to have that effect on women; they put on blinkers every time he's around and only see what they want to see." He smiled at her. "But that's a female characteristic, isn't it?"

"I wouldn't say that," protested Carly.

"Of course you wouldn't—you're a woman yourself."

"Speaking objectively," she began, and Adam grinned at her.

"Now we're moving into the realm of moonshine

again—how can you be objective about your own sex? You're a woman, so you think like one, which rules out any hope of being objective."

"You wouldn't be being the tiniest bit chauvinistic, would you?" Carly asked sweetly. "I hate to suggest it, but you're beginning to sound antifeminist." She was used to jibes about her sex around here, especially since, although there were plenty of women on the editorial team, most of the financial muscle in the firm was wielded by men, and, as always in any business, it was those who operated the levers of power and money who had the advantage. But Carly was disappointed to get that sort of needling from Adam Blake. She had thought he was more intelligent than that.

He lifted his brows. "I wouldn't call myself antifeminist, but what I've seen of most women doesn't give me much of an opinion of their brains. No man would put up with the sort of treatment my sister accepts from Roddy Shaw. Jenny doesn't use whatever brains she's got when it comes to dealing with her man." He paused, smiling wryly. "But then, some of the so-called clever women I've met haven't had much heart. I'm not certain which is worse—a woman who stops thinking when she's in love or a woman who has a brain like a knife but no feelings at all."

Carly eyed him with amusement. "Couldn't we have somewhere between the two, don't you think? Does a woman have to choose between a brain and a heart? Can't we have both? Nature certainly seems to have intended it."

"Three cheers for nature," Adam said, looking into her eyes, then letting his gaze run slowly and assessingly down over her very feminine shape. "It did a good job on you, Miss Newton, or as a feminist do you object to compliments about your looks?"

Carly laughed. "As a *woman*," she stressed, "I love compliments, and thank you for that one, but don't label me, will you? When a man calls a woman a feminist he's always trying to insult her."

"Is he? Always? You do deal in sweeping generalizations, don't you?"

She grimaced. "Okay," she said calmly. "I take back the 'always,' but quite often that is the case, you know. But after all, what does the word feminist actually mean? It doesn't have to mean I'm roaming about with a club in my hand ready to batter every man I meet over the head, nor does it mean I want to behave like a man or insist on being treated like one. I'm a woman. . . ."

"You certainly are," he said, interrupting, and she laughed again.

"I am, yes, and I want to be treated like one."

"Any time," he murmured.

"But I want my sex to be respected," Carly swept on, ignoring that. "I want to be respected as a person, and I want equal opportunities in my career and in the world at large. That's what feminism means to me."

Adam smiled at her, his gray eyes teasing. "What does lunch mean to you?"

For a few seconds she stared at him, lips parted in bafflement, then she looked at her watch. "Oh! Good heavens, I am so sorry—you had a lunch appointment, didn't you? Why, it's a quarter to one and you've got to get to the Village. You'll never do it from here inside half an hour—the traffic is always appalling at this time of day, and even if you got a taxi, which would be a miracle, believe me, at lunchtime, it would take forever to get through the traffic." Biting her lower lip, she hesitated, staring at him. "Maybe you could ring and explain that you'll be late?"

"I'll ring and explain that I can't make it," Adam said in a calm voice, looking amused. "And then maybe you'll allow me to take you to lunch? To be frank, that's why I came back just now—I decided to make an excuse to my friends and duck out of my lunch date if I could persuade you to lunch with me instead."

Carly was taken aback. "Oh," was all she could manage, but her heartbeat had increased to the speed of light, thumping like a hectic metronome inside her rib cage and making her so breathless that she had no ability to say another word.

"You don't like that idea?" he asked, watching her closely, a slight frown between his brows.

"Yes," she said, and then wished she hadn't sounded so eager, her color deepening again.

He laughed. "Well, that's a relief—I thought you were looking dubious."

"No, I'd love to have lunch," Carly said, abandoning any attempt to sound coolly offhand.

"Good," he said, turning toward her telephone. "May I make that call, then?"

"Go ahead." Carly hesitated, wondering if he would rather make it in private. "I'll just dash to the washroom, if you'll excuse me."

He was lifting the receiver and nodded to her as she walked away. Carly took several minutes to make herself look immaculate, brushing her hair until it gleamed like gold silk and taking pains with her makeup, while her mind dwelled on Adam Blake. He was so easy to talk to, such fun to be with, and whenever those gray eyes mocked her gently she felt a strange fluttery sensation in her throat. It was absurd, but she was so excited as she left the washroom to meet him that she was trembling slightly. She was acting like a six-year-old going to a birthday party, she thought, laughing at her own idiocy.

He was waiting for her, standing at her office window, looking along the avenue at the massed skyscrapers climbing skyward. Carly looked at his tall, lean figure with a very feminine appreciation and knew she was going to feel fantastic walking out of the building with him. If she had seen one of her female colleagues with him she would have felt a tingle of envy. He glanced round, saw her and smiled, a quick intimate smile, as though they had known each other for years instead of for an hour.

"Ready?" he asked, and she nodded, smiling back. "How did your friends take it?"

"I explained and they understood," Adam said, his face untroubled. "They're having a party tomorrow night and I'm invited—I suppose you wouldn't be free to come too?"

"Tomorrow night?" Carly was only making a pretense of needing to think about it, giving a little frown before she said, "I haven't anything booked for tomorrow night, I'm sure. Thank you, I'd enjoy meeting your friends."

"They'll enjoy meeting you." He waved her through the door and followed, talking quietly at her shoulder as they made their way to the elevator. "Phil Williams is a reporter working over here for a London daily paper. He's been in New York for a couple of years and loves it. His two kids go to school here and his wife says she can't face the idea of going home." He laughed down at Carly. "Their standard of living would drop

like a stone if Phil went back to England, I'm afraid.
And Helen enjoys her present life style too much to
want to change it."

"They live in Greenwich Village?" Carly asked as
they left the elevator on the ground floor and walked
out into the city sunshine.

They were having lunch at a French bistro that had
only recently opened several blocks from Carly's office,
and as they walked there Adam talked about his
friends, his home in England, how he had come to write
his book. The bistro was crowded when they arrived,
but Adam had, she discovered, rung and booked a
table while she was in the washroom, and they were
escorted to it at once by a smiling waiter. Carly was
seated facing the room and at once spotted one of the
other editors at a table at the far side of the restaurant.
The intrigued curiosity in the other girl's face made
Carly smile, and Adam looked at her questioningly.

"Something amusing you?"

"I saw someone I know," she admitted. She could
imagine the questions that were going to be asked when
she got back to the office. Jill was going to be dying of
curiosity. Authors did not usually look like Adam
Blake, so no doubt it wouldn't even enter Jill's head
that he was one of their writers.

They ordered and leaned back, talking, their eyes
constantly meeting as though each of them was still in
the process of making discoveries about the other.
Adam seemed as curious about Carly as she was about
him. He asked her how she had come to work in New
York and listened intently while she told him about
Curt and how he had rung one day and said, "Come
over here and work for me."

"Were you surprised?" he asked, and Carly laughed.

"Astonished, but then, Curt's a very surprising man. Wait until you meet him—he reminds me of a jack-in-the-box; he springs up out of nowhere and makes everyone jump. That's his technique; it keeps us all on our toes. You know that with Curt you don't have more than one chance. Your first real mistake is your last."

"He sounds appalling," Adam said.

"He isn't once you get used to him. I respect him very much."

"And like him?" probed Adam.

She made a little face. "Well, I wouldn't go so far as to say I *like* him."

Adam surveyed her. "He must think a hell of a lot of you to have made you the offer in the first place."

Carly flushed slightly. "Oh, well . . ."

His eyes mocked her. "What a modest reaction. You should have said calmly that you're a really terrific editor."

"Well, of course, I am," Carly said, and they both laughed; then she said, "And you're a terrific writer, Adam. I have to tell you that I couldn't put *Red is a Dangerous Color* down; it's compulsive reading."

"I'll match your modesty and just say thank you," Adam murmured lightly.

"Did you really do all those jobs?"

"All of them," he said dryly. "Unfortunately."

"Why unfortunately? They sound like a lot of fun."

"Most of them were dull after the first few days— that's why I always moved on to something else."

"Why did you get involved in bullfighting?" she asked, frowning. "I've never understood why anyone goes to see a bullfight. It sounds so cruel and sickening."

"It is," Adam said shortly. "And I was only twenty

when that happened. I was too young to realize what I was getting myself into. I was living in Spain at the time and a friend dared me to enter a *novillado* fight—all the fighters involved were complete amateurs, newcomers more interested in taking a risk for one occasion than in really taking up bullfighting as a profession. I thought it would be exciting to have a go at it but once I was out there in the ring it turned my stomach."

"It would have turned mine, too," Carly said with feeling.

He nodded. "In Spain there's a very romantic view of bullfighting. They talk about the glory, the moment of truth, the beauty and pathos of it all—to me it was just a slaughterhouse with an audience."

She shuddered. "You brought that out very well in the book."

The waiter brought their first course and the talk drifted on to his farm in England. "Isn't that life very quiet after all your world travels and your exciting experiences?" Carly asked.

"It's what I want," Adam said. "Another glass of wine?"

"Thank you," she said, watching him fill her glass with the white wine and too absorbed in noticing his long, powerful fingers and the way they moved to realize for a moment that he had deliberately changed the subject. When he spoke again it was to talk about a film he had seen the previous week, and the subject of his current life in England did not come up again during the rest of the lunch.

There was never a pause in their talk; they seemed to strike sparks off each other all the time, their interests and attitudes matching so closely that Carly was almost incredulous. She was very reluctant to point out to him an hour later that she had to get back to the office, but she had an important appointment at four o'clock with Curt, and she knew she dared not miss that.

"I've enjoyed the lunch very much," she said as they parted outside her office block, offering Adam her hand.

He took it but held it down between them, his thumb slowly caressing the back of her hand in a way that made a shiver run down her back.

"So have I, and I look forward to seeing you again tomorrow night. You won't forget you promised to come to Phil's party with me?"

"No," she said, looking into the gray eyes and seeing the pupils dilated like glittering jet, a wavering reflection of herself mirrored on the glaze of the iris, making her feel suddenly weak at the knees, as though the sight of her own image imprinted on Adam's eyes was deeply moving to her. "I won't forget," she promised and knew she would never forget this moment, either. How could she ever forget standing here in the New York sunshine holding hands with the most attractive man she had ever seen in her life while the bustling crowds flowed round them like a river swirling around rocks?

"It doesn't seem possible," Adam said abruptly, his voice very deep.

"What doesn't?" she asked breathlessly.

"You, me," he said, his face intent. "I feel I've known you for years, yet we only met at noon." He looked up at the blue sky as though expecting to see by the sun what time it was, shaking his head in disbelief. "How long ago is that? Three hours? Four? Now I know what Einstein's theory of relativity means—one hour with you is like a flash of light while it's happening, yet I have the distinct feeling that every second we've spent together has taught me something new about you."

Carly could not have said a word to save her life. She could only stand there, looking up at him, clinging to his hand as though to save herself from falling.

He stared down at her, then lifted her hand and bent his black head to brush his lips lingeringly into her palm. Carly half-closed her eyes in feverish shock. She had been passionately kissed before. She was no quivering adolescent, but a mature and experienced young woman more than capable of holding her own in a boardroom struggle, yet Adam's gesture made the nape of her neck prickle with reaction. Her body ran first hot, then cold, as if she was suffering from some unknown illness.

Adam released her and was gone before she realized he was leaving. "I'll ring you," he said as he went, but Carly only realized what he had said after he had been swallowed up into the crowd. She stood on the sidewalk for a moment, dazed, until the amused, curious looks she was getting made her flee into the building behind her.

She took the elevator back to her office and was walking into her room when a voice said brusquely, "What's the matter with you, for heaven's sake? I spoke to you twice."

Carly looked round blankly and met Curt's astonished stare. Flushing, she mumbled, "Sorry, what did you say?"

"Wake up!" Curt snapped. "I told you to come to my office a quarter of an hour from now—I've got to rearrange my appointments; I'm running late."

"Yes, okay." Carly smiled and wandered to her desk

in a state of dreamy bewilderment. She looked at the pile of manuscripts waiting for her and then leaned back in her chair, her arms linked behind her blonde head, and thought about Adam. It had to be a dream, she told herself. It could not be real. It had happened so fast and was so perfect. It had to have a flaw somewhere; life did not present you with a dream and not expect you to pay for it sooner or later.

The telephone rang, making her jump. Lazily she stretched out a hand and lifted it. "Yes?" she asked in a slow, contented voice.

"Why aren't you here?" Curt demanded, destroying the mood of delight enveloping her.

"Oh, sorry, is it that late?" she stammered.

"Get here," Curt snarled. "And I mean *now*."

Carly replaced the receiver and fled down the corridor.

That evening she nerved herself to talk to Louise while she was getting their supper. Louise was in a taciturn mood, and it occurred to Carly that perhaps Roddy had decided to break the news to her over lunch and that her own information would come too late, but when she broached the subject of Roddy, she realized from the look Louise gave her that he had not mentioned his marriage.

"What about Roddy?" Louise asked, tensed in irritation.

"Louise . . ." Carly had spent an hour trying to find a gentle way of breaking it to her, but now all the carefully planned sentences left her head and all she could do was plunge into it bluntly. "Roddy's married."

47

Louise stared at her. "So what?" she asked, stunning Carly.

"You knew?"

"I guessed," Louise said cynically. "After all, he's a very sexy guy. I didn't figure he would be wandering around loose for long. He's never told me he was married, but I can't say I'm surprised."

"Don't you care?" Carly stammered incredulously.

"It's none of my business. His marriage has nothing to do with me." Louise gave her a defiant, sulky look.

"But Louise—there's no future in it! Haven't you thought about his wife, his children? You can't go on seeing him when you know it will never be serious."

Louise pushed her plate away. "Look, I'm twenty-six and I've discovered that there isn't much future in any relationship I have. Most of the really attractive men I meet are married and the ones who aren't married are rarely attractive. What do you want me to do? Lock myself up and throw away the key? So Roddy isn't going to be a fixture in my life—who cares? For the present, I'm having fun with him. We spend an evening having dinner or taking in a movie and we have a good time. He's great company and I enjoy being with him. I'm not asking for the moon; I'm just asking to have a little fun now and then. What's wrong with that?"

Carly stared at her, speechless. "Don't you ever think how hurt his wife would be if she found out?"

"His marriage is his business. If he doesn't love his wife enough to be faithful to her, is that my worry? If she meant anything to him he wouldn't be dating other girls."

"That's beside the point. We're not talking about other girls. We're talking about you!"

Louise stood up. "I didn't ask you to talk about me.

Mind your own business, Carly." She walked towards the door and halted, swinging round. "And anyway, you're a fine one to talk—what are you doing with Adam Blake? It strikes me that we have a case of people in glass houses throwing stones around here."

Carly stared in shock at her. "Adam? What are you talking about? Adam isn't married!" She spoke with absolute conviction. Adam's reaction to his brother-in-law's infidelity had made it quite clear to her that the last thing Adam would ever do was cheat on a wife. She had only known him for a day, yet she already felt sure she knew him too well to suspect he could be married.

Louise laughed angrily. "Of course he's married!"

Carly began to feel oddly cold. She shook her head dumbly, denying it without being able to find the words.

"Look," Louise said, half in a brusque sort of compassion, half in mocking irritation, "are you telling me it never entered your head? He's married, I tell you, and he's got kids."

Carly swallowed. "Children?" It had to be a lie; it couldn't be true.

"Well," Louise said, as if unsure, "he has one, at least. I know that because I saw a photograph of her. Roddy showed it to me over lunch today—a snapshot of himself and Adam with a little girl riding horses on this farm Adam Blake lives on, and while he was showing it to me he said that Donna had taken it and I said, 'Who's Donna,' and he said, 'Adam's wife.'"

Carly half rose and sat down again, her legs too weak to carry her. "Oh, no," she whispered.

Louise drew a rough breath. "Look, I'm sorry, Carly," she said, eyeing her with compassion. "I thought you'd have guessed. I always guess—married

49

men have that special look, a married look, especially when they are having a fling on the side. There's a glint in their eyes because they feel they're getting away with something."

"Don't," Carly muttered, bending her head. It hurt. It hurt so much she wanted to burst into tears, but she couldn't cry with Louise standing there watching her. How could she have made such a mistake in a man? How could she have been so dazzled and bewitched that she never even suspected for one instant that he was married all the time? She had always felt she would be able to tell, too. Louise was right—men did have a married look that always betrayed them. Carly had avoided married men like the plague. She had no wish to end up as the third angle in a triangle, no desire to find herself playing the role of the 'other woman.' It offered too much loneliness and unhappiness, and however lonely she might feel when there was no man in her life at all, she was not willing to accept the pain and aching of a furtive hole-in-the-corner romance with a man who belonged to some other woman.

"They're all the same," Louise said with bitter satisfaction. "I wish to heaven the word sex had never entered the vocabulary. Hurry the day when we all become androids and are made in a factory. It will cut out all this heartache."

Carly didn't answer. She stared at the salad on her plate and did not feel like eating again for the rest of her life.

Louise slowly came back toward her and ruffled her sleek blonde head. "Don't look like that. You make me wish I'd kept my mouth shut."

"I'm glad you didn't," Carly said huskily. Tears stung behind her lowered lids and she fought to stop them trickling down her face and betraying her. How ridiculous, she told herself, how idiotic, to cry over a man you only met for the first time today. But it wasn't just a man she was crying over, it was the shattering of a dream. Carly hadn't dared to dream for years. She had kept busy with her career, excited by it, growing more and more ambitious as she realized her own abilities and brains, and for a long time she hadn't noticed how years were passing without her private life containing anything but a succession of meaningless brief relationships. Only lately had she realized how empty her world had become. Meeting Adam had been like a last chance at which she had grasped almost desperately, with an eagerness she had not been able to hide from him.

Now she felt sick, she felt humiliated, she felt she wanted to roll herself up into a ball and hide for a long, long time.

No doubt Adam had recognized her wide-eyed excitement at meeting him and had taken advantage of it ruthlessly. What a hypocrite he was, Carly thought suddenly, remembering what he had said about Roddy Shaw. How could he be so two-faced?

"All men are animals," Louise said, and Carly ground her teeth together.

"That doesn't quite cover it," she said through her teeth. "I could think up a few adjectives to describe Adam Blake that would be far more accurate, but I prefer not to use words like that."

Louise laughed shortly. "Now you're talking like a rational woman. Why don't we have some of that wine we've been saving for a special occasion and swap adjectives we think might fit the bill?"

"Why don't we do that?" Carly said. That would be

more dignified than howling her eyes out over a man who wasn't fit to live, she thought.

"Let's have a little sanity around here," Louise said. "Realism may not be pretty but it hurts a lot less than dreams."

Carly looked at her bitterly. "How true."

She had a headache the next morning. The wine partly accounted for it, perhaps, but it was mostly produced by the effect of a sleepless night and the trailing wreckage of a dream. She sat at her desk and read manuscripts with dry concentration, hating every word she read but ploughing on with the work all the same. When the telephone rang she lifted it with a brusque movement and said, "Yes?"

"Carly?" The voice sounded uncertain, surprised by the terse note in her voice, but she recognized it at once and felt a surge of bitter fury.

"Yes?" she bit out.

"Adam here," he said slowly, sounding even more surprised.

"Yes, Mr. Blake?" Carly did not allow herself to snarl or start shouting. She made her voice as cold as the frozen north, as distant as Alaska.

"Is something wrong?" he asked, very puzzled.

"Why should there be? I'm very busy, that's all. Can I help you?"

"I wondered what time I could see you this evening; could we have dinner before the party?" There was a definite note of uncertainty in his voice now.

"I'm afraid I will not be able to make the party," Carly said. "I have a business appointment this evening."

The silence stretched out between them like tightened wire. She could feel the questions beating along it from him but all he said was, "I see." There was another pause, then he said, "Goodbye."

The phone clicked and he was gone. Carly stared at the receiver in her hand in surprise. She had expected him to comment, to ask questions, to protest or show some sort of reaction at least, not just to say "I see" in a flat voice and then ring off.

She slammed her phone down violently, almost smashing it. He was certainly not a guy to waste time or words, was he? He might have said *something*. She had not expected him to break down on the phone or beg, but she had not expected him to shrug off her refusal more or less indifferently, either.

Her head began to throb again and she put a hand to it, giving a faint groan of pain. Where were those aspirins? She opened a drawer and rummaged through the papers in it crossly, found the pills and went to the washroom to get some water. She had been taking medication at regular intervals since she had gotten up, but her headache obstinately stayed there, and she felt as though a little man with a hammer was trying to break his way into her skull.

She made her way back to her desk and returned to her manuscripts. Ten minutes later the door opened and slammed shut before she had had time to look up. When she did glance up she found Adam coming toward her at a rapid pace. Carly gave a gasp of shock.

He put both hands on the desk and leaned toward her, saying through almost closed lips, "Well? What's this all about?"

"What are you doing here?" she asked in a shaken voice.

"You didn't think I would accept a brush-off over the

phone? I came round in person to discover what the hell was wrong with you this morning."

Carly leaned back, groping for her pride and self-respect, and hating him as she looked into his lean face. He was too attractive to be easy to ignore, and the fact that she had been experiencing waves of sexual awareness from the instant she set eyes on him again merely made her even angrier, both with him and with herself.

"I happen to have a strange prejudice against dating married men," she said, her voice tipped with ice.

Adam didn't give a flicker of reaction. He leaned there, his arms supporting his long body, his face only inches away from her own, the gray eyes pinning her in place, their scrutiny intent, and nothing moved in his face, not a glimmer of an expression to show her that he was taken aback by what she had said.

"I should think so," he drawled slowly. "I'm glad to hear it, but what has that to do with dating me?"

Carly was beside herself with rage. "Oh, you're good, you're incredibly good—if I didn't know different I'd believe you were as free as the wind." She paused, wanting to hit him across that handsome face. "But I do know different. You're married, Mr. Blake. And you have a daughter."

"Correction," Adam said calmly. "I have a daughter, it's perfectly true. She's nine years old and her name is Julie and I should have mentioned her to you yesterday, I know. I didn't because I wanted to get to know you better before I broke the news that I had a ready-made family back home in England. That was devious of me but, I assure you, I would have mentioned her in time. Possibly tonight at the party."

Carly was beginning to feel uncertain, rather nervous. He was too calm, his eyes too straight and direct. He couldn't be hiding anything, and she bit her lip anxiously.

"But my wife is dead," Adam said, holding her eyes. "She died just over a year ago."

"Oh," Carly whispered, all her color gone and a terrible coldness invading her. "I . . . I'm so sorry, Adam. I got the facts wrong; I leaped to conclusions."

"You got this from Roddy, I presume?" he inquired, and she nodded.

"He told Louise you were married and she told me."

"And you flew into a rage and decided to drop me like a hot potato, did you?" Adam asked, eyeing her without expression.

"I can't say how sorry I am," Carly stammered. "When I thought you were married all the time I . . ." She broke off, swallowing.

"Don't you think you might have asked me if what Roddy had said was true?"

"I should have done, I realize that now," Carly murmured, unable to meet his eyes, her glance dropping away from him. He was obviously very angry with her and who could blame him? She had given him no chance to explain or tell her what was behind Roddy's information. She had leaped to a conclusion and acted on it, and had been rude and unpleasant to him.

"I'm sorry," she said again.

"A little belated," Adam told her crisply, straightening from the leaning position. "I thought we had got to know one another very well over lunch yesterday—obviously I was wrong."

Carly felt very cold and unhappy. She had ruined her relationship with him before it had had a chance to deepen into anything more than a physical and mental attraction that had been instant and potentially very exciting. How could she have been so stupid? Perhaps her dazed incredulity at the miracle of their immediate feeling of attraction had made her swing wildly to the other extreme at the first hint that Adam might not be the dream come true she had been looking for. She had had a secret fear from the moment she set eyes on him—a disbelieving fear that Adam could not be as fantastic as she thought. She had almost expected to find out that he had some hidden flaw.

Life had suddenly handed her a wonderful present, and she had broken it with her own two hands.

Adam turned and walked to the door while she sat with bent head, aching.

"What time?" he said.

Carly looked up. "Sorry?"

"What time shall I pick you up for dinner?"

Her heart stopped painfully. "You still want to take me out tonight?"

Adam's mouth curved into a mocking yet gentle smile. "How old did you say you were, Carly? Twenty-eight or twelve? Right now you look like a little girl, and if I wasn't a man who likes to wait for the best life has to offer I'd spoil our first kiss by coming over there and kissing you so hard you would be reeling with it for hours afterwards."

Carly felt her color rushing back and laughed breathlessly. "Promises, promises."

He grinned, wicked amusement in his face. "What time?"

"Six o'clock is when I'm supposed to stop work," she said, not bothering to add that she often worked until eight.

"I'll see you here at six," he said, turning to go. "In the lobby?"

"Yes," she said to the back of his head and saw his hand lift in a brief gesture of farewell before he closed the door behind him.

Carly could have burst into song.

Chapter Three

Carly could never afterward remember much about that party; she had moved through it like someone in a dream, and the cloudy images of the dream obliterated most of what happened for her. When she met Adam in the foyer at six o'clock she felt her heart skip a beat as she set eyes on him. He was wearing a pair of black pants that were so smooth-fitting that he looked as if he had been poured into them; the way they molded every inch of his long legs and slim hips emphasized the lean masculinity of his body. His tailored white silk shirt was open at the collar, his brown throat gleaming like polished bronze against the soft material. He was looking around at the marble walls and floors, his expression ironic. Carly watched him and felt a little pang of pride as she noted how many sidelong looks he was getting from other women as they passed him. It was dangerous and absurd for her to feel possessive, proprietary, about Adam, since they hardly knew each other, yet she could not help it.

Walking over to him she slid a hand through his arm. "Hi," she murmured, smiling up at him.

His black head swung toward her at the first touch of her hand and a smile lit his eyes. "Hello," he said, his voice deep, the sound of it sending a trickling shiver down her spine.

"Where shall we have dinner?" he asked a second later.

Carly looked at his clothes and then down at her own. "I'm not really wearing party clothes; I suppose there isn't time for me to go back to my apartment and change?"

"Of course there is," he said and put a hand under her elbow to steer her out of the building. "We'll take a taxi, shall we?"

Carly laughed. "You'll be lucky to get one at this hour."

"I *am* lucky," Adam said, grinning and lifting one hand toward a yellow taxi cab, which shot through the traffic and pulled up beside them to her disbelief.

"See?" Adam teased as she got into the back and she told the driver her address. There was laughter in his eyes and he added, "I'll tell you a secret—that's the first time I've managed to get a cab all day. Usually they just ignore me."

"Don't I know it?" Carly said, starting to laugh, too. "I normally take the bus."

She was relieved to find that Louise had not come back to the apartment. While she changed, Adam wandered around and inspected the tiny place, his hands in his pockets. She came back to join him as quickly as possible and stood in the doorway staring at his profile, surprised again by his striking good looks. From this angle his cheekbones had a taut angularity, the brown skin drawn over them smoothly but tightly. There was a definite austerity in his face. Now that he was not smiling she saw power in his features, a personal force that was hidden when he looked at her because that smile of his erased the underlying strength of his personality and made her conscious only of his charm. The charm was absent at this moment; if she had never met him before she would have looked at that profile and seen a man with disturbingly attractive looks and hard, energetic features; a dangerous man, a man to walk warily with, a man whose long, athletic body and controlled face held something of the leashed power of a threat.

He did not look at all like the Adam Blake she had begun to think she knew, and the palms of her hands went moist with shock.

He must have heard the swift intake of her breath because he swung round and looked at her, his gray eyes widening in appreciation as he saw her. He whistled softly. "You look sensational!"

The words caressed her, the husky tone of his voice making her quiver in reaction, as though his voice had stroked along her nerve ends and set them jangling.

"Thank you," Carly said unevenly. She had known before they got to the apartment exactly what she was going to wear. This was her favorite dress, a pale turquoise silk that clung to her, from the scooped neckline down over the firm rounding of her breasts to her small waist and slim hips, ending just below her knees. As she walked toward him she felt his narrowing eyes watching the sway of her hips and her color heated.

It had not occurred to her before, but now she became nervously aware that they were alone in the apartment. Carly had often had a man to dinner there in the past; she liked to cook and to serve a meal by romantic candlelight with the drapes closed to shut out the New York skyline—but she had never been so intensely aware of a man in her life. Her skin felt as though it flickered with fire as Adam's eyes ran over her. Little pulses beat like miniature hammers behind her ears and at her wrists and in the hollow of her throat. She wanted to put her hand over that hollow to disguise how she felt.

"Shall we go?" she asked, her voice trembling slightly.

"What's the matter, Carly?" Adam murmured, looking down into her restless eyes with a mocking smile. "Shy?"

She laughed. "Of course not—but I thought we were going to have dinner before we went to this party."

"We are," he said softly. "Do you know that your skin is as smooth as silk?" His hand had lifted to the pale curve of her neck as he said that, the tips of his cool fingers running slowly, lingeringly, from just below her chin to the base of her throat.

Carly shivered in unspoken protest; she was torn between wanting him to caress her and wanting to wait, to have time to think. She had never been so sexually attracted to a man in her life, and the very force of her own feelings was beginning to scare her.

"Lost your tongue?" Adam asked, tilting her chin with one finger when she tried to avoid his eyes. Her blonde hair trailed over her shoulders as her head went back, and Adam moved his other hand to touch her hair, strands of it trickling like golden water through his lazy fingers.

"You're beautiful," he murmured and very slowly bent forward while she held her breath, her eyes dilated with excitement and a new sort of fear that puzzled her. His lips lingeringly followed the same path his fingers had just taken, sliding softly down her skin. Carly felt her legs go weak. Her ears drummed with blood and her eyes began to close while she instinctively put up her hands to catch his arms as if she thought she might fall down if she did not support herself.

Her fear was a dread of betraying how deep an effect he was having. She had only just met him; she wasn't rushing into bed with him after so short an acquaintance, but she knew that Adam would only have to exert the slightest pressure for her to give him anything he cared to demand. She was not afraid of Adam—she was afraid of herself, her own violent feelings of attraction, the desire she felt mounting inside her like a raging forest fire as his lips brushed the beating hollow of her throat. She knew he must feel that betraying little tremor under his mouth; he must realize that her whole body was limp with desire. But he straightened and looked down at her with a glance she could not read, his gray eyes baffling.

"We had better go now," he said, and she swallowed.

"Yes," she whispered.

"While I'm still able to get out of here," Adam said, grinning suddenly. The self-mockery, the wry admission in his face made her smile back, her heart lightening. Adam felt that way, too, did he? The control implied by his insisting that they leave when both of them felt like staying made her like him even more. Carly followed him to the door of the apartment, marveling. She had felt sexual attraction in the past, although it had never been as strong as the way she felt it now, but she had never *liked* a man almost as much as she found him attractive. Adam was someone she would like to have as a friend and someone she wanted badly to go to bed with—the combination was dynamite, she decided, smiling to herself. She felt like a child presented with a whole box of presents; she did not know which to open first. Adam constantly surprised and delighted her; it could not last, she thought.

It could not be more than a brief enchanting dream, but while she had it she wanted to live inside that dream more fully than she had ever lived before.

They had dinner at an exclusive little restaurant near the park. Carly could not have told anyone what she ate that evening. Whatever it was tasted like the food of the angels, but she never looked at what she put in her mouth. She looked at Adam and he looked at her, the flicker of a candle flame lending a soft delight to the closed little circle in which they existed. Outside that circle waiters came and went, other people ate and drank and talked, music drifted from a hidden tape, but of everything around her Carly was totally unaware. They might as well have been on a desert island.

They talked quietly, asking questions, giving answers, discovering each other with the absorbed intensity of lovers.

"There's so much I want to know about you," Adam said as they sipped strong black coffee and held hands across the table. His index finger traced a circle on her palm, wakening her blood again.

"There isn't much to know; I'm not that interesting," she said, laughing. Adam was far more interesting. He had done so much, been to so many different countries; his mind was strong and clever, his ability obviously far beyond her own. She had already found out that he spoke half a dozen languages fluently from having lived abroad so much, that he had read widely in many different disciplines, that he could turn his hand to anything from cooking a meal on a ship for a whole crew to writing a book.

"What sort of farming do you do?"

"Sheep," he said. "I have a hill farm in Yorkshire;

my land is only suitable for running sheep. I have a very experienced shepherd who has worked in the district for thirty years and knows everything there is to know about sheep."

"I've never been to Yorkshire," Carly said. She laughed. "All I know about that part of England is what I've read in the Brontë books."

"You'll love it," Adam said, his tone expressing confidence that she would be going there. "My farmhouse is three hundred years old, built of gray flint stone, with walls thick enough to keep out the battering winds in winter and to keep the rooms cool in summer. It stands on a hill overlooking a valley; I have one of the most beautiful views in the world—green fields and sheep and elm trees." He laughed, looking at her teasingly. "You'll find it very quiet after New York. At night it's pitch dark; the only sounds you hear are the wind and the calls of owls hunting down in the valley."

Carly felt a queer little shiver run over her skin. "It sounds fabulous," she said haltingly, her brows drawing together.

Adam looked at her sharply. "Something wrong?"

"No," she said. "Of course not." She looked at her watch and exclaimed, "Good heavens, it's half past nine—I'd forgotten all about that party. Will we be too late?"

"Too late? It will only just be getting under way," Adam teased. "I know Phil's parties; they go on all night and end up with breakfast." He looked around, beckoning the waiter over to ask for the check.

Carly walked to the door, frowning. It had only just occurred to her that at last she had realized the flaw in her dream—Adam lived on a remote sheep farm in

Yorkshire, a thousand miles away from her. He had told her that he was visiting New York on holiday. He was only here for a week; soon he would be flying out of her life. Even if he invited her over to his farm it could only be for a brief visit. Carly was far too busy to spend much time away from her desk, and she had no hope that she would be able to persuade Curt to give her a week off before next spring. Her work schedule was too crowded. She could not afford to stop working until she had managed to clear up all her current projects.

"Something *is* wrong," Adam said, as they left the restaurant. "What is it?"

"Nothing," she said, hiding her distress. She smiled at him. "You're imagining things." How could she admit that she was upset at the idea that she would soon be saying goodbye to him?

His friends lived in an apartment in Greenwich Village just a short walk from Washington Square in a row of terraced houses whose front steps were over-looked by maple trees. The night wind softly moved through the branches and made a whispering noise, as if commenting on who walked on the sidewalk underneath them. The houses were nineteenth century, rising four stories above them as they halted outside to look up with interest.

"You're going to like Phil," Adam promised her.

"Have you known him long?"

"We worked together years ago."

"Oh, yes, of course, you were a reporter for a while, weren't you? Why did you give that up? I would have thought you would be very good at journalism; you have such a gift for words."

"I got tired of traveling," he said, smiling. "When I was young I wanted to see the world and I did—I went anywhere, did anything I fancied—but after ten years of flying and sailing around the world I suddenly knew I wanted to settle down in one place for the rest of my life."

Carly bit the inside of her lip. "Why Yorkshire?" she asked.

"I was born there," Adam said. "I knew I belonged there. Sometimes it takes you a long time to work out who you are and where you belong, but once you know, you have to follow your instincts. I had to travel thousands of miles before I knew where I ought to be."

Carly pretended to laugh lightly, but her skin felt cold. "And now you'll stay in Yorkshire forever?"

"Forever," Adam said, guiding her toward the front door.

Behind them Carly felt New York throbbing like an overheated dynamo, the excitement and drive of it pounding away at every moment. Her own blood ran to that tempo now. The body has a clock that beats out the days of a human being's life, and Carly had found the pace of New York exactly suited to her from the first month of her arrival there. She thought of Adam's peaceful hill farm with that view of green fields and sheep and knew it was not for her. She could not imagine herself living where the only sounds she could hear were the cries of owls hunting in the darkness and the bleating of lambs in the springtime. Adam had discovered that he belonged in the quiet backwater of a Yorkshire farm, but Carly knew she belonged here, where the clamor and rush of New York filled the air day and night.

The front door opened and a woman in green velvet pants and a black top rushed at Adam excitedly, kissing him. "Adam, darling! Wonderful to see you again; I thought you never left your eyrie any more. Imagine having you here in the States at last! It's years since I set eyes on you." She was a small, slim woman in her late thirties with curly auburn hair and laughing brown eyes, her face flushed with pleasure and her voice high and excited.

"Hallo, Helen, you look as if New York agrees with you. I've never seen you look so well and happy."

"I love it here," Helen Williams said, glancing at Carly with a curious light in her eyes.

Adam introduced them. "Helen Williams, Carly Newton." He grinned. "Carly is my editor—when I was working on the paper I had a very ugly fellow editing me, I remember. Editors weren't beautiful blondes with big blue eyes in those days; they were usually irascible old guys with a strong taste for cliché."

Helen held out her hand, smiling at Carly. "They still are, on newspapers," she said in amusement. "I'm glad to know you, Carly; you must tell me all about publishing in the States. I swear that one of these days I'm going to write a book when I have the time."

"I hope you'll let me see it before you send it to anyone else," Carly said, taking a liking to the other woman on sight. Helen had a warm English voice with what sounded like a London accent buried under an acquired New York slur.

"You're English!" Helen exclaimed.

"Yes." Carly laughed at her astonished face.

"What are you doing here in New York?"

"Maybe she could tell you that inside your apartment?" Adam teased. "We could get arrested for loitering with intent to commit a crime if we stand out on your porch much longer."

Helen made a face at him. "Isn't he a tease? He's worse than my husband." She drew them into the house and closed the door. The sound of the party floated out to them from the ground floor rooms and Helen pushed a door open to disclose a crowded scene. The drumming beat of pop music came from a stereo; people leaned against walls, squatted on the floor, talked, drank, laughed, danced vigorously in the cleared space in the center of the room. Nobody seemed to notice the new arrivals; they were all too busy enjoying themselves.

Helen peered over heads and waved a hand. "Phil! Phil! Look who's here!"

A thin balding man detached himself from the makeshift bar and forced a way through the crowd to shake hands with Adam. "Good to see you, you old snake," he said, grinning. He was on the wrong side of forty with a lively, energetic face and intelligent eyes, and his smile told Carly clearly that he liked Adam and that it was mutual. They had the casual manner of very old friends, swapping cheerful insults for a moment before Adam remembered to introduce her.

Phil Williams whistled as he shook her hand. "Hallo, hallo, hallo," he said, and Helen Williams grinned.

"Down, Rover, she came with Adam, remember." Looking at Carly she said happily, "One look at a blonde and he goes weak at the knees."

Phil pretended to stagger, then caught his wife's hand and dragged her toward the dancers. "Time we showed this mob how to dance, Helen," he said, looking at her with a smile, then looked back at Adam and Carly. "Grab a drink or a peanut and enjoy yourselves!"

Adam looked down at Carly. "Drink? Or dance?"

"Dance," she said, her mouth suddenly dry at the thought of dancing with him.

He took a step closer and caught her hands, then lifted them to his shoulders, still holding them tightly in his fingers. "We think alike on every subject," he said, low mockery in his eyes.

Under his intent gaze she felt nervous and shy, her face very warm. They began to dance, their bodies moving in a rhythm that had as much to do with the hidden awareness between them as with the beat of the music. Carly was intensely conscious of him, the animal warmth of his skin heating her own as their bodies brushed lightly against each other, the muscled strength of his lean figure tautly graceful. Someone changed the music and a slow, romantic mood entered the room for a while.

"Turn the lights down," Phil Williams called out and there was laughter as someone obeyed.

In the warm, smoky shadows Carly drifted back into that dream, her cheek against Adam's, her hands held in the grasp of his long fingers, the silk of her dress whispering as it stroked along the moving body beside her. Distantly she heard the muted chatter of guests in the background; she heard the clink of glass and the clatter of plates as someone helped himself to some of the cold food laid out at the back of the long room. She had taken in a quick glimpse of that room as she had stood talking to Phil Williams near the door; it was high-ceilinged and hung with sketches and paintings of seascapes with towering waves and white-sailed ships of the nineteenth century. For the party it had been stripped of furniture, the carpets taken up and the cold tiled floor polished so that the guests' feet slid and skated a little as they danced. Carly could imagine that, elegantly furnished in the style of the period in which it had been built, it would be a beautiful apartment.

Adam drew back his black head a little to look at her, his brows curving in amused assessment of her. "Enjoying the party?"

"Yes," she said frankly, smiling.

He took one hand from hers and caressed her warm cheek with a slow, sensual movement, holding her dazed eyes. "Is Carly short for Caroline?"

She shook her head. "It isn't short for anything."

"It was invented just for you, was it?"

"Just for me," she said, smiling again.

"Do you know you have a dimple when you smile?" His index finger found the tiny hollow in her smooth skin and she quivered as he touched it. He moved closer, his thighs brushing hers, his chest touching the rise and fall of her breasts. Carly felt too weak to stand alone, letting her slim body slacken against him as she danced.

He put his cheek against her own again and whispered into her ear, "I want to make love to you, Carly. I want you so much it hurts."

She couldn't have answered him if she had tried. She was hurting, too, aching with the aroused throb of desire deep inside her body. Her senses clamored for the satisfaction she needed so much.

If they had been alone in her apartment the need tearing at both of them would have swept them away at once, but their mood was suddenly destroyed when Phil turned up the lights, changed the music and shouted,

"Come on, everybody, have some of this food before Helen has a fit of the sulks. She spent hours getting it all ready—you might eat it."

People turned to the cold buffet and started helping themselves, while the noisy music made Carly and Adam draw apart, their faces still flushed, a restless frustration in their eyes.

"What about you two?" Phil demanded, appearing beside them.

"We just ate," said Adam. "I couldn't eat a thing. Could you, Carly?" His glance touched her, but did not linger, as though he found it hard to meet her eyes.

"Not me," Carly said, forcing a smile.

"Sorry, Phil," Adam said.

"I should think so—Helen will never forgive you. Surely you can manage a leg of chicken?"

"Don't even mention it," Adam said, grimacing.

Carly hated the idea of food. She felt as if she were floating on a cloud so high above New York that she couldn't imagine how she was going to get down again; the idea of anything so mundane as food was totally horrifying to her in her elated, excited frame of mind.

Phil eyed Adam. "Well, go and dance with Helen and let me have a chance to swoon over this ravishing lady you've brought here to tempt me."

Adam laughed. "You don't imagine I'm fool enough to let Carly spend any time alone with you, Don Juan?"

"Who, me?" Phil asked, looking flattered. "You know I only start to get dangerous when the moon is full."

"It's full tonight," Adam said. "Shove off and dance with your wife and stay away from my girl."

"She wants to dance with me, don't you, Carly?" Phil asked her, giving her a wink at the same time.

"Then I can tell her all about your dark past and give her some hints on how to handle you."

"That's what I'm afraid of," Adam flung back. "I know what a liar you are, but Carly doesn't; she might believe all your horror stories about me."

"Don't you think she ought to know that you're first cousin to Bluebeard?" asked Phil, and Adam laughed and flung up his hands, stepping back.

"Okay, you win, but I hope Carly has enough sense to know when she's having her leg pulled."

"And beautiful legs they are, too, if I may say so," Phil murmured, eyeing her wickedly.

"And you can cut that out," Adam said as he walked away, laughing, to find Helen Williams.

"Can I have this dance?" Phil asked, grinning at Carly.

"My pleasure," she said.

His face sobered now that Adam had gone. While they danced he said, "He's a great guy, all kidding apart. I have a lot of respect for Adam; he hasn't had an easy life. His parents died when he was in his teens, did he tell you? He lost family and home in one fell swoop. He had to make his own way in the world without any help, and he did a fantastic job of looking after himself. He was a terrific reporter—I can't think why he gave it up; he was cut out for it."

"He told me he was tired of traveling around the world."

Phil nodded. "Yeah, that's what he told me. I can understand that. He hadn't had a home since he was fifteen."

Carly hesitated, dying to ask questions but not sure she ought to talk about Adam behind his back. They had talked so much about so many things, yet Adam had never once mentioned his wife to her after their exchange in her office, and she had not liked to bring the other woman into the conversation since he obviously did not want to talk about her. But she wanted very much to know about the dead woman, to get some glimpse of what sort of relationship Adam had had with his wife.

Phil looked down at her searchingly. "He was married; did you know that?"

She nodded. "She died, didn't she?"

Phil looked away from her, his mouth straight and hard, and nodded without saying anything.

There was a little pause, then he said, "He's got a kid—a little girl, Julie. She's very pretty, takes after her mother, with big green eyes and curly hair. Black hair, the same color as Adam's, but much finer and softer. She's a lovely little girl, Julie. Adam adores her; he really dotes on that kid. She thinks the sun shines out of him, too. I'm surprised he didn't bring her with him to New York."

"Does he have someone to look after her?"

Phil nodded. "A housekeeper who lives in the village. When Adam isn't there she sleeps in the house with Julie. She's a very friendly woman with grandchildren of her own and she's good with Julie; Adam trusts her absolutely."

"That's nice," Carly said, her mind absorbed.

"It can't be easy for him, bringing up a little girl without a wife," Phil observed, frowning. "Helen and I have our children always on our minds—kids are a heavy burden to carry even when there are two of you. When you're a man on your own, it must be a nightmare, especially when your child is a girl. Adam's wonderful with Julie, though; he seems to know by instinct how to treat her."

Adam had said very little about his daughter, either, Carly thought. Obviously there were hidden places in his life that he was not yet ready to reveal to her, and she sighed, looking away.

"That's a deep sigh," Phil said slowly, watching her averted face. "I'm not bugging you, am I, telling you all this stuff about Adam?"

"No," she said, shaking her head, but her spirits were oppressed by what he had told her. Why had Phil looked so grim when he spoke about Adam's wife? How had she died? How did Adam feel about her now? The fact that he had never mentioned either her or Julie suggested that Adam was a man who locked his emotions inside himself, despite his apparently open nature.

"How long have you known Adam?" Phil asked.

"How long?" Carly looked around, her blue eyes wide in surprise as her mind went blank. How long had she known him? It seemed like an eternity, but as she unscrambled the chaotic tangle of time inside her head she laughed. "I met him yesterday," she said in tones of incredulity. Only yesterday—it was unbelievable!

"Good lord," Phil said on a low whistle. "Well, I knew Adam was a fast worker, but this beats his record."

Carly stiffened. "Does it? What *is* his record, or is that a leading question?"

Phil laughed. "Don't get the wrong idea!"

"I won't," Carly said through her teeth.

She got an uncertain look. "I was only kidding."

"Were you?" Noting Phil's obvious uneasiness she

softened and smiled. "So am I," she said. She might only have known Adam for a few hours but she already felt sure that he was not the type to rush every female he met straight off her feet.

"You can trust Adam," Phil said quite soberly.

"I know." And even if she had not been so certain, she would have wanted to trust him, because there comes a time when trust is essential. If you start questioning the truth of other people's words and actions you can get lost in a maze of uncertainty and unhappiness. You have to take people at their face value most of the time, she thought. It was the only way to live without tension and suspicion eating away at you.

Adam appeared behind Phil and tapped his friend on the shoulder. "Okay, chum, that's your lot. I want my girl back."

Phil made a regretful face. "Some people have all the luck."

"Helen won't like that remark much," Adam warned, and Phil laughed.

"And you would drop me right in it, wouldn't you?"

"Right in it," Adam promised, grinning back.

Phil gave him a pretended punch. "Go on back to Yorkshire, you rat," he said, then said to Carly, "Watch him, Carly; he's a dangerous guy in a clinch."

"I'm sure he is," Carly said and got a mocking smile from Adam.

For the rest of the party Carly found herself mostly with Adam, although from time to time they talked to some of the other guests, had a drink or nibbled some of the little party tidbits placed around the room in bowls. Adam and Carly had stopped talking so much; a new mood had succeeded their exploratory questioning of each other. Their eyes talked quite a lot, however. Carly preferred not to think too much about what that dialogue implied. It was an involuntary and silent conversation, paralleled by the touching of hands, the brush of bodies as they danced, as though their mental exploration of each other had moved on into new territory and become a sensual consciousness beating beneath the skin, in their veins, along their nervous systems.

The night wore on without her realizing it. Once she said to Adam, "I've got to go to work in the morning, you know."

"Take a day off," he advised.

"I can't do that!"

"Why not?"

"Curt would kill me."

"Dorsden? Are you scared of him?" He eyed her with amusement and she knew he was not in the least impressed by Curt.

Carly laughed. "Petrified."

"I don't believe it."

"It's true, I assure you."

"Flutter those long lashes at him and he'll be eating out of your tiny little hand," Adam teased.

"Not Curt," Carly said. "He eats nails for breakfast. If I offered him my tiny little hand he might very well eat that."

The other guests began to leave and Carly yawned, looking at her watch, and then at the window which was lightening with pale gray dawn. "Adam, I really must go."

"Have breakfast first," Helen Williams said, overhearing her. "I'm going to start cooking the eggs now."

"I really can't stay, I'm sorry." It was five o'clock

and Carly hoped she could catch a couple of hours sleep before she had to go to the office.

"I'll call you a cab," offered Helen, but Phil said he would drive them into the center of Manhattan. Even at this hour the traffic was beginning to build up, and Carly sat in the back of Phil's car with heavy eyes, her head drooping onto Adam's wide shoulder as the car swung round a corner.

Phil said reminiscently, "I remember when we first came to New York, Helen and I once took a drive in Central Park in the early morning—it was an amazing experience."

"Why don't we do that?" Adam asked, looking down at Carly.

"I doubt if there will be a horse and carriage available at this hour," Carly said.

"Couldn't we see?" he asked, and she thought of Curt, then nodded.

"Why not?"

There was one horse and carriage waiting at the Plaza entrance to the park, and Phil pulled up beside it and grinned at them. "Enjoy the ride," he said, as they climbed out of his car. He drove away, waving, and the sleepy driver helped Carly into the swaying carriage. Adam swung himself up beside her.

"This is strictly for the tourists," Carly said.

"So, I'm a tourist," Adam retorted. "I haven't set foot in Central Park in years."

The carriage moved off at a walking pace, jogging from side to side, the harness jingling. Adam leaned back, his shoulder touching hers, staring at the skyscrapers climbing up into the pale morning with delicate trails of mist swirling around the top floors, reminding Carly of a mountain range.

"It's a marvel New York doesn't slowly sink into the Hudson with all this weight on it," Adam said.

"It's built on rock," Carly reminded him, pointing to the jagged black rocks scattered here and there in the park. The mist clung a little down here, too, shining drops of it dripping from leaf to leaf and splashing down into puddles on the paths.

The horse was having difficulty pulling his load along and Carly watched him anxiously. "Can't we get out and walk?" she asked Adam. "I'm afraid that horse isn't going to make it; he looks far too old to be pulling so much weight."

The driver turned his head, hearing what she had said, and told her happily that the horse was just fine. Carly was not, however, convinced.

Carly watched the horse, frowning, and Adam watched her, tender amusement in his face. His hand searched for hers and lifted it to his lips. She started nervously and looked round at him, finding those gray eyes fixed on her with intent intimacy.

"I think I'm falling in love with you," Adam murmured huskily.

The words made her heart miss a beat. She thought for a moment she had misheard him, and her eyes, wide and disconcerted, said as much. Adam smiled, giving a wry shrug.

"Incredible, isn't it? At my age! Thirty-six years old and I find myself feeling like a twenty-year-old in love for the first time. I haven't felt like this since I was very young—in fact, I'd forgotten what it felt like."

"What *does* it feel like?" Carly was still trying to believe her own ears; what he was saying had knocked her sideways. She had known the minute she saw him that he was the sexiest, most attractive man she had ever seen, but it had never occurred to her that what she had felt had had any echo inside Adam. She had been telling herself she liked him more than any man she had ever met, but here was Adam bypassing all the preliminary phrases a man and woman might use at the start of a relationship and arriving right at the heart of the matter in a way that shook her. She was stunned by the express-train rapidity of it, thrown almost into a panic, her heart beating in her throat like a bird trapped in a closed room. She had to make herself smile, talk as normally as she could, but all her nerves were prickling with fire and excitement.

He held her hand against his cool cheek, his skin slightly rough on her palm. "Words fail me."

"I don't believe it," she teased in an unsteady voice. "Words are your business."

"That's why they're failing me—all the words have been used so many times before; they're worn out, tarnished, faded and shabby. I need some new words to describe how I feel about you, but I can't find any good enough." His lips moved along her fingertips, brushing them lightly. "Just three fit the bill. I love you."

Her lashes fluttered against her cheek in a tremor of nervous shock. The horse trotted slowly on and the driver whistled quietly to himself. She hoped he wasn't listening. Adam was speaking in a low, husky voice and she had to listen intently to hear what he said, but she did not want a stranger overhearing. All around them New York was waking up to a misty morning, but here, in the park, they seemed to be enclosed in their own world far away from city streets, a place of black branches gleaming wetly behind thickset leaves, of birds sleepily greeting the dawn, a leaden sky arching high above, straining between the skyscraper tops like gray canvas stretched from one to the other.

"We've only known each other for two days!" she whispered, and Adam half-groaned, half-laughed.

"Do you think I don't realize that? It's crazy. I must be out of my mind; I never imagined I believed in love at first sight. This has never happened to me before. I feel like someone who was walking along a street when a truck hit him."

She was so nervous she began to giggle, stifling it with one hand. Adam looked down at her and she looked up, her lids flickering quickly and shyly. Carly could hardly believe what was happening, either. She wasn't a tongue-tied adolescent, she was a hard-working, intelligent woman of twenty-eight, but suddenly she felt like a lovesick schoolgirl. Adam was right—it was some sort of madness that had hit them both.

Adam smiled at her with that heart-turning tenderness, as though her giggling delighted him. "I love you," he murmured, kissing her hand again. "Especially when you smile like that."

"That's a very big word to start throwing around after two days," Carly stammered. "Love." Repeating it made her realize it more fully.

"Enormous," he agreed. "But it's the only word I can come up with—nothing else is adequate for how I feel." He took a long, deep breath, his face taut. "What about you, Carly? I know I'm rushing you, but I'm only in the States for such a short time, I have to cut a few corners. If you need time to make up your mind, I'll understand."

Carly asked warily, "Time?" She moistened her lips

with the tip of her tongue; her mouth was so dry she found it hard to speak at all. "Is this a proposition?"

Adam's face altered. In the pale morning light, it looked like the face of a statue, the lids stiff and opaque, the mouth a straight line. She felt anger coming from him and was taken aback.

"I'm not talking about propositions," he said harshly, letting go of her hand as though she had disappointed him. "Of course I want to make love to you! My male instincts work the same as anyone else's. I want you so much I was tempted to skip the party and stay in your apartment." His eyes blazed suddenly, naked desire in them, and she caught her breath, looking away. "But you knew that, didn't you?" He bent closer, speaking in a quick, angry voice, but so softly she could only just make out the words. "You knew how I felt, Carly. You felt the same, didn't you? We both knew we wanted to stay there and make love."

She swallowed, hot color rushing up her face, and looked away, unable to speak.

Adam laughed briefly. "Yes," he said, still watching her. "We both knew. But sexual satisfaction comes very low on the list of what I want from you, Carly. I want to share my whole life with you, not just spend a few hours in bed with you. I want to wake up in the mornings and find your hair on my pillow, and come home at night and find you waiting for me. I've found you after giving up hope of ever finding someone like you—I don't ever want to lose you again."

She sat listening, knowing that he was saying what she had felt herself from the minute she saw him, but there were other worries on her mind and she frowned with uncertainty. How much of what they both seemed to feel was real? And how much had both of them been looking for someone to love? Before she met him she had been dreaming hopelessly of a man like him, of a personal happiness she knew she had not found. Had Adam been doing the same? Had they both leaped at the first faint chance of finding love? Was the way she felt real or illusory? Self-deception was so dangerous; you could talk yourself into imagining you felt an emotion you did not really feel at all.

"I know it's too soon to make a definite decision," Adam said. "But I haven't much time with you. One thing life has taught me is to take what I want and think about it later. Instinct works better than intelligence where emotion is concerned. I want to marry you, Carly. I don't want an affair with you for a few days. I want you in my life forever. I don't want to say goodbye to you."

Carly hadn't been thinking in terms of marriage; she had been thinking strictly of a brief dream snatched from the realities of daily life, and she was speechless. They were coming back towards the Plaza, the horse clip-clopping wearily, sending misty waves of breath floating into the air, encouraged by the sight of the end of the drive. Carly looked around her at the gray, mist-shrouded towers of New York, needing the sane contact of ordinary life at that moment to convince her that she wasn't dreaming. Was it happening? Had Adam just proposed to her? Or would she wake up in the apartment to hear Louise yelling that it was time to get up?

"What are you thinking?" Adam asked impatiently.

"I'm dazed," she admitted.

His voice deepened and roughened. "You haven't told me how *you* feel about *me*."

She thought of her career, her ambitions of becoming a top editor, of how much she loved life in New York, of the excitement and adrenalin of the city. A few weeks ago her head had been totally absorbed by thoughts in which Adam had had no place. How could she have imagined she was about to meet a man who would hit her like a tidal wave and change her world?

"Carly," he muttered, taking her face between his hands and looking down into it, his eyes passionate. "Carly, am I wrong? I would have sworn you felt the way I did; was I way off beam?"

"No," she whispered. "You're not off beam. But . . ."

"But you need time?" His gaze was wry but gentle, and she nodded.

"It's so soon," she said, and Adam sighed.

"I could have asked you this yesterday, when you sat in your office and looked at me with those big blue eyes, just like a child's, and laughed at me. I knew then; I knew without a single doubt, Carly. It happened on sight for me."

She looked at him restlessly, a troubled mixture of piercing happiness and doubt inside her.

"But if you need more time, you can have it," Adam said. "As much time as you need."

The carriage slowed and halted and they climbed out. The driver accepted the money Adam handed him, touching his hat with a curious grin that made Carly look away, rather pink. Had he been listening or not? She walked a few steps on and Adam caught up with her.

"I have an appointment with Curt at ten o'clock," she said, looking at her watch. It gave her something to do to cover her embarrassment. "I'd better go home and have a shower and some breakfast." She looked up, smiling. "I had a fantastic time, Adam; I loved the party, and meeting your friends."

"And me?" he asked, a little mockingly. "Do you love me? That's the question I want answered."

She looked at him helplessly, and Adam bent his head, taking her mouth fiercely, demandingly. Carly trembled as his hands slid round her, one forming itself to the small of her back, the other pressing along the yielding indentation of her spine, pushing her toward the strong arc of his body as it bent towards her.

Carly's eyes closed as a shock wave of pleasure hit her. An intense sensuality flowed through her, and her arms enfolded his neck as she gave herself up to the demand of his kiss. She was trembling violently, feeling the deep piercing of sexual excitement inside her with a sense of helpless abandonment. Adam pulled her closer and his kiss deepened. She knew she had been waiting for the touch of his mouth against her own for hours, that her body had been aching for closer contact. Their eyes had been meeting all the time at the party, and the frustrating touch of their hands and bodies had been unable to relieve this burning sensual need.

Adam drew back suddenly, breathing much faster. His face was darkly flushed and his eyes were glittering. "If you don't walk away this very minute, I'll lose my head," he said, in light self-mockery.

Carly wondered how she was going to be able to leave, feeling as she did, but she somehow managed to smile back and nod. There was a row of taxis near by. She walked over and claimed one of them, giving Adam a brief glance and a wave as the cab passed him. He stood on the sidewalk staring after her in the New

York morning, a first gleam of sunshine penetrating the mist to show her his face before she lost sight of him.

When she got to the apartment she found Louise still asleep. Carly had a shower, dressed slowly and went into the kitchen to drink some black coffee. Oddly, she did not feel sleepy now. She felt very awake and alert. Her mind was tossing like a troubled sea as she thought about Adam's proposal.

Even if he gave her a much longer time to consider the idea, she could not imagine herself living on a farm in Yorkshire. What would she do all day? Housework and washing and cooking? She would have to uproot herself from the exciting, stimulating world she had known for years, abandon her career for good and become an ordinary housewife, with a view of green fields and sheep. Adam had told her that his nearest neighbor lived half an hour's walk away across the fells. Adam would probably be out all day working in the fields and she would be in the house alone, with nobody to talk to but the sheep.

Carly could not face it. It was too far removed from what she knew. She had been working in the publishing world for years, and she knew she was good at her job, and that she loved it, needed it.

She had no real doubt about what her decision would be; if he had asked her to live in London, she would have jumped at it without a second thought. She had never felt this way about any other man. Adam was offering her an impossible choice, though.

She put her head in her hands, her body wrenched by a deep painful sigh. *What am I going to do?* she thought.

Chapter Four

$\mathcal{A}$re you up early or did you come home late?"

Lifting her head quickly, Carly rearranged her expression before she met Louise's eyes. The other girl stood in the doorway surveying her like a tired bird inspecting a far from edible worm.

"Hallo," Carly said in what she hoped sounded like a bright tone. It did not seem to convince Louise, who strolled forward, yawning and running a hand through her tousled hair.

"What's wrong? You look as if you've been in a traffic accident. Trouble with the boyfriend?" She touched the coffee pot. "This still drinkable?"

"Yes, I should think so." Carly watched Louise pour herself a cup of black coffee and sip it with half-closed eyes.

Louise looked at her, nursing the cup between both hands. "Well? Aren't you going to tell me? If I'm prying—say so."

"You're prying," Carly said, smiling.

"Okay," Louise said, apparently not taking offense. "I wondered if I could help, that's all. I'm an expert on love affairs that go wrong. I ought to be—most of mine do."

"I have to work this out on my own," Carly said flatly.

"I suppose we're talking about Adam Blake?"

Carly glanced at Louise in a sharp way, frowning. "It isn't what you think!"

"No?" Louise smiled drily.

Shaking her head, Carly said, "He isn't married anymore—his wife is dead."

"Oh," Louise said, her expression surprised. "Is that what he said? I'll check that out with Roddy, if you like; if that's what's bugging you."

"I don't need to have it checked out," Carly said impatiently. "I take Adam's word for it." A faint smile touched her face. "He isn't lying to me." How could he be lying when he had asked her to marry him?

"Then what *is* bothering you?" Louise caught her glance and held up a hand, palm forward. "Okay, okay, we'll drop the subject."

"You're still seeing Roddy, then?" Carly asked, trying not to show her own disapproval too strongly, and Louise made a little face.

"I doubt it."

"Oh?" Carly was not going to force Louise to discuss it, any more than she wanted to discuss her own private worries.

Louise drank some coffee, staring at the window. "I just don't want any more heartache," she said. "All I ever get from men is heartache. I'm tired of it. So I told Roddy last night that I don't want to see him again. We were having dinner when I noticed that there was a tiny darn in his shirt cuff—beautiful little stitches; someone had done a wonderful job. It was barely visible. And I thought of his wife taking all that trouble to darn his shirt and I felt sick." She looked defiantly at Carly. "And don't say I told you so."

"I wasn't going to."

"Well, that's good." Louise put down the coffee cup and went to the door. "The last thing I want is to have you telling me I've done the right thing. I've done the only thing I could do—taken steps to see I don't get any more heartache. From now on I'll just moon over movie stars and forget about true-life romance."

"Don't be so defeatist," Carly said, smiling.

Louise walked out without answering, and Carly gave a deep sigh, then glanced at her watch and got up stiffly. She might as well make tracks for the office. She had a lot of work to catch up on today and a grueling interview with Curt timed for ten o'clock. Talking to Curt was like riding on a roller coaster; you never knew when the next bend would hit you, but your stomach was in your mouth half the time just anticipating it.

She managed to do quite a bit of work before joining Curt in the boardroom that morning. He was there already, flicking over papers in a large portfolio, and he glanced up as she walked into the room. Every time she saw Curt she felt surprised at how small and slight he was; thinking about him, talking to him on the phone, remembering his vitality and throbbing energy all made him somehow seem a towering figure. All that dynamism was visible as he nodded to her now.

"Carly, I wanted a word; glad you're here first. How did you make out with this English writer? What's his name? Blair?"

"Blake," she said. "Adam Blake."

"Will he be available for publicity?"

Carly thought of Adam and smiled, a secret tender little smile which Curt observed with apparent disgust.

"No," she said. "I doubt it." She knew Adam too well now to expect him to be ready to go through the hoops of the publicity circus.

"Have you tried to persuade him?" Curt had a suspicious look now, his beady eyes narrowed.

Carly looked into his face calmly. "I wouldn't dare. You try, Curt; you're tougher than I am and you'll need to be tough if you try to take on Adam Blake."

Curt looked interested, ruffling himself like an angry bird. He was always attracted to trials of strength, his ego enjoying the chance of defeating an opponent in any sort of contest in or out of the boardroom. He could not be happy if he was not on the move, going somewhere, aiming for new heights, new reaches for his power. Curt was not the type to accept the status quo; he always looked for something more than he already had and that was what made him so formidable. He was never satisfied.

"When can I meet him? How long is he over here for? Get him on the phone and fix a lunch."

"I'll try," Carly said, and she knew she would enjoy watching Curt locked in battle with Adam. They were the two strongest men she had ever met. It would be some war.

"What do you mean, you'll try?" Curt growled, stabbing an index finger in her direction. "When I say fix it, I mean, fix it. Do it now, then get back here."

Carly walked to the door, hiding a smile. Although Curt meant exactly what he said, there was always an element of play acting in his behavior. He was very conscious of his reputation as one of the hard men of publishing; he encouraged it and nourished it with everything in his power. The tough act was both genuine and deliberate. Curt liked to live up to his legend; after all, he had created it himself, and it was an extension of himself. No doubt in the beginning it had been entirely natural, during the period when Curt was driving himself up the ladder of success, but now that he had reached the top he was still going and still remembering to terrify people when he felt they needed it.

She found the number of Adam's hotel and called him. It took several minutes before he came on the line, and the sound of his voice made her stomach drop like an elevator going too fast.

"Hallo, Carly."

"Hi, how are you this morning?" she asked, trying to sound calm and level-headed and not as if her knees had suddenly turned to jelly. His voice was so deep and warm, and the low, husky note of it had an intimacy that made the hair on the back of her neck prickle.

"I feel fantastic," Adam said, laughter in his voice. "It's these dreams I've been having."

Carly was rather stupid this morning or she would not have repeated "Dreams?" in a weak voice.

"About this ravishing blonde," Adam teased, and she felt her face go bright pink, making her glad he was not there to witness the effect he had on her.

Hurriedly she said, "Curt asked me to ring you."

Adam laughed again, very softly, almost as though he had indeed seen her blushing like a schoolgirl. "Oh?"

"He wants to meet you," she stammered, and then pulled herself together and said more calmly, "he asked me to tell you he was looking forward to talking to you and hoped you would be able to have lunch with him. When would you be free this week?"

"Today," Adam said promptly. "For lunch with you—I'm not so sure about lunch with Curt. He isn't a beautiful blonde." He paused and said teasingly, "Or is he?"

"Not that I've noticed lately," agreed Carly. "I'm sure you'll enjoy meeting him, though; he's a very clever man, and very interested in your book, Adam. There's a lot to talk about."

"I suppose I can spare a precious lunch," Adam accepted wryly. "So long as you promise to have dinner with me this evening."

She hesitated for the briefest beat of time, her face troubled. She wanted to be with him, and she knew it, but at the back of her mind she felt the pressure of the decision he had asked her to make and she ached with doubt and unhappiness. Why did she have to fall in love with a man whose life style was so far removed from her own? Why was this impossible choice being forced upon her? If only Adam lived in New York or London; if only he did not live far away from anywhere civilized!

"Thank you, I'd love to," she said and was amazed to hear her own voice sound so casual, betraying nothing of the inner turmoil disturbing her.

"Good," Adam said, a smile in his voice, and she realized that she was picturing his face, recognizing already the expression that would go with that tone. She felt she was on a nonstop express train bearing her away at great speed into the night, into a darkness she had not anticipated and that terrified her. They had known each other such a short time, but already she had been through a hundred different moods with him. She had pictured falling in love as some sort of glorious golden sunset, a tranquil halcyon future stretching in front of her. Instead, love was a constant surprise, a bewilderment and bewitchment, and Carly found herself flashing from the lighthearted gaiety of drinking champagne to the aching sense of loss that came whenever she contemplated saying goodbye to Adam.

"Could you join us here at twelve?" she faltered.

"Fine," he said.

There was a pause, then he murmured, "Thought about my proposal, Carly?"

She felt her mouth go dry. "Yes," she whispered.

"Any answer yet?" He sounded so casual, so sure of himself. Of course her dazed response to him from the start must have told him how fiercely attracted to him she was. He did not sound as if he was worried about her answer.

For some reason, that annoyed her. "No," she said very clearly. "You aren't rushing me, are you, Adam?"

"Yes," he said with amusement, and she found herself laughing, too.

"Well, don't," she said. "I'll see you later."

When she had hung up she went back to the board-room and found it full of people talking, interrupting each other. Carly squared her slender shoulders as she paused in the doorway. Sometimes she felt tired when she contemplated the mimic warfare of the world she lived in; there was so much in-fighting, so much back-stairs conspiracy and intrigue. The world of corporate publishing was like a tank full of piranhas at times. You had to walk very warily if you did not want to be stripped down to your bones. The politics of big business seemed to Carly to have little to do with books, but once the ugly reality of money intruded into any scene you couldn't avoid this sort of pressure.

She sat down next to Louise, who gave her a sidelong look, her mouth wry. Louise was a cynical realist; she professed to be merely amused by all the intrigue around them, but Carly remembered that the definition of a cynic was a romantic who had been disillusioned.

"Have I missed anything?" Carly whispered to her.

"Not a thing," Louise whispered back.

Curt turned his dangerous eyes on them. "If you've got anything to say, maybe we could all hear it," he bit out.

Carly smiled. "Sorry, Curt."

He eyed her for a few seconds, then turned back to the marketing director. "Well, go on," he said impatiently.

While the marketing director was talking Carly lost track of what he was saying, her mind wandering, and it was only when Curt asked her a direct question that she started, her eyes flying to his face, her mind recalled from the distant regions into which it had traveled.

"Sorry, Curt, what did you say?"

"What's the matter with you this morning?" Curt asked irritably. "If you've got one of those feminine problems why didn't you stay in bed?"

Everyone looked down, some of them grinning. Carly sat upright, her teeth tight. "I haven't," she said. "What did you say?"

"I asked about the production date on the Grafton book—are we going to make it?"

"Yes, by the skin of our teeth."

Curt nodded and turned his attention to someone else, to her great relief. Louise smiled at her furtively, grimacing.

As they left the boardroom Carly muttered, "Why does he do that? Why do they all do that?"

"Do what?" asked Louise vaguely.

"Pick on the fact that I'm a woman and try to imply that that makes me a weak little creature who is always collapsing under the strain of doing a job? If a man's attention is wandering, Curt doesn't ask him if he has one of those male problems today, does he?"

"Haven't you heard? Men don't have problems—it's only women who get them." Louise shrugged, her face scornful. "Ignore it. I do."

"I do my job as well as any man," Carly said. "It isn't fair to throw my sex in my face all the time."

Louise laughed. "Who ever said life must be fair? Carly, you haven't figured out how the world works. When Curt's in a temper he picks on any weakness he can see—in your case, it just happens to be your sex, but if you were a man he'd make digs about how much you drink or what sort of love life you have—or don't have, as the case may be. Curt is a fighting animal; he has no qualms about looking for everyone's weak spot. His instinct is to locate the chink in your armor and go straight for it."

Carly looked at her, frowning. "Sometimes I'm not sure I like Curt."

"Only sometimes?" Louise mocked, her face amused.

"Well, at times he can be quite endearing," Carly returned rather defensively.

"So can Dracula," Louise said. "But if he taps at the window after sunset, don't let him in."

Carly was still laughing at the picture of Curt as Dracula when she went into her office and stopped dead. Adam turned from the window and smiled at her.

"Hallo, Carly. You're late—you did say twelve, didn't you?"

She had forgotten he was coming; once she had got involved in the hectic pace of the boardroom discussion he had gone out of her head. She walked toward him, apologizing. "I'm so sorry; we ran late with our conference."

He nodded, looking around the office. "I've been amusing myself by memorizing the place where you work; it's very tidy for an office."

"I like it tidy," Carly said, glancing around. She had a large, square room with large windows on one wall and rows of filled bookshelves on two others. On one wall she had pinned various items ranging from current covers for books to little memo sheets holding notes on ideas the junior editors came up with and scribbled down for her to consider. The only sign of disorder was in the piles of manuscripts and proofs that were everywhere, but even those Carly tried to keep in some order.

Adam took a step nearer and caught her face, framing it in both hands and lifting it toward his own. "I've missed you."

She felt her heart skip a beat. "We only left each other a few hours ago," she said lightly.

"Every minute we spend apart seems like a lifetime," Adam said, his gaze focused on the warm, pink curve of her mouth, and she felt her lips trembling as though he had touched them.

Her own eyes ran over his strong-featured face, a faint sigh drifting from her. He was far too attractive; she felt pulses beginning to hammer all over her body as she looked at him. It was hard to remind herself that he was the intruder in this frenetic world of hers; she felt that it was the busy, noisy world outside that was intruding on their intense awareness of each other.

"Don't you feel the same?" he asked huskily, watching her, and she could not lie to him. Her widening blue eyes confessed the truth, and Adam smiled tenderly.

He bent slowly toward her and her hands flew up to

grasp his shoulders in a gesture of restless passion; her mouth lifted to meet the promise of his firm, male mouth.

Before it touched hers, the telephone rang, making her jump as if she had been stung.

"Ignore it," Adam muttered, searching for her lips.

Carly drew back, shaking her head. "I can't." She groped for the phone and whispered shakily, "Yes, Carly Newton speaking."

"What time is this English guy getting here?" Curt demanded in his brusque way, and Carly sighed.

"He's here now."

"Well, bring him along—I'm waiting." The phone crashed down at the other end and Carly looked at Adam with a wry smile.

"That was Curt."

"Who cares?" Adam said impatiently, reaching for her again, and she eluded his grasp.

"Curt doesn't like being kept waiting; we had better join him before he starts eating the desk."

Adam surveyed her oddly, a deep, smoldering heat in his gray eyes. "You're very elusive this morning," he half-accused, and her eyes slid away from his stare, her face warm.

"This is the office," she said incoherently.

Adam's brow curved upwards. "You don't mix business with pleasure, is that it?"

"That's it," Carly said, walking towards the door. "Coming?"

The lunch was a fascinating occasion for Carly. For the first time in her experience of Curt she saw him faced with an immovable object, and it amused her to see him grappling with Adam's calm refusal to cooperate on every proposal Curt came up with. A few he conceded, but Adam had no intention of becoming part of the three-ring circus with which Curt wanted to launch the book.

"Surely a good book sells itself?" he asked Curt calmly.

"You're living in the past," Curt retorted. "Today you have to advertise to sell, and publicity is essential. Why, if Moses came down from the mountain with the Ten Commandments today he would need a good press agent to sell them to anyone."

Adam grinned. "That may be your opinion—I can't say it's mine."

"You want your book to sell well, don't you?" Curt demanded, glaring at him.

"I've written the book," Adam said. "As far as I'm concerned, my part of it is finished. I've got other matters on my mind. I can't spare the time from my farm to come over here and tramp around the United States selling it."

"You can get a farm manager," Curt threw back.

"I've got one, but I work there, too."

"If this book sells, you won't need to work again," Curt said, giving him a charming smile.

"I like working on the farm," Adam said coolly. "That's why I bought it. I don't like being away from it for long. I dislike living in a city and I dislike traveling."

Carly stared at the beautifully cooked steak on her plate and could not bring herself to eat it. What Adam was saying did not surprise her, but it brought her own dilemma into clear focus. Adam would not want to live anywhere but on his remote farm, and Carly could not face the idea of living so far from her own established way of life. She was a city dweller. She liked to be surrounded by other people, to have theaters and movies and good restaurants available whenever she wanted them. She enjoyed the constant bustle of city life. She was afraid of the empty silences of the countryside, the dark nights and quiet dawns, the sense of being far from the throb of human activity.

Curt stared at Adam, his eyes distended, disbelief written all over him. "You *like* the country?" he demanded with the expression of one who thinks he has met a lunatic.

"I couldn't live anywhere else," Adam said, smiling, the crooked twist of his mouth full of charm and amusement as he observed Curt's incredulity.

"Don't you sometimes feel you'll go crazy, stuck out there miles from anywhere?"

"No, never."

"But what do you *do?*" Curt asked, as though Adam lived on a desert island in the middle of the ocean, which, in Curt's eyes, no doubt, he did.

"I read, listen to music, work, write—I'm very busy," Adam said. "I'm up at five, winter and summer alike. There's a great deal to do on a farm, you know."

"I thought sheep just went around eating grass," Curt said.

"Sheep are prone to a hundred different ailments," Adam said drily. "We have to make sure they don't contract any of them. We *work* at sheep-farming, Mr. Dorsden."

"Curt," he was told impatiently. "But what do you do in the evenings? There can't be much entertainment available."

"I go to bed at ten, usually. Farming is a tough life. I do paperwork sometimes. But mostly I relax with a good book or do some writing." Adam glanced at Carly suddenly. "I have friends, too," he added. "I have a social life on weekends." His brow had creased and his eyes were very serious. He was talking to her now, not Curt, as if it had suddenly occurred to him that the picture he was painting of his life was not a very alluring one. "It may not be a very sophisticated life, but it is a satisfying one."

Curt grunted disbelievingly. "Well, I certainly don't envy you, Adam. I'd go nuts if I was forced to live like that. Wouldn't you, Carly?"

The question threw her and she looked at him in open-mouthed consternation before she looked quickly at Adam. He was watching her with somber intensity and Carly trembled, searching for some noncommittal way of answering Curt.

"I've never lived on a farm," she said at last, her voice uneven and ragged. "I wouldn't know."

"Oh, come on," Curt insisted. "I know you, Carly—you love New York, you love city life—it would drive you round the bend to live in a dead-and-alive place like this farm."

Carly had a feeling that Curt had dragged her into the argument deliberately, but he couldn't suspect what was going on between her and Adam. Could he? Surely even Curt's razor-sharp intelligence could not read the secret behind their friendly exchanges over the past hour? Meeting his hooded gaze, she wondered. Curt had once told her with a dry smile that he could read cards by looking at their backs. Had he intuitively picked up her relationship with Adam?

She would not put it past him to have guessed at something and to be using her as a battering ram to get under Adam's guard.

Adam was still staring at her intently. He was suddenly very pale, his skin stretched tautly over his cheekbones and his mouth very straight and hard. The gray eyes were fixed, the dark pupils gleaming with rigid attention as he watched her.

"What made you decide to take up farming, Adam?" she asked quickly, steadying her voice.

There was a brief silence, then he said, "I came to a decision suddenly. I'd done so many different things and none of them gave me what I was looking for. One day I just woke up and knew what I wanted, so I set out to look for the sort of farm I knew I could manage with a small staff. I knew very little about farming—that was a few years ago and I had a lot to learn. Now I know enough to realize how little I know. Back then I knew almost nothing."

Curt was interested. "You're obviously a man who knows what he wants." Curt approved of that. He was that sort of man himself.

"Yes," Adam said, his eyes on Carly. She looked away.

They parted from Adam outside the restaurant where they had eaten. The crowds rushed past them as they stood chatting on the sidewalk and Carly was grateful for the fact that Curt was doing all the talking, his dominating presence making it unnecessary for her to say a word.

She was kept very busy all afternoon with a protracted meeting, and when she got back to her office she found a note on her desk from Sue-Ann saying that Adam had called and would see her at six-thirty in the lobby.

There had been a string of other phone calls and

Carly had to make some in return. She was aghast to look up and see that it was past six-thirty as she put down the phone after her final call. Where had the time gone? She had been running like mad all day to try to keep up with events, and she seemed to have done so little.

She flew into the washroom and got ready but she was a quarter of an hour late as she emerged from the elevator to find Adam pacing to and fro across the marble floor, his whole body vibrating with angry impatience. He swung round at the sound of her heels clicking towards him on the floor. Carly did not know him for a second. His face was dark with blood, his gray eyes leaping.

"I thought you had stood me up," he broke out harshly.

"I'm sorry; I was kept busy and didn't notice the time." She paused as their eyes met, drawing a shaken breath. "I'm very sorry, Adam," she repeated in a pleading little voice. He looked like a stranger, the hard lines of his face alarming.

He compressed his mouth, taking her elbow and guiding her out of the building. "I've booked a table," he said. "Shall we go and have a drink first?"

"If you like." Carly was still shaken by the sight of his taut face. The charming man she had fallen in love with had vanished and a tense stranger had taken his place.

Adam glanced around him as they walked, his brow dark. "How can you stand living in this madhouse?"

"You get used to it," Carly said lamely.

"I wouldn't want to," Adam retorted. He shot her a glance she could not quite read. "Was Dorsden right? Do you like living here?"

Carly hesitated, biting her lip. She had no real option but to tell the truth, however. "Yes," she almost whispered.

"You *like* it?" Adam sounded incredulous. His eyes lifted and moved around the New York street—the hooting streams of traffic, the hurrying crowds, the rearing skyscrapers climbing up into the blue sky, the heat and dustiness of city air pressing in on them. "You like all this?" he asked, half-begging her to deny the fact.

"Yes," Carly said, feeling defiance flooding into her. "It's exciting." She threw him an overbright smile. "I'm a city girl, I suppose."

They turned into the restaurant where they were going to eat and sat down at the bar. Soft music trickled out of the stereo system behind them as Adam ordered their drinks.

He nursed his glass, his head bent. "It never occurred to me that you might prefer this world," he said. "You didn't tell me that."

"Didn't I?" Carly looked back over their long, searching conversations, frowning.

He grimaced. "I suppose I should have picked it up."

"I thought I had told you everything about myself," Carly said in a light tone.

"You probably did and I preferred not to hear what you were saying," Adam said. "Have you ever noticed that we only hear what we want to hear? We ignore the things that don't fit."

"It's human nature," Carly murmured.

They drank in silence for a moment and she waited for Adam to say something more, but when he did speak he changed the subject. They finished their drinks and went in to dinner without bringing up the issue of city life again. Over the meal they talked about films and music and publishing, but Adam steered clear of anything resembling a personal remark. Carly obediently followed his lead, grateful for a breathing space in which she might think clearly.

Adam managed to get a taxi and they drove back to her apartment. She looked hesitatingly at him as they stood outside the building. The sky was a deep, warm blue tending to purple, and the uneven lines of the other buildings looked like battlements, while a silvery half-moon slid behind them and reappeared from time to time.

"Coffee?" Carly suggested.

"I'd like some," Adam said, to her regret. She needed to be alone to think, yet she knew she did not want to say goodnight to him. Her mind was in a ridiculous state of tossing confusion.

To her relief, there was no sign of Louise. The apartment was empty and dark. Carly gestured to the small couch. "I'll make some coffee," she told Adam, and he watched her walk toward the tiny kitchenette. Her hands were shaking as she made the coffee, every nerve attentive to the sound of Adam prowling about, as he had in her office, like a strange animal in a strange place. The place where one lives is very revealing, and Carly was somewhat nervous of what her apartment was telling him about her. She wondered what he would make of the jumble of objects—would he guess which belonged to her and which to Louise?

When she carried the coffee through she found him stretched out in a relaxed attitude on the couch, his hands behind his dark head and his long body casually disposed in front of him. Putting the tray down she poured the coffee and sat down next to him.

"So this is where you are when you're not in that office of yours," Adam said. "You like books, don't you? I've never seen so many in one small space."

She laughed. "I read for pleasure as well as for work."

"One taste we share in common," Adam answered, and her eyes moved away nervously as he skated close to bringing into the open the subject on both their minds.

He talked about the various countries he had visited during his long travels, but as they finished their coffee he put his cup down and turned to her, taking her cup out of her hand and putting it on the table. Carly's eyes flew to his face anxiously.

His smile disappeared, wiped out of the gray eyes as if it had never been there. "Don't look like that—what have I ever done to make you look at me that way?"

The grating sound of his voice fueled anger in her, too, as though the emotions beating beneath the surface of their quiet conversation had altered their chemical makeups suddenly.

"Why are you shouting at me?" she asked, her voice rising.

"I'm not shouting," he shouted.

"Oh, no, of course not," Carly snapped. "I'd hate to hear you when you were."

His hands grabbed her, his fingers hooking into her flesh and making her gasp with the violence of that grip.

"Let go," she broke out, struggling to free herself.

Adam refused to release her, and the way he held her, staring at her with a grim satisfaction that said louder than words that he was making her aware of his masculine strength and her own feminine weakness, made Carly even angrier.

She was conscious that what was happening was taking place on two levels. On the surface there was this warring hostility, but beneath that was the real emotion that had sparked off his trial of strength. Emotion that has no other outlet finds what channel it can, and their feelings were erupting into a barbed exchange that looked like dislike and anger but that actually had far more complex origins.

"You haven't been honest with me, have you?" Adam demanded harshly.

"What are you talking about?" she fenced, knowing perfectly well what he meant.

"You're hiding your thoughts from me; do you think I don't know that now? I thought I had a pretty good idea what sort of woman you are, but now I realize I was being overoptimistic."

"How could you expect to know me very well after three days?" Carly asked more calmly. "Be sensible, Adam."

His face darkened. "Don't patronize me, damn you."

"I wasn't!" The idea had never entered her head, but she was overlooking the existence of his male ego; Adam was prickling with touchy pride at this moment, ready to lose his temper at the slightest excuse.

"You let me make a fool of myself," he grated.

"I did?" Carly was stunned, bewildered.

"You let me charge ahead and propose to you like an idiot," he ground out. "I suppose it amused you to have me rushing at you like a bull at a gate only to knock myself out and sink to my knees."

"Adam," she began, her face softening as she saw his furious glare. "You can't think . . ."

"Can't I?" He would not let her finish that sentence.

His temper had rushed away with him, the glitter of his eyes coming closer as he dragged her towards him.

"I don't enjoy feeling like a fool," he muttered as his mouth moved down to take hers, his body pressing her down against the cushions as she fought to escape the force of his kiss. Carly was so angry she refused to close her eyes, staring up at him as she struggled, her slender body twisting and turning like an eel in his hands. The angry, silent duel their eyes fought ended abruptly as the demanding hunger of his lips broke through her defenses.

Her lids fell and her body weakened, her helpless surrender seeming to placate Adam slightly, the deep bite of his fingers easing on her shoulders, his mouth warming and softening as it moved against her own.

Carly felt his hand slip gently down her arm, settle on her waist and then move upwards, making her heart race as it closed over the smooth uplift of her breast. His other hand had begun to play with her hair, his fingers running upward into it, massaging her scalp in a soothing movement, like someone gentling a horse.

She was clinging to the hard curve of his mouth, kissing him back restlessly, passionately, allowing him to probe the moist warmth of her own mouth without protest. Her arms slowly crept round his neck to draw him closer. If he was going away soon, Carly knew, she would always regret it if she did not feed the famished hunger of her senses, allow herself to express the desire and emotion she had felt almost from the moment she set eyes on him.

She was so intent on kissing him back, stroking his thick black hair, touching the muscled nape of his neck with her fingertips, that she did not notice that Adam was unbuttoning her blouse until she felt his fingers moving against her bare skin. A piercing thrust of sexual excitement went through her and she groaned, intense pleasure pulsing inside her.

Their bodies had somehow tumbled backward. She was lying along the couch with Adam covering her, his thigh moving restlessly against her own. His mouth left her lips and made a slow, sensuous journey down her throat until it was softly caressing her breast, her white flesh swelling at the stimulation of that touch, her nipples hardening, the delicate tracery of blue veins under the skin more prominent as blood filled them. Carly heard her own voice moaning huskily, but the sound was almost obliterated for her by the thunder of her heart and the drum of aroused blood in her ears.

Adam took one of her hands and laid it on his chest, raising himself to look down at her. Carly felt the movement but she did not open her eyes; her lips parted breathlessly, moist and tingling from his kisses.

"Touch me, Carly; I want to feel your skin against mine," Adam whispered unsteadily. "We've talked so much about so many things, but we still won't know each other until our bodies have talked without saying a word."

Tremblingly she undid his shirt and slid her hand down the firm rib cage, feeling his warm skin, the muscled tension of his body, the deep inner beat of his heart, through every pore of her hand.

Their bodies moved in total harmony, in an exchange of passion that had no need of words and said more than words could ever do, the warmth of skin on skin, the tangling intimacy when the mind drowns in sensual satisfaction. Carly felt feverish with desire, aching for the moment when they would end this tantalizing frustration.

Adam's lips moved hotly against her throat, his voice muffled. "When something is so right there can only be one answer, Carly. Don't you know that?"

She did not want to talk or to listen. She wanted to stay locked inside this heated excitement forever without having to face the underlying problem with which her feelings for Adam presented her. Her hands moved over his bare shoulders, finding the column of his neck, the vital strands of his black hair clinging to her fingertips as she caressed him.

Adam sensed her refusal to listen. His head was raised; he looked down at her flushed face. "Carly, we belong together, don't you see that? I know I'm rushing you but I have so little time. I've got to get back to England in a few days and I want you to follow me as soon as you can."

She lay still, sighing, her face distressed. "I can't," she stammered.

He stared at her restlessly. "All right, you need more time—I'll wait, darling, if I have to." A smile came into his eyes, tenderness in the curve of his mouth. "You're worth waiting for, Carly."

She should have accepted that, but honesty forced the words out of her. "I can't marry you, Adam!"

Adam's face hardened, but he said nothing, staring at her with the smile dying out of his eyes.

"I've thought about it over and over again—Adam, I couldn't bear to give up my career. I've spent years training for this job. I've only been doing it for a year; it's exciting, don't you see?"

"More exciting than marrying me," Adam said harshly.

"You make it sound simple, but it isn't," Carly faltered.

"Isn't it? It seems very simple to me. The question is an easy one—do you want to be my wife?"

"If you lived here in New York—yes," Carly admitted, her voice low and unsteady. "I wouldn't hesitate for a second."

His eyes flashed; he moved closer. "There you are, then—you admit you feel the same way I do!"

"But you don't live in New York! You want me to chuck my career and forget any idea of having a separate life. Do you know how long it took me to work my way up the ladder in publishing? Do you think anyone just walks into a job like mine?"

"You're saying your job matters more than I do," Adam ground out.

Carly closed her eyes, then opened them again and looked at him in unhappy defiance. "Would you give up farming and come and live in New York for me?"

"That's different," Adam snapped.

"And what's different about it?" Carly bristled, knowing what he would say.

"I'm a man," Adam said flatly. He began to do up his shirt, sitting up, his face averted from her.

"That's rank sexism," Carly accused angrily. "Do you really believe that? That because I'm a woman my job isn't important to me? It is, believe me. I'm good at it and I enjoy it. I'm as good as any man in my field."

Adam stood up, the repressed fury inside him evident in the savage movement of his body as he turned towards the door. He didn't try to argue, and Carly got up, too, buttoning her blouse and smoothing her ruffled hair.

As he moved to the door, she said huskily, "Where are you going?"

He turned to look at her with bitterness. "You think

I'm staying to hear you giving me a lecture on feminism?"

"I'm not talking about feminism, I'm talking about us—do you think it was easy for me to decide? If you didn't despise my job, you'd realize how hard it was for me to make up my mind. If you really loved me, you wouldn't expect me to throw up everything I've worked for and follow you to the other side of the world." His mouth tightened, and she quickly added, "Not after three days, Adam! We barely know each other. If you knew anything about me, you'd realize how I feel about my job."

"If you loved me, you wouldn't hesitate," Adam bit out.

"Be reasonable—we only met three days ago!"

"Three days, three minutes—what difference does time make? I knew the minute I saw you. I knew you were the woman for me. If you felt the same way you wouldn't need to think about it. You would just put your hand in mine and come away with me."

Carly looked at him in silent uncertainty, her face confused and unhappy. He gave her a twisted, angry smile.

"There isn't any more to say, is there? There seems no point in arguing about it; if you don't know now, you're unlikely to be any wiser this time next month. Let's face it. You chose your career."

She watched him walk to the door in frozen silence. It opened and closed and Carly still just stood there, her face stunned. All those hours of talking to each other had left them in the dark about how they really felt. Adam hadn't realized how strongly she felt about her career—and she hadn't realized that Adam would brush aside her ambitions as lightly as cobwebs.

He was an old-fashioned chauvinist, she told herself. No doubt he believed a woman's place was in the home and couldn't imagine why she should want to succeed in a career, anyway. Well, if that was how he felt, he wasn't the man she had begun to fall in love with. How could she have been happy with a man who dismissed her job without hesitation?

She marched into her bedroom, her face set, and went to bed with a heavy heart. She couldn't get to sleep; she lay aching with misery, hearing Louise come home an hour or so later and move around softly before she, too, went to bed. It was long after the apartment was silent that Carly finally fell asleep.

When she got to the office next day she buried herself in her work, refusing to think of Adam. The phone rang, people wandered in and out, and she got some very curious looks as she spoke tersely and impatiently when she was interrupted.

At a quarter past eleven, Sue-Ann tapped on the door and came in, grinning from ear to ear, and Carly looked up, her brows pleated in a frown of irritation. "What is it now?"

"A delivery for you," Sue-Ann said, her eyes full of amusement. "This should put you in a better mood." She stood aside and Carly threw a brief, annoyed look past her, her face altering as she saw the boy in the doorway. He was struggling manfully with a huge basket of long-stemmed dark red roses. With a sigh of relief he put it down and handed Carly a small envelope. She had flushed to her hairline and only just remembered to fumble in her handbag to find him a tip. He vanished, smiling.

"Aren't they just gorgeous?" Sue-Ann breathed with delight.

Carly looked at the roses and couldn't find any way of saying anything. Her heart was hurting inside her. Sue-Ann gave her a quick look and discreetly went out, closing the door. Carly hurriedly opened the envelope. For a second she just stared at the one word written on the tiny card inside it. *Goodbye.* Adam had not signed it, but her trembling lips formed his name as she read the word.

She ran back to her desk and tapped out his hotel number. The switchboard girl was laconic. "Mr. Blake? Oh, he checked out an hour ago, flying back to England."

Carly put down the phone, her skin ice cold now. She stared at the massed red roses, their perfume filling her whole office, and tears rose to her eyes.

Chapter Five

If he really cared about her, he would be in touch sooner or later, Carly told herself, but as the weeks passed and she got no sign from him she began to realize that when Adam had walked out that night he had gone for good. Sometimes she struggled with a painful desire to lower her own pride and get in touch with him. She had the address of his farm in Yorkshire, and she had the perfect excuse, as his editor, for writing to him on some apparently neutral subject, but her pride would not allow her to do that. Adam would see through any excuse she made and would know her real reason for contacting him.

She had phone calls from Roddy Shaw once or twice and casually brought up Adam's name, just for the pleasure of saying it. Roddy was vague about him. Carly gathered he saw little of Adam, although they were so closely related.

"Adam rarely leaves that farm of his," Roddy told her, sounding rather pleased about that.

"Is he writing another book?"

"I wish he was," Roddy said impatiently, then paused and said, "If he did another one, you'd be interested, would you?"

"Very," Carly said with a dry note in her voice. She would be very interested in anything about Adam, but she could not tell Roddy Shaw that. In fact, she would die rather than let Roddy Shaw guess as much.

Adam had signed his contract a week earlier and Carly sat with the document on her desk, staring at the strong, flowing signature as though it might tell her something about him.

Nothing had changed between them, of course; her decision would be the same if he repeated his proposal now. Carly loved her job; she did not want to give it up, but she loved Adam, too, and she did not want to lose him, either. She spent hours puzzling over the problem, looking for some way out. If she went back to England and got a job in London she would be close to him—but you couldn't marry a man who lived in Yorkshire and then commute to an office in London. Adam was right in one sense: If she married him, she would have to forget her job. She had to choose between her career and Adam, but Carly wanted both of them.

One evening she was miserable enough to attract Louise's attention. "What's wrong with you these days?" Louise asked her. "Do you know how rarely you smile lately? You used to wear a smile so often I found it quite infuriating, but now you look like someone waiting to be taken out and shot."

"Do I? Sorry," Carly said, forcing a smile.

It didn't seem to convince Louise. "Come on, can't you tell me? We've known each other long enough."

Carly hesitated, then found herself pouring out the whole story. Louise listened, watching her face.

Looking incredulous, Louise suddenly interrupted, "He actually proposed?"

Carly nodded.

"After only knowing you for two days?" Louise stared at her as though she had never seen her before.

"Amazing, isn't it?"

"That doesn't cover the situation," Louise said. "I've

heard of fast workers but that is ridiculous. Was he quite sane, do you think?"

Carly smiled reluctantly. "Adam always seemed ultrasane to me, Louise."

"What did you say to him?" Louise asked curiously. "I gather you refused or you wouldn't still be around."

Carly looked down, sighing. "How could I marry a man I'd only known for such a short time and go off to live at the back of beyond, give up my job, forget about a career. . . ." She broke off, sighing again and Louise said drily, "I see."

Carly looked up. "What do you see?"

"You regret it," Louise said. "Don't you?"

"I don't know." Carly moved restlessly. "It was such a hard choice to make."

"You wanted to have your cake and eat it, too," said Louise.

Carly laughed. "I suppose I did."

"You certainly did, I'd say. You want your career and Adam, too, right?"

"Right," Carly said with a wry little smile.

Louise whistled under her breath, almost soundlessly, her face thoughtful. "Do you want some advice or should I keep my mouth shut?"

"I'd be glad of some advice," Carly said.

"Go after him," Louise told her bluntly.

"I can't do that!"

"Why not? In your place, I'd be running. Men like that don't grow on trees, you know."

"He wanted me to give up everything and follow behind him like some lady in the Old Testament," Carly said impatiently. "Ruth, wasn't it? Where thou goest I shall go—that stuff. Do you believe in that in this day and age?"

"When it is a man like Adam Blake talking—yes," Louise said, grinning.

"He would never have dreamed of giving up *his* way of life for me," Carly pointed out.

Louise eyed her as though she had taken leave of her senses. "Of course he wouldn't—they never do. Okay, Carly, it isn't exactly a fifty-fifty arrangement, but aren't you cutting off your nose to spite your face? You want him, so go after him and put up with the fact that he's something of a male chauvinist."

"What about my job?"

"Jobs aren't hard to find—men who love you enough to want to marry you are," Louise said wryly. "I wish I'd been in your shoes. I'd have been saying yes, please, before he had finished asking the question."

Carly met her eyes, frowning. "You would?"

"What do you think? Carly, he asked you to share his life. Weren't you the one who said a while back that she sometimes felt lonely?"

Carly nodded slowly. She had felt more alone than ever since Adam had walked out that night. The emptiness of the days and nights alone stretched out in front of her like a desert and she had no zest for her work these days.

"You're crying for the moon if you want to have everything your own way. If a choice was easy it wouldn't be a choice at all. It would be obvious, as simple as pie. What you have to do is ask yourself which you want most—a career or the man you love." Louise hesitated, grimacing. "I'm taking it for granted that you do love him." Her tone held a question, and Carly gave her a little smile.

"Yes."

"Then you need your head examined if you let him go without trying to get him back."

"You'd write to him?" Carly asked, and Louise gave a shrug.

"I'd go after him to Yorkshire. You can't say on paper what you can say face to face."

"I don't know," Carly murmured. "It's such a huge step to take. How do I know it would work out between us?"

"Even if you had known him for a year you couldn't be sure about that. I've known married couples who split up after ten years together. Marriage is a lottery however long you take to make up your mind before you take the plunge."

Carly nodded. That was true. "I'll have to think about it," she said, though. She still did not feel she could burn her bridges.

"You want to have children, don't you?" Louise asked, and Carly opened her eyes wide.

Louise saw her face and laughed shortly. "Hadn't that occurred to you?"

"No," Carly said. "No." How could that aspect of it have escaped her? She thought of a child with Adam's dark hair and gray eyes, her heart wincing with a peculiar mixture of pain and pleasure.

Louise hesitated, then said, "Don't let your pride stand in your way, Carly. You'll regret it later if you do."

A week later, Roddy Shaw got in touch with Carly at the office to ask how the production of Adam's book was going and if she had a definite publication date yet. Casually, Carly said, "There are one or two points I'd like to discuss with Adam, actually, before I send the manuscript off to the printer. The text has been copy-edited now, but there were a few queries."

"I'll pass them on to him if you give them to me now," Roddy said, and she hesitated.

"I ought to talk to him, myself." She was sure Roddy had no idea that Adam had ever proposed to her, but she felt uncomfortable as she insisted.

"He's away at the moment," Roddy returned.

"Away?" Carly was taken aback. "Really? I thought he never left his farm."

"He doesn't leave it very often," Roddy agreed. "This is a special occasion. An old friend of his is getting married and Adam has gone to Greece for the wedding."

"Greece?" repeated Carly. She pretended to laugh. "That's a long way to go for a wedding."

"As I said, this is an old friend—someone Adam knew when he was on his travels, I suppose. I don't know the lady."

"It's a lady?" Carly asked, a little chill feathering her skin. Stupid to be taken aback—why shouldn't Adam have friends of the opposite sex? And this particular friend was getting married, after all, and had invited Adam to the wedding . . . He couldn't be involved with her or his presence would be out of the question.

"Yes," Roddy said with an underlying note of curiosity, as though her unhidden interest in Adam had aroused questions in his mind. "I'll talk to Adam when he gets back."

"When will that be?" Carly pressed.

"As he's going so far he's taking a short holiday at the same time," Roddy told her. "He'll be staying in Crete for a week and he's due back on the twenty-eighth."

"Okay," Carly said calmly. "Lucky Adam—Crete must be fascinating, but I suppose it's quite hot at this time of year."

"Adam isn't the type to spend his holidays on the beach. If I know him he'll go in for the tourist trips around Knossos. He's staying a short drive from there, anyway. Adam takes everything seriously, even his holidays."

Carly hung up and sat staring at the telephone. She was due a holiday; why shouldn't she take it in Crete?

The idea sent excitement drumming through her veins and she got up and walked restlessly around the office. If she turned up in Crete while Adam was there he would know she had come deliberately. Don't be so obvious, she told herself, what is he bound to think? She halted and smoothed back her blonde hair, her blue eyes overbright.

Did she care? What did it matter if Adam knew the minute he saw her that she had followed him there? She thought of her pride as some heavy weight trailing after her, hampering her, and angrily kicked it away.

Going back to the desk she called a travel agency and was able to book a flight to Crete and a week at a hotel near Knossos. It was the best hotel available, so with any luck she could find herself staying at the same hotel as Adam.

Curt was indignant when she told him. "You can't take a week off at a moment's notice!"

"I'm due for a holiday," she pointed out. "And I need one now. I'm very tired, Curt. If I don't have some time off I'll grind to a halt."

He stared at her gloomily. "Is this why you've been going around like a duck in a thunderstorm for weeks?

I thought you were having a bad attack of the love bug."

She laughed. "You make it sound so romantic."

"There's nothing romantic about sex," Curt informed her. "Women just have the wrong attitude. When a man feels frustrated he does something about it; a woman just sits about moping."

Carly eyed him with disfavor. "You want us to imitate men, is that it? You really think we should rush out and tackle the first attractive man we see and jump into bed with him?"

"Why not?" Curt asked. "You're always talking about equal opportunities for women, but that's one opportunity you never seem to take."

"It's been bred into us that a girl waits to be asked," Carly retorted. "A system dreamed up by men, I'd like to point out."

"So change the system," Curt said cheerfully. He gave her a sly look, amusement sparkling in his eyes. "Or can it be that you secretly prefer the system just the way it is? All this talk about feminism is misleading, in my opinion. It begs the question about in-built instincts, doesn't it? A woman's instinct is to let the man do all the chasing; very few women go out and do any chasing on their own account."

"If we did you would turn round and say we were unwomanly," Carly mocked him.

"And you would be," Curt came back. "Before you can start chasing men you have to grow another skin, Carly. Women are born with one fewer than men."

She laughed. "I can't argue with that; I've always thought men were pretty thick-skinned."

"And that's another female characteristic," Curt told her. "Women always have to have the last word."

She looked at him demurely before going out of his office. "A gentleman always let's us have it, too."

Curt said something very rude as she closed the door. She wondered what he would say if he knew that she was in fact taking a leaf out of his book and doing some chasing on her own account? Although he had pretended to encourage the idea she suspected that Curt would be shocked. He liked sex the way it was arranged at the moment. He loathed what he called "pushy ladies." Curt had that much in common with Adam; he was a good old-fashioned male chauvinist. Sylvia Dorsden was very clever in the smooth way she managed her husband; Curt didn't even have a clue that he was being managed. He thought he did all the managing in his home, but Carly had visited him there and she had seen how Sylvia twisted him round her little finger. Curt was the type of man who had a simple view of the world and his wife made sure he never suspected that the decision-making was not all his province.

She decided not to tell Louise why she was going to Crete. Her holiday came as something of a surprise, but Louise merely told her to have a good time and forget about work for a while.

"You need a break," she said. "Come to that, so do I. But why go all that way? Why not a week on the beach in Florida?"

"I'm dying to visit Greece," Carly lied and hoped with fingers crossed that Roddy would not be in touch with Louise while she was away. She did not imagine he would; she gathered that Louise had heard nothing from him since she ended their brief relationship.

She was very nervous as she drove from the airport on Crete to the hotel, sitting back nervously as the battered taxi skidded and roared along the dusty roads. The driver was a young man with curly black hair and a broad grin who seemed to find it amusing that Carly should gasp with horror at his speed and the way he cut in on other vehicles. "Don't worry, miss," he flung over his shoulder. "I know what I'm doing." He had, to her surprise, a strong American accent, and his use of English was fluent.

"Your English is very good," she told him, and he looked pleased, throwing her another smile, the casual way he looked away from the road sending her heart back into her mouth.

"I spent a year in Chicago," he told her. "Nice place, Chicago."

"Why did you come back to Crete?" Carly asked, closing her eyes as he went through a set of red traffic lights.

"My mother," he said, shrugging violently. "You know what mothers are, miss."

"Yes, I know what mothers are," Carly said, smiling. She had a mother of her own who liked to keep track of what she was doing, and who wrote all the time to say how much she missed her and wanted to have her back home. Mrs. Newton had urged Carly to spread her wings and fly to the States, but she would have been very happy to see her daughter come flying home. Carly came from a casual, cheerful family. Her parents understood her desire to get on in her career, and they were far from being possessive, but it was reassuring to know that they would be glad to see her and were always happy to hear from her.

"You an American girl, miss?" asked the driver, again swiveling his head to look at her, bringing the angry blare of a horn from another car as he brushed past it.

"English," Carly said, gulping. "Don't you ever look at the road when you drive?"

"Not when there is a girl as pretty as you to look at," he said, grinning.

"How many accidents do you have?" asked Carly, and he laughed.

"Oh, me, I am a wonderful driver." She wasn't sure she believed him, but he got her to the hotel safely and insisted on giving her his telephone number in case she wanted a taxi in the future.

She checked into the hotel, looking around her nervously as she followed the receptionist to the elevator, but there was no sign of Adam. The young woman showed her to a room on the first floor overlooking a dusty garden full of pale statuary. A swimming pool was the central point of attention for the other guests. Carly glanced down from the window and saw half a dozen people in the blue, blue water, while a handful of others lounged beside the pool, sipping drinks under striped beach umbrellas.

Casually, she murmured to the receptionist, "A friend of mine is staying here, I believe—a Mr. Blake, from England?"

The girl turned blank dark eyes on her. "Blake?" she repeated without a hint of recognition. "I do not know the name. The porter will bring up your luggage in five minutes, Miss Newton. I hope you enjoy your stay with us." She moved to the door, a thin, sallow girl with flat slippers on her feet that made no sound as she walked out of the room. Perhaps Adam wasn't staying at this hotel, after all? Roddy had only told her that it was a hotel a short drive from Knossos, and this was the best hotel in a wide circle of the old city, so Carly had concluded that she would find Adam here. Had she come all this way for nothing?

The hotel lay in a steep valley lined with hills cloaked in pine forests. The permanent music of cicadas filled the air, and the grass, bleached by the hot sun to the color of ripe corn, made a dry whispering sound as it bent in the breeze. Under the shadows of the pines the earth was bare and sterile, but between them crept a tangling mass of thyme and rosemary and low shrubs whose spicy scent pervaded the hillsides, mingling with the smell of the pines. Little paths wound upwards, dry and dusty, baked hard by the habitual sun, and here and there were clumps of olive trees and laurels.

Heat shimmered in the distance, turning the horizon into a burning glass. Carly felt tired and sticky after her long journey. Her head had begun to ache and perspiration trickled down the back of her neck, making the thin material of her dress cling damply to her skin.

The porter struggled in with her luggage, accepted his tip with a smile and left. Carly unpacked before her clothes could crease and then decided to go down to the pool for a swim. The water looked so inviting.

Changing into a tiny black bikini, she eyed herself ruefully in the mirror as she fastened the clip of the brief top. She was going to look pale to all the suntanned guests lounging around the pool; her skin had a city pallor that would take days to disappear. Shrugging, she turned to pick up a beach towel and a cotton robe and left the room.

Her arrival went unnoticed for a moment. Those guests who were not in the water were lying with closed eyes, basking like lizards, their heads partly shaded by the striped umbrellas. Their skin glistened with suntan oil, and Carly bit back a smile as she thought that they looked like steaks waiting to be barbecued.

A small boy was bouncing up and down on a short diving platform. "Mommy, Mommy, watch me!" he yelled.

A sunbathing young woman lifted a languid hand. "I see you, darling," she murmured without looking.

Carly dropped her cotton robe and towel on one of the spare loungers and walked towards the side of the pool. The sun glinted down on the water, dazzling her.

The little boy was looking as if he might burst into tears. His round face took on a sullen defiance. Leaping into the water he began to swim under the surface while Carly watched him casually, half-smiling.

He stayed under for so long that her smile vanished and a frown took its place.

She dived into the pool and swam toward where she could see his body glimmering through the sunlit water. Plunging down toward him, Carly caught him round the waist and started to haul him up to the surface. He struggled weakly. As they burst out of the water he was spluttering and coughing, water pouring from his nostrils. Carly towed him back to the side and helped him onto the surrounding tiles. He lay on his face, heaving as he gasped for air, and his mother came running to join them, her face horrified.

"What happened? Johnny, are you okay? Did he hurt himself?" She went on her knees beside him, stroking his wet hair and bending down to look at his face.

"I was okay, Mom," Johnny panted, throwing Carly an accusing look. "She interfered; why didn't she leave me alone? I was only swimming under the water; I was doing fine."

His mother looked at him and then at Carly, who smiled, spreading her hands.

"He stayed down there so long I thought he might have hit his head."

"I didn't. I was fine; why don't you mind your own business?" the boy growled, his lower lip sticking out.

"I'm sorry," Carly said. She knew the child had been in difficulty. He had only been half-conscious as she towed him to the side. But if he didn't want to admit that, she wasn't going to make him do so.

His mother gave her a faintly worried glance. "It was very kind of you, thank you, but Johnny's been swimming since he was tiny; he swims like a fish."

"I can swim better than I can walk," the boy boasted.

"I'm sure you can," Carly soothed. "Sorry—but it's best not to hold your breath under water for too long in case you run into trouble." She got up and walked away, diving back into the water. A moment later she saw mother and child leaving the poolside, an air of gloom about them. Flicking back a strand of wet blonde hair, Carly turned onto her back to do a back crawl down the pool, cannoning into someone as she shot away.

"Sorry," she apologized automatically.

The young man grinned at her. "Not your day, is it?"

She flushed slightly. "It doesn't seem to be," she agreed.

He winked. "The kid was in trouble, wasn't he? I didn't spot it until you brought him up out of the water, but he was coughing up half the pool as he came. You probably saved his life. By the time any of us noticed he could have drowned."

"I think he was trying to impress his mother," Carly murmured, treading water as she listened.

"He thinks the sun shines out of her," the young man agreed. "But she doesn't pay him enough attention; he spends most of the day in the pool on his own."

"She's very pretty," Carly said, having noticed that much about the other woman.

"Yes," he agreed slowly, his glance traveling over Carly's blonde hair and oval face, something in his amused inspection making her flush a little and laugh. "I didn't say a word," he exclaimed, meeting her eyes again. "You're English, aren't you? So am I, in case you hadn't noticed the accent."

"I had; I'm very quick that way." Carly laughed, rather liking him. He wasn't exactly good-looking, but he had a direct, frank way of looking at you that made him easy to like.

"James Mortimer," he introduced himself. "Are we going to continue this conversation in the pool or shall we go and have a drink while we talk?"

"I'd like a swim before I have a drink," Carly said, turning onto her back again in readiness. She enjoyed swimming with the sun pouring down on her face.

"You didn't tell me your name," James said.

"Carly Newton."

"What would you like to drink, Carly Newton? I'll order while you have your swim."

"Something long and cool and refreshing, please."

"Right," he said, splashing to the side. Carly swam to one end of the pool and turned back again, catching sight of James toweling himself lightly beside the little

127

group of sunbathers. She did another couple of laps before climbing out. James was just moving away and gave her a little wave. "Be back with the drinks in a minute!"

Carly padded over to the lounger on which she had left her towel. She dried herself, rubbed in some oil delicately and then stretched out.

When James returned Carly accepted the glass he offered and sipped tentatively at the drink. James watched her, his hands on his lean hips. He was tall and thin and very brown. With his brown hair and eyes, he looked like a study in monochrome.

"Like it?" he asked.

"Delicious," Carly admitted.

He apparently took that as an invitation, because he suddenly flung himself down on the lounger next to her and turned onto his side to smile at her.

"Where do you live?"

"New York," she said, and took another long drink of citrus juice. It was ice cold and very refreshing.

"New York? I've never been there. You work in the States, I suppose? What do you do?"

"I'm in publishing," she said and saw him look surprised and curious.

"Really? What sort of publishing?"

Carly always found that when men heard what sort of job she had their reaction was to be fascinated, ask a lot of questions and then vanish swiftly. Her job alarmed them; it made her sound too formidable and scared them off.

She started to talk about her job deliberately; that should convince James Mortimer he was wasting his time. Instinct told her he was exactly the type of man to retreat in the face of what she imagined to be her high expectations. James stared at her as she talked, his expression altering.

"You must be very important," he said, and Carly met his eyes and saw that he was laughing at her. "Do I have to pay to talk to you?"

Carly burst out laughing. He thought she was trying to impress him! She had found him very pleasant, but suddenly she really liked him. How could you fail to like someone with such a strong sense of humor?

"What do you do?" she asked him.

"I'm an unemployed actor," he said.

Carly wasn't sure he wasn't joking. She stared at him intently, trying to work it out. His eyes were bright and dancing, his smile teasing.

"Are you really?"

"Really," James said. "I'm between jobs so here I am." He paused, grinning. "I was invited over here for my brother's wedding; he wanted me to be best man badly enough to pay my fare."

She felt a tremor of surprise run through her. "Wedding?"

James caught the look on her face and gave her a curious glance. "Yes, does that make you go weak at the knees? Why is it that the word wedding has that effect on women? My mother's a perfectly normal woman most of the time, but when Bob told her he was getting married she burst into tears. Bob was horrified; he thought she was against the idea until she told him she was so happy she had to cry."

Carly laughed. "Your mother sounds like a lovely lady."

"I like her myself," James said smugly. He cocked an eye at her. "I take after her; have you noticed that yet? Noticed how lovely I am, I mean."

"I've noticed you're an idiot," Carly told him sternly.

"Is that kind?" James became mournful.

"When is the wedding?" Carly asked casually. Could it possibly be the same one that had brought Adam here?

"It was yesterday," James told her. "The bride wore white, my poor brother wore a dark suit, and I did not lose the ring although I was afraid I might, but that was only because Bob kept threatening to kill me if I did and he made me nervous."

Carly smiled. "Was it a big wedding?"

"Enormous; the bride is a local girl and has five thousand relatives living in Greece—they all seemed to come to the wedding. That was why Bob was so eager to have as many of his own friends and relatives around as he could talk into coming over here. Poor old Bob felt very outnumbered."

Carly felt her skin chilling with excitement and nerves, but she hid it from James as well as she could. "Were the bridesmaids pretty?"

"I didn't notice," James said, grinning at her.

"I suspect you're a liar."

"Who me?" he said in mock affront.

Carly got up and walked to the edge of the pool. She felt James watching her as she poised to dive, her slender body pale by comparison to his bronzed one, the black bikini more or less dry now after she had been lying in this sunshine for half an hour. As she dived she heard James say, "Oh, hallo, Adam, I didn't see you there."

Carly went down, down, down into the water as if she was drowning, her mind so shaken that she almost crashed into the tiled floor of the pool and only just pulled up in time. She broke the surface, her blonde hair plastered to her head, and shot a look across the pool.

James was still lying on the lounger, but there was nobody with him, he was quite alone. Seeing her staring toward him, he raised an arm in a lazy movement, waving. Carly automatically waved back. Had she imagined hearing him say Adam's name?

You're going out of your mind, Carly Newton, she told herself as she turned onto her back and swam several lengths of the pool at crawling speed, her eyes fixed on the burning blue of the sky.

When she calmed down, she clambered out of the pool and joined James again, picking up her towel and starting to dry herself while he watched admiringly.

"Have dinner with me?" he asked suddenly.

Carly looked up, startled. "Oh, thank you, but . . ."

"Why eat alone when you can have company?" he interrupted, not allowing her to finish her attempt at a polite excuse.

She looked at him in rueful amusement. He was persistent but friendly, and it was as hard to brush him off as it would be to shoo away an appealing puppy that was following you.

Her hesitant expression spoke for her. James grinned. "Go on, say yes; it can't hurt you."

She laughed, relaxing. "Thank you, I'd love to have dinner with you." He was right; why shouldn't she have company over dinner? She was here alone and if she had guessed wrongly and Adam wasn't staying at this hotel she would be on her own at dinner, anyway.

"Seven-thirty in the bar?" James suggested.

"I'll see you then," she promised, collecting her robe and tying the belt loosely around her slim waist.

She had to wait for a moment or two before the

elevator arrived, and several other people joined her. She walked into it when it did come and stood at the back behind several latecomers. Between their heads she glanced casually into the hotel foyer and suddenly saw Adam. Her heart turned a somersault, her eyes focusing on him with intent excitement for a second, until she realized he wasn't alone.

He was talking, smiling down at a girl in brief blue shorts and a low-cut white cotton tee-shirt. Carly felt a sliver of ice inside her at the intimate way they were talking, especially when she saw the other girl casually lean her shoulder against Adam's, and a moment later saw Adam put his arm round the girl's waist to guide her past some guests who were in their path.

The elevator doors closed and Carly stood rigidly, her body aching with jealousy and pain. In delayed replay she saw it again, Adam and the girl in blue shorts, an indefinable warmth in the way they looked at each other. They were not chance-met strangers, you could see that at once. They knew each other very well.

Carly muttered, "Excuse me, please," as she pushed her way out of the lift at her own floor. Head up, struggling to look calm and at ease, she walked across the corridor and let herself into her room. Only when the door was shut did she stop pretending. She leaned on the door, facing the situation she had got herself into: Adam was obviously here with someone else. He was not alone at the hotel, and she had been a fool to follow him here.

I can't bear it, Carly thought, putting her hands over her face. She did not know which pain was the worst: the fact that Adam was here with another woman or the fact that she had made such a fool of herself by coming here in pursuit of him.

I can't stay, she thought. I'll have to find another hotel, take a plane to another island, get out of here before he sees me. Rushing over to the wardrobe she began to get out the clothes she had unpacked and hung up before she went down to the pool. She flung them on the bed and got down her suitcase, but as she tremblingly began to pack she paused, her face undecided, confused.

Suppose he saw her checking out? He would realize she had both come here and was leaving hurriedly on his account.

She walked to the window and back again, pacing the floor like a caged animal, biting her lip. What was she to do?

Her mind kept coming up with decisions and discarding them, but as she calmed down and thought more, feeling less, she realized she had to face it out, make Adam think it was sheer coincidence that she was here in Crete. She mentally rehearsed their meeting; she would be very calm and polite, smile, say a few surprised words and then walk away and not look back. If Adam suspected something he would not be sure he was right if she seemed coolly offhand. She was going to have to act as she had never acted in her life.

Chapter Six

Carly took extra care in dressing for dinner that evening; she meant to go down like a ship with all flags flying. Adam was not going to see her stricken with pain and humiliation; he was going to see her smiling and relaxed and sure of herself. Every female instinct she possessed came to the fore. She brushed her hair until it shone, hanging around her oval face in a smooth golden bell. She brushed soft glittering blue onto her lids, put on mascara with a hand that was perfectly steady, outlined her lips in warm gleaming pink. Her dress was a straight black shift, simple, but beautifully cut and styled, the material hanging perfectly and making her look slender and cool and sophisticated.

Surveying her reflection in the mirror, Carly dabbed perfume behind her ears, at her wrist, in the hollow between her breasts. A tantalizing fragrance drifted around her as she moved to the door.

When you have put yourself into a difficult position the only thing you can do is smile defiance in the face of the enemy, she told herself, and something hardened inside her. Adam? The enemy? That hurt, but Carly pushed her unhappiness aside. All that mattered tonight was that she should go through with this embarrassing encounter without seeming to be a fool.

James was waiting for her in the bar. She paused in the doorway, glancing around the softly lit room, and he waved to her. There was nobody with him and Carly walked across to join him, her body swaying on her very high heels.

James gave a low whistle of admiration. "You look fantastic, a real knockout."

She smiled. "Thank you; you look very nice, too." He did, she thought, his thin body shown to advantage in a pale, lightweight suit something between blue and gray. The shade emphasized his tan. She sat down beside him and he beckoned to the smiling Greek waiter.

"What will you have to drink?"

She asked for another of the citrus drinks she had had earlier, and the waiter nodded, going back to the bar.

James leaned back. "By the way," he began and stopped dead as his eyes moved to the doorway. Carly followed his stare and felt her body jerk as if it had touched a live wire. Afterward she hoped her face had not betrayed that instant of shock. It seemed a lifetime before she was able to switch on a polite, surprised smile, the smile she had rehearsed in front of her mirror until she thought she had it perfect. Now it felt stiff and unreal, stretching her mouth until it ached.

"I was going to tell you," James said rapidly at her ear. "A couple of friends are joining us; I hope that isn't going to ruin your evening." He grinned at her in self-mockery. "I know you would rather be alone with me, but fate is against us."

Carly laughed lightly. "How tragic; how shall I ever bear it?"

Under her laughter she was aghast. Adam and that girl were going to join them? How was she going to get through an evening at the same table with them? She had thought she would only have to put on her act for a few minutes, but now it seemed the ordeal was going to be prolonged beyond endurance.

Adam was walking toward them. Carly looked away from James, still wearing her stiff painted smile, and let her eyes fleetingly touch Adam's face.

"Good heavens," she said aloud in tones of unconvincing amazement.

James looked at her, raising one eyebrow.

"It can't be," Carly said, wishing she had taken acting lessons while she was at school. She knew she must be putting on a truly abysmal performance and convincing nobody.

Adam stood in front of her, looking down at her, his face hard and calm, his gray eyes moving over her with one flick of his thick dark lashes.

"Hallo, Carly," he said in that deep voice.

James had his mouth open. "I don't believe it! You two know each other?"

"Slightly," Carly said.

"Yes," Adam said.

Their voices chimed at the same instant and there was a brief beat of time when they looked at each other, the other two excluded from that tense, hostile exchange of glances.

Looking away, her body throbbing with pulses born more of pain than excitement, Carly smiled at James. "I'm editing Adam's book; he's one of our writers."

"I'd no idea you had written a book, Adam," James said incredulously. "How mind-boggling—what is it? A thriller?"

"An adventure story," Adam said.

"I can't wait to read it. And Carly is your editor? Isn't that amazing?" There was the slightest trace of suspicion in his eyes as he glanced at her, and Carly felt herself stiffen.

"We've only met a few times," she said quickly. "Adam was in New York a few months ago."

The girl standing beside Adam was staring at her oddly, her eyes narrowed in scrutiny. No doubt she was jealous, Carly thought. The way the other girl had her hand casually linked around Adam's arm hinted at possessive awareness. Carly knew she was going to dislike the other girl. Already she didn't like the way she was clutching Adam's arm. She stared back, the little hairs on the back of her nape bristling with dislike.

Tonight the girl was in a very pretty rose-pink dress, the skirt full, the waist tightly held by a wide sash. She looked young and gay, and she made Carly feel dull and depressed. Her dark hair was softly curled around her face and her eyes were beautifully shaped, wide and expressive.

I hate her, Carly thought, her teeth tight. She isn't as young as she looks on first sight; she just dresses young. There was maturity and experience in the carefully made-up face. Carly was glad to see faint lines running from the eyes and mouth, a betraying confidence in the body movements.

"If you know Adam, I guess you know Jenny," James said.

"No," the other girl said. "We've never met, although I've heard of Carly." She held out her hand with a polite but unfriendly smile. "Hallo."

Carly took the hand, shook it without pressure. "Hallo."

Their smiles were false, artificial, but James seemed unaware of the fact.

Adam had talked about her? Carly couldn't believe it. What had he said to this other girl? How dare he talk about her to another woman? She looked at him with resentment as he took a chair next to her, and she found him staring at her, his face all angles and tight lines, no sign of the charm she had been shown in New York visible in those strong features now.

The waiter darted up and Adam and Jenny ordered drinks. Carly had barely touched hers, but James asked for another glass of whiskey and cola.

"How can you drink that?" Adam demanded. "God knows what it's doing to your insides."

"I like it," James retorted.

Jenny made a face at him, a real smile in her eyes now. "What you like isn't necessarily good for you."

"Yes, Nanny," James mocked, and Jenny laughed.

"When are you going back home?"

"Trying to get rid of me?"

"Any sign of a job yet?" Jenny asked without answering the teasing remark.

"If there was, I wouldn't be sitting here twiddling my thumbs. I'd be on the first plane home."

Jenny put her hand on top of his, smiling reassurance, her face warm. "Poor James, why did you choose such a tough profession?"

"I didn't choose it—it chose me," James said.

Carly looked sideways through her lowered lashes and found Adam watching her. Her heart missed a beat and she was angry with herself for caring whether he looked at her or not.

Under cover of the light banter going on between James and Jenny, he leaned toward her and said very quietly, "What are you doing here?"

The moment had come and she summoned up all her

reserves of courage, turning to look at him, her lashes lifting and her blue eyes open wide in calm unconcern. "I'm taking a long overdue holiday."

"At the same hotel as me?" Adam asked that between his teeth, his hard mouth curling back in sardonic disbelief.

"How could I know you were here?" Even to herself her casual tone seemed to carry conviction. Adam's gray eyes probed her face, his brows meeting in a straight black line.

"Sheer coincidence?" he asked with that same incredulity, however, and Carly shrugged.

"Sorry; bad timing, isn't it?"

His frown deepened. "You sound very flip."

Carly laughed, a silvery little sound that made her wince inside. You sound like a silly idiot, she told herself, but it was better than sounding like a woman who has made a monumental fool of herself by chasing after a man who has forgotten she exists.

"Do I? Well, I *am* on holiday, I suppose."

"You didn't know I was here?" Adam pressed.

"When I saw you walk into this bar just now I was stunned," Carly said with the conviction of one who is actually telling the truth. She *had* been stunned, every nerve end rippling with panic at the sight of him, and the way she said it seemed to convince him at last. He leaned back in his chair and lifted his glass to his lips, swallowing the contents at a speed that astonished her.

"Hey," James said, catching sight of this, "you really needed that, didn't you? Have another one."

Adam put down his empty glass with a little crash. "No, thanks. I'm hungry. Shall we go and eat?"

Carly stumbled to her feet, her own drink still half-drunk. Jenny and Adam walked away together and

James took Carly's hand, swinging it between them lightly.

"Maybe this wasn't such a good idea after all," he said with faint concern. "Do I get the impression you and Adam don't hit it off?"

"Do you?" Carly hedged, walking quickly after the other two.

James came with her, his long legs keeping pace easily. "Would you rather we made an excuse and left? We could always eat somewhere else this evening."

"No, of course not," Carly said. "Your imagination works overtime, James; you should watch that."

James looked down in surprise at the crispness of her voice. "For such a sweet little girl you can be very tough-talking, can't you?" he asked. "But then, I suppose I should have expected that. You wouldn't be capable of doing that high-powered job of yours if you were as sweet and innocent as you look."

Carly wasn't sure she liked that, but she didn't bother to argue. The little exchange with Adam had stiffened her backbone enough to take her through this dinner, and she was intent on staying in a fighting mood.

They had a table by the window looking out over the garden. The sun was very low on the horizon, coloring the sky with flashes of crimson and gold that gave dramatic effect to the deep, smoldering blue of approaching night. As Carly glanced toward that unbelievable sunset the coppery ball of the sun vanished, swallowed in abrupt darkness, and she drew a surprised breath.

Adam was watching her averted profile. She forgot momentarily that she hated him and turned with eager, parted lips to say, "Did you see that? Wasn't it marvelous?"

Adam's eyes were steady and cold. "Yes," he said, and a trickle of ice slowly ran down her back at his voice.

She drew back, her face altering, and looked away, meeting Jenny's eyes across the table. The other girl was frowning, too, and her eyes were remote. Oh, this is going to be a wonderful evening, Carly thought grimly. I'm going to have the time of my life, I can see that.

The meal was one of those uneasy social occasions when everyone present is aware of discomfort but keeps smiling and hoping that the evening will end as soon as possible. On the surface they were all ultra-polite, talking about Crete, the weather, the wedding at which they had been present, publishing and books, James's hopes for the future. They kept falling into unhappy silences, until one of them managed to dredge up some other topic that seemed safe enough to avoid argument. Carly listened, speaking only when forced to, one finger pushing the stem of her wine glass as she bent her head in a pretense of being absorbed by her meal. The fact that she barely touched a mouthful of the food was betraying, however. She felt Adam look at her plate, and she flushed slightly.

"Don't you like Greek food?" he asked.

"Very much," she stammered. "I'm just not hungry —it's so hot. Is it always this hot here?"

"They're having a heat wave. Last night was so warm I didn't sleep at all, so I went down and swam for an hour until the dawn came and it was cool enough to go back to bed." James laughed as he told them this, his brown eyes very bright. "And do you know, the water in the pool was warm, too."

"I took a cold shower several times in the night," Jenny said.

"You should take lukewarm showers," Adam said. "Cold ones wake you up and make the blood circulate even faster, so they're self-defeating in the end."

Carly stared at her salad of octopus and tiny pink shrimps bedded down on limp lettuce with huge Greek tomatoes arranged around the plate. She gingerly put a piece of octopus in her mouth. It tasted like slightly chewy chicken with a salt flavor, not unpleasant, but not a taste she could rave about.

"How is it?" James asked. He had had a dish of lamb flavored with spikes of rosemary, and his appetite was better than hers, it seemed, since he had finished his meal.

"Strange," Carly said, smiling at him. "I thought I ought to try something very Greek while I was here."

"If you don't eat it, you'll hurt the waiter's feelings," James warned. "He's beginning to look at you accusingly already."

Carly sighed, forcing herself to eat a little more. Adam refilled her glass, and she watched the brown, sinewy hand moving, her heart beating painfully. She was bitterly aware of him, conscious of the width of his shoulders in the white linen jacket he was wearing, the muscularity of his lean body as it moved beside her, his thigh inches away from her own and that close body warmth flowing between them, although she took great care never to let her knee brush against his despite his close proximity.

She ate as much as she could, and the waiter removed her plate, eyeing her sadly.

"Go and stand in the corner," James teased. "You're a naughty girl."

"It was really very nice," she faltered, flushing.

A huge bowl of fruit was placed in the center of the table and they all took what they wanted from it. Carly chose a peach, the pink and gold skin like velvet to her fingers, velvet with a brushing softness on her skin, a faint roughness like the down on a child's cheek. She peeled it with care, listening as the others talked. The neat ribbons of skin slid to her plate while she watched, glad of having something to do to keep her mind occupied as well as her hands.

"Coffee?" Adam asked her a moment or two later, and she started, her eyes flying to him, a transient sadness in them.

"Yes, thank you." Her voice was soft and husky, and Adam looked into her eyes and frowned again, but differently, this time. What was he thinking? Carly wondered, but she looked away and didn't let herself think about that too closely. If she could get through this one evening she could avoid him for the rest of her week there. Why had she come? Why had she been such a fool?

The sound of his voice was so bitterly familiar to her. She heard the intonation of it without listening to the words. She would know the sound of Adam's voice anywhere; it beat in her blood and was the one voice in the world she had yearned to hear for weeks, but now that she heard it she merely ached with pain. Why was life so surprising, so bewildering and unexpected? Things never happened as you wanted them to, as you dreamed they would. Dreams lay apart from real life. You were crazy if you let yourself follow a dream. All you did was run into the stone wall of life and hurt yourself.

James was teasing Jenny. Carly listened without

hearing, and then suddenly her whole mind jerked awake.

What had James said? Had she misheard him?

"My mother-in-law is looking after them," Jenny said. "She's very good with them; in fact, she spoils them, especially Andrew. He's her pet and he knows it. Children always know things like that, don't they? You can't hide a thing from them."

Carly looked at her intently, her face drained of color. Jenny was looking wry, her mouth twisting.

"It's good for kids to be spoiled for a little while," James decided happily.

"My mother-in-law is an expert on spoiling little boys," Jenny told him. "She spoiled my husband from the day he was born." She sounded as though that made her angry, and into Carly's mind came a picture of Roddy Shaw. What had Adam said about his sister, Roddy's wife? What had he called her? Holding her breath and trembling a little, she looked at Adam. He was watching the other woman with a sardonic expression on his face.

Was Jenny his sister? Carly looked back at her, searching her face now for signs of some likeness between her and Adam. The same coloring, and surely there was a similarity in their bone structure. It was an indefinable resemblance—she would have missed it entirely if she had not been looking for it—and maybe she was reading far more into a mere similarity of coloring than she was wise to do, but Carly was eager to believe her own eyes. If she had been capable of it, she would have laughed at herself. You can convince yourself of anything if you really try.

James was laughing. "Oh, Roddy's okay," he said, and Carly closed her eyes, almost sick with relief.

Jenny smiled, but there was a hint of determination about her, a feeling of gritted teeth, as though she was defiant. Roddy Shaw was not a man any woman would feel easy about; Jenny could not be blind to his wandering eye, and no doubt she had had to watch him ever since they were married. Carly did not envy her. All the same, Jenny had strength in that very feminine face, a possessive, wary look that suggested that Roddy was unlikely to get away with much.

"He's fun," James added. "I like Roddy." He was being rather too insistent about it. Carly got the feeling he did not mean it.

Jenny looked at him and smiled again, her face relaxing now, and Carly saw James wearing a satisfied expression. Yes, James had been lying, but he had done it to please Jenny, and now that he saw he had pleased her he was happy. He's nice, Carly thought. I like him more and more. He has a kind heart, and he likes Jenny without being in the least interested in her sexually. He treats her as though sex did not exist, in fact, which is a rarity. Most men are immediately aware of your sex, even if they're not attracted to you. They have one way of looking at a man, quite another of looking at a woman, whatever her age or appearance. James had shown definite signs of sexual awareness with Carly, but he treated Jenny as though she was his sister. How long had he known her and Adam? Carly got the feeling it was an old acquaintance. Perhaps Adam was as well-acquainted with the groom as with the bride?

"If we've all finished our coffee, shall we go?" Adam asked, and Carly got shakily to her feet with the others. She was so disturbed that she almost tripped, and Adam, moving fast, steadied her, his hand at her waist.

"Too early to turn in yet," James said lightheartedly. "And it's still far too hot to be able to sleep. Why don't we go for a drive? It will be cool in the car, especially if we drive up into the hills."

Adam looked at Jenny, who raised her brows questioningly.

"What do you think?" he asked.

"Up to you." Jenny shrugged.

Slowly, Adam turned his head and met Carly's eyes. "What about you? Fancy a drive in the hills?"

Dry-mouthed, she whispered, "It sounds very pleasant." An hour ago she would have turned the idea down flat and gone to bed, glad to have escaped from his company, but now she needed to snatch a moment alone with him. She was realizing that the conclusions to which she had jumped had caused her to behave in such a way that Adam had now a completely false impression. Her plan of admitting frankly that she had come to Crete to see him had gone badly wrong, all because of her own stupidity.

"There you are, then, we're agreed," James said, grinning at them all.

"You've got a car?" Carly asked, and he explained that he had rented one for his trip to Crete.

"The bus service is far from adequate; they're few and far between and always crowded, and they take hours to jog along the roads. Apart from that, I don't read Greek, so I can't make out the timetables." James grinned at her. "Luckily, car rental here isn't that expensive."

"James is penniless," Jenny said, laughing at him. "As always."

"I manage," he protested. "With a little help from my friends."

"What friends?" Jenny mocked, taking his arm and walking beside him out of the hotel.

Carly walked after them, aware in every fiber of her being that Adam was keeping pace with her, his long stride making it easy for him to stay in step at her side.

She swallowed and threw him a nervous look. "I didn't realize Jenny was your sister."

Adam's black head swung towards her and a look of surprised disbelief crossed his face. "Didn't you? I thought I'd mentioned her to you often enough."

"You did," she said, trying to smile and failing lamentably, her lips quivering. "I just didn't connect that Jenny with this one."

His brows shot up. "Why not? How many do you think I know?"

She could hardly explain that jealousy had blinded her to the obvious. Flushing, she said, "Stupid of me not to realize."

"Yes," Adam said drily, then he walked in silence for a few seconds while Carly wracked her brains for something, anything, to say to end this gulf between them.

"You see . . ." she began, and at the same instant Adam started to speak, too.

"What are you . . ."

They both stopped and said, "Sorry."

"Go on," Carly said.

"It doesn't matter—what were you going to say?" Adam answered.

"Nothing," she said. "What were you?"

"Nothing," Adam said, and suddenly smiled at her, a smile that made her feel as though the sun had come out again, illuminating the starless Greek night for Carly as though it was broad day.

She smiled back, wordless with delight.

"Do you want to know what I was really going to say?" Adam asked quietly. "I was about to ask if it was really sheer coincidence that you arrived here while I was here." His gray eyes gleamed with teasing amusement. "Now accuse me of being conceited."

"You're conceited," she said, laughing, then added soberly, "No, I knew you were here."

Adam stopped dead in his tracks and turned to look down at her. Above them the dark pine trees whispered in the night wind, the whirr of cicadas permanently sounding in the shrubberies.

"You knew?" he asked huskily.

"Roddy told me."

Adam's hands caught her elbows, moving her out of the shadows into the yellow light spilling from the hotel behind them. Carly looked up at him, her face uncertain, her blue eyes glittering a little as if tears were dammed up behind them.

"Why are you here?" He paused, and then as she opened her mouth to answer he said roughly, "No, don't tell me, I don't care why—it's enough that you are." He glanced behind him at the disappearing figures of Jenny and James as they walked into the small parking lot, then looked back at Carly and touched her cheek with his fingertips gently.

"I've missed you," he said huskily.

"I've missed you, too," Carly admitted in a shaky little voice.

She heard him draw a long, deep breath. "Why did you act so offhand when we met tonight?" he demanded.

"I don't know," she said, not wanting to admit the truth.

"Women baffle me," Adam said in an impatient tone. "They're a law unto themselves. I'll never understand them if I live to be a hundred."

James called from the open car door. "Are you two coming or not? We're waiting!"

Adam hesitated, his expression shifting, then said, "We had better go, I suppose." He turned to walk toward the car and Carly kept up with him. He shot her a quick look. "Do you like James?"

"He's very nice," she said defensively.

"Then you won't want to see him getting a punch on the nose, will you?" Adam muttered. "So don't flirt with him anymore."

"I didn't. . . ."

"You did. I saw you with him down at the pool this afternoon, flirting like mad."

"You saw us. . . ."

"Clearly."

"I didn't realize you had seen me." She had even told herself she had imagined hearing James say his name but obviously she hadn't imagined anything. Adam had been there.

"Did you see me?" Adam asked, looking sharply at her, and she shook her head.

"I see," Adam murmured.

"What does that mean?"

"It means that you weren't flirting with James to annoy me," Adam said. "I wondered if you might have been. I know the tricks women like to play."

"I don't play tricks!"

"Then you're one of the wonders of the world," Adam said. "I've never met a woman yet who didn't go in for elaborate games to get what she wanted."

"You don't know *me*," Carly said angrily.

"I realized that in New York," Adam bit out. "I was dumb enough to think I did for a while. I thought I'd found my own personal miracle, but I was wrong, wasn't I? I'd just met another woman."

He walked forward, leaving her stunned and angry, and by the time she caught up with him he had taken a seat in the car. Carly climbed in beside him in the back seat, the doors slammed and James started the engine.

"What kept you?" he asked, his tone mischievous, and when they gave him no answer she heard him laughing softly to himself as the car drove out of the parking lot and headed along the dusty road towards the pine-clad hills. James drove fast, far too fast for the winding, narrow, rutted road, and Carly found herself bumping about, sliding across the seat and almost flung forwards into the space between James and Jenny by the speed with which the car accelerated.

Adam caught her, an arm around her shoulders clamping her against him, and said impatiently, "Slow down, James. This isn't a racetrack."

"Sorry," James said cheerfully, slowing a little.

Carly wasn't sure if the fast-beating hammering she could hear was her own heart or Adam's. She was held close to him, her head near his shoulder, the silken strands of her hair tumbling down his sleeve.

He knew she had come here deliberately to see him but he was still talking to her with terse contempt. He had not forgotten her refusal in New York nor was she going to find it easy to talk to him here. She had the impression that Adam had closed the valves of his attention, shuttered his mind against her. He was angry with her and not ready to give her another chance to turn him down.

Rejection always hurts; she should have remembered that, she thought. And for a man it hurts more than women sometimes realize. The male ego is fragile, easily dented, and Adam was protecting his ego from her now as he threw her another barbed, hostile glance.

Carly sighed. How was she going to soften that stony face of his?

Then she remembered his admission that he had missed her and her breath caught. Maybe the wall between them was not so high, after all.

They drove high into the hills, between pine forests through which the night wind breathed like a human voice, full of melancholy and hushed awe. Occasionally they saw little stone houses glimmering white in the darkness, thin cracks of light creeping through their closed shutters.

It was rough, desolate country, almost uninhabited, and the car bounced and crashed over ruts in the dusty, stony road.

James parked at the summit of a hill and they all got out of the car just as the moon drifted from behind a bank of dark cloud, sending pale light spreading gently across the sky and giving them a hazy picture of the valleys below. The pool of moonlight turned the land into a silvery lake, a gleaming mirror that hid the houses and trees and gave back to the sky the light it threw down at the earth.

"Look at that," Jenny murmured in a delighted voice.

"Worth driving up here to see, isn't it?" James asked her, and they walked away across the rough grass to look at the view from the far side of the hill.

Carly stared at the moonlit sky, her heart beating in her throat. Adam stood just beside her and she felt his eyes on her averted face.

"Why are you here, Carly?" he asked brusquely.

"You said you didn't want to be told."

"Now I do—have you come to end it?"

Her head swung round in baffled surprise. "End it? End what?"

His mouth twisted in sardonic mockery. "The frustration."

She caught back a stifled cry of surprise.

Adam turned her toward him and his hands bit into her soft flesh, her arms held immobile at her sides. "It drives you crazy, doesn't it? I've been eaten alive with it ever since I left New York. I knew it was unfinished between us while that frustration was nagging away under my skin."

"You're hurting me, Adam," she whispered, struggling to free herself from that cruel grip.

"I want to hurt you. I've thought about hurting you quite a bit since we last met. A man who has been made to feel a fool has to soothe his ego somehow. I was so sure you felt the way I felt—and you let me go on thinking that. I didn't make a fool of myself; you made a fool of me, and you'll never get the chance to do it again, Carly. If you've come here expecting to get me on my knees again, you can forget it. I've no intention of losing my head over you this time."

His quick, harsh words sank into her mind and embedded themselves like thorns, making her want to cry.

"Adam, you've got it wrong—I didn't . . ."

He wouldn't let her finish. One hand clamped down over her mouth, silencing the stammered words.

"Don't lie to me, Carly. We both know what happened. I'll never go on my knees to you again. If you want me so much that you've come all this way to get me you had better get that straight right now. From now on, you'll do all the begging. I don't expose myself to being laughed at twice."

"I didn't laugh at you! How can you think I would?"

"Women always laugh at men when they've lured them into making fools of themselves." His face was dark, savage with pain and anger, and Carly fought with the desire to burst into tears. She had imagined their meeting so differently; she had had such high hopes of this trip. Now the stark rage in his face made her heart sink.

She made a desperate attempt to reach him, leaning back with her blonde hair falling down her back, silver in the moonlight, her eyes wide and gleaming pleadingly. She said, "Adam, I came to find you—don't you understand?"

"Well, you've found me," he said with a bitter smile. "I'm flattered, of course, that you should want me enough to take so much time off from work. I know how important your job is to you. It must have been quite a sacrifice to you to spare some precious time just to pursue me to Crete, and I'm quite ready to make it worth your while; don't misunderstand me."

The scathing tone made her color run hotly into her face. He looked at her with cold mockery.

"How long have we got? How long are you here for?"

Her stiff lips parted and whispered automatically, "A week."

"A week?" he repeated in sardonic derision. "A whole week? We mustn't waste any of it, must we? Why don't we go straight back to the hotel now and get to bed?"

Carly flinched from the ice-tipped words he flung at

her. "Do you have to talk to me like that? How can you . . . ?"

"How?" Adam repeated in a thickening voice, bending toward her. "I'll tell you how, Carly. I've had months of wanting you, waking up in the night from dreams of you, missing you and hating you so much I wanted to kill you. Believe me, I'm only showing you the tip of the iceberg. The part you aren't seeing is the time I've spent since we last met."

"We only knew each other three days," Carly flared up, trembling. "That wasn't long enough. . . ."

"It was long enough for me to fall hopelessly in love with you, long enough for me to be pretty sure you felt the same—long enough for you to leave a very painful hook inside me that's been festering ever since. If you had asked me to wait, to give you time to be sure, I'd have understood, but you didn't, did you, Carly? You had no intention of marrying me, however long I was prepared to wait, because your job was more important to you than I was!"

She could not think of a thing to say to him. It was true, but the truth was so partial, so fragmentary, that her mind was choked with all she wanted to say in her defense, and she could not get out a syllable of it.

"You were playing with me," Adam said bitterly.

"No! I just . . ." Her stammered words died away as she was faced with his accusing eyes, and then she made a monumental mistake. On the point of tears, she whispered, "I'm sorry."

Adam looked as if she had slapped him in the face. His hands dropped from her arms and he swung away, his body tense with suppressed anger, leaving Carly aghast, realizing that she had admitted, by saying she was sorry, that Adam's accusations were true.

James and Jenny were still laughing and talking in the shade of a twisted olive tree on the edge of the hill. Adam called to them in a cool voice, "Shall we go? That wind is getting quite strong."

"Coming," James called, and a moment later they were back in the car and driving away toward the hotel.

Carly was silent all the way back. When James had switched off the engine, she opened the door beside her and stumbled out onto the warm tarmac, walking a little ahead of the other three as they made their way into the hotel.

"Good night, thank you for dinner and the drive," she said to James with a set smile.

"Glad you enjoyed it," he said, looking at her closely. "You look pale; jet lag catching up with you?"

"Something like that," Carly said, conscious of hidden irony. Something was catching up with her, but it wasn't jet lag—it was something far more dangerous and far more permanent.

She turned to the stairs and fled, hearing the elevator doors part with a swish as the others reached them. Carly made it to her own room before the tears started. That was one thing to be grateful for, she thought, as she sank down onto her bed and cried like a frightened child with her hands over her wet face.

Chapter Seven

She hadn't thought she would sleep but somehow she did, and overnight her mind must have been working on the problem of what to do about Adam, because morning found her in a calm, determined mood. Adam's fury last night indicated that he felt very deeply about her, whatever he had said, and Carly wasn't giving up without a fight. She had come all this way because she knew she loved him, and she wasn't going to let Adam himself stop her.

When she had had breakfast in her room she went downstairs and found Jenny by the pool. Her wet bikini told Carly that she had been swimming, but now she was sipping a glass of fresh orange juice and staring at the sculptured shadows under the pine trees at the far end of the hotel garden.

She looked up in surprise as Carly halted beside her. Her face froze. "Oh, good morning."

"Hallo," Carly said, and sat down on the chair opposite. A waiter at once came up to ask what he could bring her, and Carly shook her head, smiling.

When he had gone, Jenny asked stiffly, "Sleep well?"

"Not very." Carly stared frankly into the other woman's eyes. A flash of surprise crossed Jenny's face.

Carly smiled coaxingly at her. "You said Adam had told you about me."

"Did I? That was a mistake."

"He didn't tell you?" Carly's face fell. She had been

hoping that Adam's sister could give her some clues about how Adam really felt.

"It was a mistake for me to admit he had." Jenny finished her orange juice and stood up, and Carly leaned forward to catch her arm.

"Don't go—I want to talk to you."

"Well, I don't want to talk to you. I don't see that we have anything to talk about."

"Not Adam?" Carly asked with a rueful look. Jenny stared at her, frowning.

"I don't discuss my brother behind his back."

"I'm not asking you to betray any secrets," Carly said hurriedly. "I'm just trying to understand him."

Jenny bit her lower lip, her face uncertain. After a moment she slowly sat down again, leaning across the small white table between them, sunlight dancing over her wet skin.

"Adam told me what had happened in New York; he told me he wanted to marry you and you turned him down. Why can't you leave him alone? Haven't you hurt him enough?" The words were low and rapid, accompanied by a direct, hostile stare.

"I don't want to hurt him at all," Carly assured her. "But I don't understand him and . . ."

"You don't understand *him?*" Jenny interrupted. "I don't understand *you.* What do you want from him? A cheap affair? You won't get it. I know my brother; that's not his scene at all."

"That's not what I want, either!"

"Then what *do* you want?" The other girl stared at her scornfully, her brows rising.

"Can't you listen and let me tell you?" The blue eyes appealed to the other woman, and after a pause Jenny shrugged.

"Okay, I'm listening."

"Did Adam tell you we only had a couple of dates before he asked me to marry him? I knew him exactly three days—that's all. Would you rush into marriage that fast?"

Jenny hesitated. Carly held her eyes, forcing her to be honest, although she could tell from the other girl's expression that Jenny wanted to side with her brother at the expense of sincerity.

"Would you?"

Jenny looked away. "That's not an easy question."

"It isn't an easy question when a man you've fallen for very badly demands an answer right there and then and flings off in a temper when you just can't give it yet."

Jenny laughed wryly. "He's not an easy guy."

"Boy, is that an understatement," Carly said. "Your brother is a very tough guy indeed to understand; that's why I'm asking for your help."

Jenny pushed her empty glass around with one finger, looking down. "Has he ever talked to you about his first wife?"

"No," Carly said, stiffening. "What was she like?"

"That's another tough question to answer; I barely knew her. All I know is what happened and what Adam has told me, which isn't much, but it may explain why he reacts the way he does. She was very much younger than Adam. They met in Spain; she was on holiday there and when she went back to England they kept in touch. Donna was an only child, very spoiled, her parents were wealthy and gave her everything she asked for."

"Nice for her," Carly said and knew she was jealous, jealous of a dead woman she had never met. She despised herself but she couldn't help it; Donna was a part of Adam's life, and Carly felt shut out of that past he had never talked about.

"Adam saw her whenever he could, but there were other men around; Donna was a Venus flytrap where men were concerned. But it seems she chose Adam, because they were married a year after they met and then Julie was born." Jenny looked up, smiling grimly. "She arrived early, so I guess they had to get married."

"Oh," Carly said, choking back the hurt. She had known they had a daughter; why should it hurt more to know they had anticipated their wedding day? Irrational, she told herself, and very stupid.

"And then Donna started dating other men. She was a born flirt, couldn't help herself, I think. There were scenes, Adam was very angry, he was bitter and resentful and felt trapped. So he left her and Julie, and there was a divorce."

Carly looked up, astonished. "I'd no idea!"

"He hates talking about it." Jenny sighed, looking away across the pool. "A lot of what I know is largely guesswork. Adam keeps his thoughts to himself."

"But he said she was dead!"

"She is—she died of pneumonia a year after the divorce and Adam flew home to England, forced Donna's parents to hand over Julie to him and bought his farm." She looked back at Carly. "And now for the guesswork on my part—did you know our parents died while Adam was still at school?"

Carly nodded. "That was a terrible blow, for both of you, I guess."

"It broke up our family. My aunt took me to live with her but Adam wouldn't stay there; he quarreled with Aunt Kay from the start. She had never had any children and she was very old-fashioned. She tried to be too strict with him. Adam rebelled and ran off; he kept in touch with me, wrote every week, but he refused to come back or go on with his schooling." Jenny sighed. "When Mum and Dad died I think Adam was a lot more upset than I was, but he had already learned not to show it. I think Adam started searching then, searching for what he lost when our parents died. He thought he'd found it with Donna and it all blew up in his face. Then when he met you . . ." She broke off, giving a shrug.

Carly smiled with a blinding, bewildering rush of joy. "He thought he had found it at last?"

"Something like that," Jenny muttered. "My brother is one of the last romantics; he's the type to follow a dream for years without giving up."

"But he has given up on me?" Carly asked, her mouth a warm vibrant curve.

Jenny looked at her searchingly. "Do I gather you haven't given up on him?"

"No way," Carly said lightheartedly. "Do you know the trouble with your brother? He has no patience."

"That's true," Jenny agreed with sudden amusement.

"He rushes things and he doesn't give anyone a second chance," Carly said. "But he's going to have to learn how to, Jenny." She stood up and walked to the edge of the pool. Jenny watched as she dived into the water, her slender body cutting through it like a pale arrow as she swam toward the far end.

When she hauled herself out of the pool a while later, Jenny had gone, and Carly stretched out on a lounger, shading her eyes as she looked up at the sky. The languid heat of the night had passed into a welcome coolness toward dawn, but now the sun was building up the same sweltering temperatures that had made her feel so uncomfortable yesterday.

Voices caught her attention. Turning, she saw James and Adam talking at the entrance to the hotel. They were wearing jeans and shirts, so obviously they were not intending to swim. James looked over and waved a hand.

Carly got up and walked across to join them, meeting Adam's narrowed eyes calmly. She saw a flash of surprise pass through them and wondered what he had expected to see when they met—fear and nervous wariness? She smiled at him deliberately, a teasing look on her face.

"Aren't you taking a swim today?" she asked, dividing the question between the two men.

"We're driving to Knossos," James told her. "Why don't you come? It's quite an experience visiting the site of the old Cretan palace."

Carly looked down at her slender body in the tiny bikini. "Will you wait while I dress? I'd love to come."

"We'll wait," James promised, grinning as he also inspected her from head to toe. Carly moved away, but she knew that Adam had not failed to absorb how she looked, although his dark face had not been very revealing.

She ran up to her room quickly and took a shower, dried herself and searched through her clothes for a pair of jeans and a cotton tee-shirt. The bright yellow jeans hugged her figure so tightly they looked as if they had been molded on her, and her small, high breasts strained against the thin cotton of the white shirt.

Her blonde hair was vigorously brushed, her skin left innocent of makeup apart from the merest touch of pink on her lips. Giving herself a quick look she smiled, deciding she would do, then hurried to the door.

She found Jenny with the two men, and, as Carly approached, the other woman gave her a quick look and a comparatively friendly smile. Her frigid attitude had obviously thawed since they had talked earlier, to Carly's relief. She wanted Adam's sister to like her; Carly believed in family, and she knew that any hostility inside the family unit could be poison to a marriage. Friends come and go in anybody's life, but the members of a family stay forever. Carly could remember her own mother saying wryly, "I'm not sure I like my sister, but I'm stuck with her, so I haven't any choice; I have to love her." Mrs. Newton had laughed as she said it, making it clear it was a joke, but there had been a lot of truth behind what she said, all the same.

"Ready, Carly?" James asked cheerfully. "We thought we would have lunch at a little taverna on the road to Knossos. It's half past eleven now, so we'll drive through the hills before lunch and after lunch we'll stop at the old palace."

"That sounds wonderful," Carly said, ready to fall in with any plan if it gave her a chance of talking to Adam. She had no idea what she was going to say to him, only that she wanted to be with him. Any doubts she had had about the future had gone out the window as she'd listened to his sister and realized all that had gone into making Adam the man he now was. His life had been emotionally wounding ever since he was an adolescent, and Carly meant to make it up to him. She had thought him so strong and self-assured when they met in New York, but Jenny had given her new insights into his character. Carly felt protective, maternal, as she looked at his hard, masculine face. It was so hard to reach past the mask he chose to wear, but somehow she was going to do it.

James turned the car toward the hills, but as they were driving along the rough, winding roads the sky clouded over suddenly, taking them by surprise. Carly looked up, frowning.

"I've never seen a sky that color before; it's almost yellow."

"A storm coming," Adam said tersely.

The smoky umber of the skyline rumbled with thunder, as though his comment had summoned up an answer, and lambent lightning flashed far away.

"There goes our trip to Knossos," James complained.

Rain began to come down in a fine drizzle, clouding the road ahead as though it was plunged into mist. The windshield wipers began to click to and fro, and James peered through his rainy windshield, sighing. "Shall we go on or go back?"

"We might as well have lunch at the next taverna we come to," Adam advised.

"Right—the next one I see, we'll stop," agreed James. The tires hissed on the wet road and the car began to crash through a series of potholes masked by puddles.

"This road's terrible," James yelled to them above the drumming of the rain on the car roof. Carly caught a glimpse through the curtain of running water of the thick yellow mud on the surface of the road. "Hey, I think there's been a landslide here," James said, slowing to a crawl as the car skidded. "There are rocks all over the road."

"Pull to one side," advised Adam.

Jenny was pale. "I don't like this," she murmured.

"James, stop driving until this rain has stopped—it's too dangerous."

"I would if I wasn't afraid the points would get wet," he told her over his shoulder, leaning forward as he tried to steer his way between mud and rocks. "I haven't spotted any other cars for miles, and if the engine stalls we could sit here for hours before we were rescued. Do you want to spend the day sitting in this car in the pouring rain?"

"The storm center's coming closer," Adam warned.

Carly could hear the crash of thunder so loudly it seemed to be centered overhead, and she flinched, instinctively moving closer to Adam. He was leaning against the window beside him, staring through the rain, and seemed oblivious to her.

"Is that a house behind those trees?" he asked James suddenly.

"Where?" James followed the direction of his pointing finger, screwing up his eyes. "It's some sort of building," he agreed. "A barn, I think."

"Drive under the shelter of the trees; there's a stony track leading to the barn, and the trees will keep the worst of the rain off the car."

"Okay," James said obediently, pulling off the road. The vehicle bounced and protested as it ran over the rough cart track. James pulled up under one of the trees and switched off the engine. Rain filled the air with a persistent rushing that made Carly feel very nervous.

"I suggest we shelter in the barn," Adam said, pulling open his door. He dived out and shot through the streaming rain to the ramshackle old stone building a few hundred feet away.

James groaned and cast a look at the two women. "I

suppose we have no choice—here goes!" He followed Adam, his head bent.

"We're going to get soaked," Jenny complained as she and Carly tore through the downpour. The air was split with lightning and a shudder went through Carly as she almost fell inside the shadowy barn, her white cotton tee-shirt clinging to her body and so wet that it molded her like a second skin, the material almost transparent. That fact only dawned on her as, panting breathlessly, she paused in the shelter of the door, running a hand over her streaming hair, the movement lifting her high breasts so that they tautened under the wet material. Adam watched her, his eyes narrowed to slits, and hot color ran up her face as she realized she might as well be naked. Hurriedly she dropped her hand and moved to look out at the rain-soaked landscape.

"I wonder how long this is going to last," James groaned beside her. "Look at that rain!" He jumped as thunder rolled close at hand. "My ears are splitting. The storm must be right overhead."

"Come away from the doorway," Adam said, his hand closing round Carly's arm and pulling her back.

"I've got a funny tingling at the back of my neck," Jenny said in a worried voice. "Do you feel strange, James?"

"You're not going to turn into the Wolfman, are you?" he asked, grinning, but Jenny didn't seem amused.

"I feel odd," she said, and Adam frowned.

"You're not going to faint, Jenny?"

"It isn't that sort of feeling; it's—" She broke off, giving a rueful shrug. "I don't know what I feel; it isn't like any feeling I've ever had before."

"Imagination," James said. "Or a drop of rain trickling under your shirt."

"Maybe," Jenny agreed, but doubtfully. "If it didn't sound silly, I'd say it was a ghost walking over my grave."

Carly watched her, a little shiver flicking down her own spine. "I know what you mean; strange, isn't it?"

"Hey, you two are scaring me," James mocked. "Maybe this place is haunted."

That amused him, and he began to laugh, capering towards Jenny with his arms raised, making ghostly noises, and at that moment the earth shook. Jenny screamed. Carly's heart stopped and her ears drummed with appalled disbelief. The barn was moving and the air was full of a confused mingling of sounds: the rumbling beneath their feet, the crashing of brick and stone, the tearing and splintering of wood, the ear-splitting sound of glass shattering, and Jenny screaming above it all. Carly lost awareness of the passing of time. Adam got her by the waist and pushed her bodily out of the toppling building, shouting, "Run, get out of here!" Her heart was too large for her chest; she was suffocating with fear, running in panic without her legs seeming to move at all. Around her she could hear the sounds of the world being torn apart; a great pine bowed and fell a few yards away, the trunk snapping like a match stick, the branches rippling and sighing as it fell. Instinctively, Carly veered out of its path and collided with Jenny. Both of them stumbled and fell. Carly was dazed by the violence with which her head hit the rainsodden stony ground. Her outstretched arms scrabbled in muddy earth in a convulsive attempt to get back on her feet.

All she felt was helpless panic. There was nowhere safe in the world; she was out in the rain and the storm with nowhere to go. The sky was still tearing with electric flashes that lit the rainy horizon.

A strong arm lifted her, and, as she started to run again in blind fear, held her, and Adam's voice said, "It's stopped; stand still. You're safe, Carly."

She flung her head back, her eyes wet, although she hadn't known she was crying. Her saturated hair hung in rat tails down her back, and she knew she looked a mess, her yellow jeans smeared and streaked with mud, her top a sodden rag. Adam put both arms round her and she clung, her face buried in his chest.

"Don't cry," he whispered, his head bowed so that his lips were close to her ear. "I've got you; you're safe. Darling, don't cry."

"I'm not," she managed to say in a voice choked with salt, and she felt him smile although she couldn't see his face. His hand covered the back of her head in a protective gesture, pressing it closer to him.

The rain poured down around them, gushing and gurgling into streams that ran over the stones like a small river. Carly felt safe, her body curled into Adam's in a childlike gesture of trust, the fear she had felt gone because she blindly believed Adam would not allow anything to happen to her.

When she had stopped shaking she moved away slightly, breathing in a more controlled fashion, the frantic heaving of her body slowing. She saw James and Jenny sitting on the ground, their hair plastered to their heads by rain, shivering convulsively and very pale.

"Do you think there'll be another quake?" James asked of nobody in particular. His voice was hoarse and nervous.

"God knows," Adam told him. "But I'm staying put; we're in the safest place out in the open here."

Jenny was staring in appalled silence at the destroyed barn. It was a tumbled mass of masonry and ripped wood with wet straw blowing around in the wind.

"We could have been killed," she said thickly.

"We weren't," Adam told her. He released Carly and went over to his sister, bent and patted her shoulder comfortingly. "Don't start fretting; you're alive and there isn't going to be another quake."

"I could use a drink," James muttered.

Adam straightened and grinned easily at him. "Sorry, I can't oblige; it didn't occur to me to bring a bottle of whiskey out with me."

"I want to get back to the hotel," Jenny cried miserably. "I want to get the first plane back home to my children. If I'd been killed . . ."

"You can fly home tomorrow," Adam reassured her.

"I want to be home now; I'm frightened! What if there's another quake?"

"I told you, don't think about it." Adam glanced up at the sky and grimaced. "The storm's moving away; that flash came from much further off."

James slowly stood up, slicking back his damp hair. "We could sit here for hours; why don't we drive back to the hotel and risk it? Given a choice between getting pneumonia from hanging around in wet clothes and having to drive through an earthquake, I think I'd plump for the earthquake."

Jenny hesitated, biting her lip. "What do you think, Adam?"

"I think James is right. The sensible thing would be to drive back, but we'll wait for another ten minutes—if there *is* going to be another quake it will probably come quite quickly. If there hasn't been one for a quarter of an hour we can risk driving back."

The fallen pine tree suddenly shifted and murmured, making Jenny jump violently.

"Don't worry, it's only settling down," Adam soothed.

"My nerves are shot to pieces!" Jenny whispered.

"So are mine," James agreed. "I've always wondered what an earthquake was like; now I know, and I'm glad we don't get them in England."

Adam walked away while they stared after him. He made his way to the car and got into the driver's seat. They heard the engine start a moment later, and James gave a low sigh of relief.

"I thought it might stall after all this rain."

"We're lucky no tree fell on the car," Jenny pointed out, walking over to join Adam. Carly and James hurried after her, and they all got into the car. Adam backed into the road carefully, the tires sliding on the thick yellow mud.

"This is not going to be a pleasant drive," he murmured as he turned back toward the hotel. The rain had stopped now and the fine mist had begun to dissipate, blowing away in front of them in unwreathing coils as the sun unbelievably appeared and shone down with a humid sultriness. Jenny craned to stare back at the ruined barn, her neck muscles visibly tense.

"I'll never forget that place."

Carly knew exactly how she felt; she never would, either. It was the place at which she had known with an intense finality that she belonged to Adam and with Adam and that her career would never mean as much to her as this man whom she had known for such a short time, but whom she loved more than she had thought possible.

While she had been shuddering with fear and clinging

to him blindly she had been thinking how close they had come to being killed and asking herself what it was that she had put before the way they felt about each other. Without Adam, her career, however exciting, would always leave a blank space in her life; she would always be aware of that lonely emptiness in the night, that sense of isolation in the midst of busy New York. She would be giving up a good deal if she married Adam and went to live on his remote farm, but if she chose to stay in New York she was choosing to be alone, however many people lived and worked around her. When it came down to it, she wanted Adam more than she wanted anything else. He mattered more; he was more important.

As they drove back to the hotel they saw other wrecked buildings, with people standing outside them staring in stunned horror at the destruction which the earthquake had brought. Carly wondered if many people had been killed; they saw no sign of such tragedy but the threat of it hovered in the air and people looked frightened and pale. They heard the wail of sirens as they got back to the gates of the hotel parking lot, and Jenny looked back over her shoulder, wincing.

"Ambulance," she murmured. "Adam, we must book a flight at once; I'm not staying here a moment longer than I have to. I have my children to think of."

"We'll book flights as soon as we can," he promised.

They found the hotel in a state of hysterical confusion, the ground floor full of anxious, alarmed people milling about, talking to each other with unsteady voices. The elevator was out of operation, since it was dangerous to use it during a threatened quake, they were told. They were advised not to go to their rooms until it was certain there would be no repeat of the earth tremors, but Adam coolly insisted on going up to change out of his wet clothes. It was an hour since the first quake, he pointed out, and if there was going to be another one it would surely have struck by now. James stalwartly followed suit, but Adam took his sister's door key and Carly's and said he would bring down dry clothes for them to change into.

"I'd rather you didn't take the risk," he said quietly before he left.

Jenny huddled in a chair, shivering in her soaked clothes. "I feel like a refugee."

Carly felt slightly sick but oddly at peace. She had resolved her problem, and with her mind clear she felt no further worry. Whatever the problems in front of her, she would at least know she was doing what, at the bottom of her heart, she knew she wanted to do.

Adam returned in dry pants and a thick sweater, then handed Jenny a pile of dry clothes and Carly another, grinning at them.

"You can use the washroom over there to change in."

There was a shower there, intended for use by people who had been swimming in the hotel pool but were not staying at the hotel. Both women showered and dried themselves, dressed in warm clothes and brushed their wet hair until it was more or less dry.

When they rejoined Adam and James they found them in the bar drinking stiff whiskies. There was a carnival atmosphere in the hotel now. Frightened people were flinging off their terrors and throwing themselves into a party spirit to hide the moments of panic they had felt. The management put on a special dinner that evening, followed by a Greek exhibition dance performed by men in traditional costume who invited guests to join them on the floor. Carly laughed as Adam and James linked arms with the other men and danced in a long line to the rhythmic strumming of the bouzouki music.

Later, the band played more modern rhythms, and as they danced, Adam looked down at Carly and said, "Forgive me for the way I spoke to you yesterday?"

"Yes," she said, her arms round his neck as they moved to the slow waltz that the band was playing.

He laughed, his eyes teasing. "Just like that? Don't I get any furious recriminations?"

She shook her head, smiling back.

"You're very forgiving."

"I love you," Carly said, and put her head on his shoulder. She felt his arms tighten round her in a movement of possession. Against her hair he whispered, "Darling."

They were silent for a moment, then Adam said huskily, "I understand how you feel about your job, Carly. I'm glad you came to find me. Even if I can only have you now and then when you have time, I'm glad. I realized during the quake that if all I could hope for was a few brief days from time to time, I'd rather have that than nothing at all. The only thing that matters is that we love each other."

Carly trembled, her eyes wet, hiding them against him and hearing the deep, quick beating of his heart under her cheek.

She couldn't bring herself to speak for a moment, so moved was she, and Adam misinterpreted her silence and took a long, harsh breath above her head.

"Carly," he began, and the stifled sound of his voice held an anxiety that got through to her.

She lifted her head and looked at him, her mouth trembling in her attempt to smile.

"I don't want to be what Curt calls a pushy lady, Adam," she said huskily. "So will you please quickly ask me again to marry you before I'm forced to propose myself?"

Adam looked down into her eyes, his face still and intent, his eyes searching her upturned face.

"Do you mean that?"

She nodded, her heart making a painful music in her ears.

"What about your job?"

She shrugged helplessly. "I've decided nobody can have everything—it's just a question of what you really want."

Adam's mouth relaxed and curved into a smile, his eyes tender and warm. "Sure? I'll give you more time to think it over, if you like; I don't want to rush you this time. I've learned my lesson. I wanted you so much I tried to grab you and run off with you, but that was damned selfish. I was treating you as though you had no life, no mind of your own. You should have got it through to me that I was behaving like a louse."

"I seem to remember I did try," she murmured. "It just made you angrier to have it pointed out."

He made a self-derisory face. "I was in a state of frustrated fury. I'd found you at last when I had begun to think my dream woman didn't exist, and when you refused to just walk away with me there and then I was beside myself with temper."

"I did notice that," Carly teased, putting up a hand to touch his cheek.

"I love you, Carly Newton," Adam said, watching

her intently. "Would you like me to go down on my knees in the old-fashioned way or shall I just ask you—will you marry me?"

"I wondered when you'd get around to asking," Carly said, her blue eyes very bright. "I thought I'd have to do it myself, after all." She paused, very breathless suddenly. "Yes," she said.

"Yes, you will?" Adam asked, his body tense as they moved together on the dance floor.

"I will," she said, then laughed in elation. "I feel so strange—as if I'd just learned how to fly without wings."

"That comes later," Adam said, his eyes mocking, and her cheeks filled with excited color.

He watched her blushing and grinned. "When will you marry me? How long do I have to wait?"

"Until I've talked to Curt and been released from my contract—I'm on three months' notice."

"Three months! I can't wait that long!"

"I don't imagine Curt would release me any sooner; he has to find someone to take over, remember, and that won't be easy. We'll be weeks sorting through the various candidates and deciding who is the best."

Adam sighed. "Well, I suppose after waiting so long I can wait another three months."

Carly smiled at him. "It won't be as long as it seems at this moment." Three months would pass, she thought; it might seem like eternity tonight, but once she was back in the frenetic whirlpool of New York she would find the days passing faster and faster, and, whatever the problems of living with Adam on a sheep farm miles from any town, she knew she was going to be happy with him. She had finally admitted that during the earthquake. Nothing was going to keep her away from Adam anymore.

"I'll even learn to like sheep," she said, not realizing she was talking aloud until she heard Adam laughing, and their eyes met as they shared a moment of deep happiness.

Chapter Eight

*C*urt was staggered when Carly went into his office, the morning she returned to work, and announced her resignation. She saw a whole variety of expressions chasing through his eyes before he said a single, solitary word: surprise, suspicion, anger, calculation. Waiting for him to say something, she wondered which emotion would be uppermost when he did speak.

"Who's poached you?" he demanded. "How much have they offered? Haven't you got any sense of loyalty? I took you out of a dead-end job back in Britain where you had no prospects and taught you everything you know, and this is what I get for it!"

"Curt," she interrupted, seeing that he was working himself up into a long speech on the topic of treachery and stabbing in the back, one of his favorite subjects, convinced as he was not only that everyone had his price, but that everyone wanted his job and his firm. Like some Borgia prince, he saw conspiracy all around him. It was what kept him on his toes, forever alert to the threat of danger. Carly even thought he enjoyed it. If life became calm and secure, Curt would soon grow bored.

"You can't trust anybody," he went on mournfully, giving her a reproachful glare. "I thought you were different. I thought you were one of the few people I could trust, but you're all the same. Who approached you? A holiday, you said you needed! So where were you, really? Who have you been in a huddle with, cooking this up?"

"I haven't . . ."

"Have you signed anything yet? Your contract has a three month get-out clause and I'm not releasing you until . . ."

"I'm getting married," Carly said, and he stopped, mid-rant, his mouth open.

Satisfied with his silence, she went on, "And I'm leaving publishing altogether. I haven't been poached by anybody, Curt."

He shut his mouth with the snap of a bulldog closing his teeth on a vanishing tail. "So where does it say that if you get married you have to give up your job? Who's the guy? I'll talk to him if he's some old-fashioned guy with ideas about a woman's place being in the home. Now, don't you worry about it, I'll take him out to lunch and have a few drinks and talk to him like a father. . . ."

A Godfather, no doubt, Carly thought, eyeing him with amusement. Curt meant to make her intended husband an offer he had better not refuse.

"I'm marrying Adam Blake," she told him, and Curt looked so horrified she had to bite her lip not to laugh.

"That English guy? That . . . " He paused to think of an epithet sufficiently loaded to describe Adam. "That writer," he ended in a disgusted voice. Curt remembered Adam well; he always remembered people he found impossible to dominate. They were his failures, the battles he had lost, a permanent reproach to him.

"That's Adam," Carly agreed, and Curt ground his teeth.

"What do you want to marry *him* for?"

"I love him," she offered.

177

"He lives in England, doesn't he?" Curt dredged his memory, a scowl knitting his brows. "On a goddamned sheep farm!"

"That's right, in Yorkshire."

Curt slowly shook his head, starting to grin. "You plan to marry a sheep farmer and go and live in the middle of nowhere?" His grin spread from ear to ear. "You'll be back within a month," he concluded, with unhidden satisfaction. "It will drive you cuckoo. You're not a country girl, you're a city girl; you'll never settle down on a farm at the back of beyond."

Carly hoped her face looked calm and unworried, but she knew that despite having made up her mind to marry Adam, her own doubts and uncertainties were still there at the back of her mind, and Curt's words sent a nervous tremor through her.

Aloud, she said, "Sometimes you're faced with a choice, Curt. Obviously I'd like to have my job and marry Adam, too, but that isn't the way things are. Adam lives on a farm, not in New York."

He looked her up and down assessingly. "You're a lovely girl; you could do better than this guy. New York's full of attractive men; you just haven't looked hard enough. I tell you what I'll do—we'll have some dinner parties, introduce you to a few people. . . ."

The idea of Curt as a matchmaker made her want to laugh out loud, but she suppressed the desire and said quietly, "I've made up my mind, Curt. I'll get Sue-Ann to type my resignation and you'll have it later today."

Curt gave her a narrow-eyed, considering stare. That wasn't the end of it, she knew. Curt would return to the attack when he had had time to view the problem at more leisure. It was flattering, in a way. It meant that Curt saw her as a success, a credit to his genius for picking the right people. If she wasn't doing her job as well as Curt demanded, he would let her go without a second's hesitation; he would probably have fired her long ago, in fact. Curt had a personal interest in her career, though; he had been the one who saw her potential long before she had achieved anything. She was a constant reminder to him and everyone in sight that Curt Dorsden had an unfailing nose for talent. He didn't want her to stop advertising his genius like that.

Adam called her that evening to ask how the interview with Curt had gone. His voice sounded fuzzy and distant, as though he was talking to her from the bottom of the sea. She missed some words, caught others. It was a very unsatisfying way of talking to him, but it was better than not talking to him at all.

"Still sure about it?" he asked, just before he rang off, and the phrase came to her as clear as a bell.

"Certain," she said, and Adam asked, "What? I didn't hear you."

"I love you," Carly shouted, and she heard him laugh.

"I love you, too; talk to you soon. . . ."

He was gone, and she put the phone down, feeling both elated and depressed. She wished the next three months were over; they were not going to be easy. Curt would see to that. He wasn't going to let her go without a form of siege warfare that might go on for weeks until he accepted that she wasn't going to change her mind. Curt was a realist; he would start looking for her successor before it became too urgent, so that she could work with the new editor for a while in order to help him or her settle into the job. But she guessed that Curt would put off making up his mind for as long as he dared.

179

Louise, at least, was entirely on her side. "You never did a wiser thing," she assured her. "I knew the minute you got back. Before you went away you looked like somebody who needed a blood transfusion, but you came back bright-eyed and bushy-tailed."

Carly laughed. "Am I that obvious?"

"Love's wonderful," Louise teased. Her face sobered and she gave a faint sigh. "I envy you; I really do. Why don't I meet someone like Adam Blake? The trouble is, I never get out and meet anyone except people in our business and I know all of them and can't stand the sight of any of them."

"Tell Curt," Carly said. "Maybe he'll arrange some dinner parties for you," and she told Louise what he had offered to do to find her a marriageable prospect in New York.

"I don't believe it," Louise said, collapsing in hysterical laughter. "What would he do, order one of his friends to propose?" She gave Carly a wry stare a moment later. "He's worse than my mother—she's been nagging me for years to marry the boy next door. She likes him, so why shouldn't I, is her attitude."

"But you don't like him?" It was the first time Louise had ever mentioned any boy next door, and Carly was interested.

"Certainly I like him, I've known him all my life, but why should I marry him just to please my mother?" Louise got up and drifted off to the kitchen, leaving Carly wondering if, had her mother not pressed her so hard to do it, Louise might not, in fact, have married the boy next door. Sometimes, just by pushing someone in one direction, you can send them running in the opposite one.

She followed Louise and watched her making coffee, her face intent. "Is he nice?"

Louise looked round. "Who?" But she knew perfectly well who Carly was talking about, and her face had a faint flush.

"The boy next door."

"Oh, him," Louise said, turning away. "He's like apple pie; you always like it, but it's always the same, and you don't get any particular thrill out of eating it."

Carly knew just what she meant. Louise got down the coffee mugs and poured each of them a cup. As they went back to sit down and drink it, she said casually, "But I'm saving him for a rainy day. Maybe some day I'll go and get him."

Carly's eyebrows rose. "If somebody hasn't got him first," she pointed out, and Louise laughed.

"Who? Tom? You've got to be kidding. He's the faithful type; he's been proposing to me since we were in high school."

"Even the faithful type gives up sometime," Carly warned and got a frown. She left it there and Louise didn't mention the subject again.

While Curt was trying to think of a way to persuade her to change her mind his attention was focused on her, but Carly knew when he finally gave up, because he became briskly intent on choosing her replacement and showed no further interest in her. The uncomfortable spotlight of Curt's personal interest was switched off, and, although he was perfectly friendly and polite, she knew she barely existed for him anymore. Curt behaved as though she had already left. Carly found it both a relief and slightly hurtful. Maddening though he could be, she liked Curt, and, although she had decided to leave her job, she *was* human; she didn't enjoy realizing she wasn't indispensable and that, when she had gone, she would soon be forgotten altogether.

The woman who was taking her place was someone she knew slightly, having met her in a business context in the past. Isobel Donaldson was an experienced editor, a year older than Carly, very capable and lively. Curt made the final choice, of course, but Carly felt Isobel was the best candidate, although she decided not to press her name too strongly. Curt would like Isobel better if he thought he had made the choice without being influenced.

Sylvia Dorsden threw a farewell party for Carly before she left, and Curt presented her with a wedding present, a very beautiful silver teapot with a matching cream jug and sugar bowl. Carly was delighted with it, and overwhelmed by Curt's generosity. She had not been expecting anything so magnificent, but then, Curt loved to astound people. As she gazed at his present with enchanted eyes, he smiled happily, satisfied by her expression.

"I'm speechless, Curt," she stammered, looking at him. "How can I ever thank you? They're beautiful."

He waved her thanks away with a smile. "Just remember, if you ever come back to New York and want a job—call me."

Carly was touched and surprised. She saw that Curt was not as angry with her as she had supposed; he had merely decided to accept her decision and find someone to replace her. She hadn't become an invisible person to him, after all. It was merely that Curt's practical nature meant that he dealt with life on a day-to-day basis, which focused his whole mind on the matter in hand. He had forgiven her, and he was making sure she knew it.

She stood for a second, very close to tears, then kissed him, and everyone laughed as Curt looked startled and a little pink.

"Thank you," Carly said.

"Yes, hey, where's that champagne?" Curt hurriedly muttered, looking around for help in this emotional situation. Curt did not like emotion. Sylvia Dorsden gave Carly an amused smile as Curt's glass was filled, and Carly smiled back, her eyes bright with threatening but happy tears. She had hated the thought of leaving New York under a cloud. She hated the thought of leaving New York at all—but that would have been a very painful way to go, to end her happy time in the city with a feeling of gloom.

"When do you join your husband-to-be?" Sylvia asked her later, as they chatted in the middle of the lively party.

"Next week; I'm flying to England on Monday and going to see my parents, then I'm going up to Yorkshire to join Adam."

"When's the wedding?"

"We plan to get married in three months," Carly said.

Sylvia looked startled and curious. "Why wait so long?"

"My mother has plans for a big family wedding, for a start," Carly said drily. "But apart from that, there are problems on Adam's side. He has a little girl I've never met and . . ."

Sylvia's lips pursed and she whistled. "Oh, oh, that's not going to be easy—how old is she?"

"Nine," Carly sighed.

Sylvia gave her a sympathetic look. "He's divorced?"

"Her mother is dead," Carly said flatly.

"Dead?" Sylvia surveyed her for a moment, her eyes intent. "When did it happen? How long ago?"

"Just over a year."

"And she's had her father to herself ever since?"

Carly nodded and Sylvia clicked her tongue.

"That's tough. You're right—you do have problems. A little boy would be bad enough, but a little girl—you're going to have to be very clever with her, Carly. She may be only nine, but she's bound to feel jealous and possessive about her father, especially as she's had him to herself for so long."

Carly squared her shoulders. "I know," she said in a low, disturbed tone. She knew; it had been keeping her awake at night for a long time, but she would face it once she got to Yorkshire and saw exactly what the problem was. She might find it didn't exist, after all.

She had already packed up most of her private possessions and sent them off to England in a large packing case to be delivered to her family home. She and Louise had stood there staring at it before it was picked up, their faces wry.

"Doesn't seem much to show for nearly two years in New York, does it?" Carly had said.

"Travel light, they say," Louise offered. "I wonder if I'd have much more if I left." Her eyes flicked round the room, her brow creased, touching on the various items she owned with speculative irony. "I think I'd throw most of this junk away."

"Maybe *things* are junk anyway," Carly said. "It's what happens to you that matters, not what you own."

"Comforting thought, if it wasn't for the fact that

nothing much seems to happen to me, either," said Louise. "When you've gone, I'll have to tidy the apartment before Trudy moves in, I suppose."

Trudy was taking over Carly's share of the rent. She was an advertising secretary, a very quiet girl with dark brown hair and eyes like molasses, who had seemed to Louise the most congenial of those who had shown up to view the apartment. Carly suspected that Louise had deliberately picked someone likely to be domestic and willing to keep the apartment tidy.

"Starting the way you hope Trudy will carry on?" she teased, and Louise had laughed.

"Why not?" She had paused, then said, "I'll be sorry to see you go, Carly; we've had some good times."

"I'll keep in touch," Carly had said lightly.

"You do that; I'd like to hear from you from time to time." Louise had turned away. "I'll make us some coffee."

Carly watched her vanish, smiling. She would miss Louise, just as she would miss this apartment, the office, Curt and Sue-Ann and everyone else. But most of all, she knew she was going to miss New York. It had been not merely the background of her life for the past two years, it had been almost like a constant companion to her, a living presence that gave a pulse of excitement to her waking moments. She could not imagine how she was going to cope with living on a farm miles from any human habitation, with only the wind in the trees, the sheep and the birds for company.

She flew to England on a dull winter day, leaving the New York weather threatening snow and everyone going around huddled in thick winter coats, the knife-like winds whizzing down the streets and slicing into people as they hurried to work. Carly had not been home for a long time, but she had a fairly shrewd idea what to expect, and England did not disappoint her. As she left the plane in London, a fine chilly drizzle sent her scurrying to the airport bus waiting at the foot of the steps, and it rained solidly as her taxi took her from Heathrow across London to get a train down into Kent.

Several times in the train Carly looked up to find one passenger or another regarding her with suspicion, her smile of pleasure in the sight of the rainy green fields obviously making her seem something of a screwball. She felt like saying to one man, "It's so good to be home again," but his air of nervous distrust changed her mind. Instead she just grinned at him. He shot out of his seat and moved up the train out of her reach, but watched her from his safer vantage point all the way through Kent, clearly waiting for her to become even more dangerous. His eye kept lifting to the communication cord, in case he needed to pull it.

Carly kept her gaze on the landscape floating past, the wet green pastures between low, tangled hedges, the oak trees and elms beneath which moved black-and-white cows at a slow, ruminating pace, which she felt to be the exact pace of English life. Her mind found it hard to adjust to that steady, thoughtful rhythm after the rush and tension of New York. She felt her veins drumming with adrenalin. Impatience and restless energy were such a way of life for her now; how was she ever to adjust to moving and talking at a slower speed? Despite her pleasure at the sight of her own country, at the familiar climate and weather, she was still mentally in a hurry; she was dying to get home and see her mother. She wanted to urge the train to go faster. It stopped at stations, and when people had got off and got on, did not start off again at once but sat there in the mild, damp air, the dripping of raindrops from the platform canopy and the cheerful exchange between the driver and a station guard the only sounds for several minutes. Nobody was in a hurry, it seemed. Time was passing, but people read their newspapers and gazed out at the neat row of poplars sighing outside the station fence, seeming quite happy to wait. Carly shifted her feet and looked at her watch and then out the window. Were they never going to start off again? The doors slammed, the train moved, rattling over a high embankment between forests. At last, thought Carly; only one more stop and she would be home.

When she climbed down out of the train the rain had stopped, and the sun was coming out in a wind-fretted blue sky. Standing on the platform, inhaling Kentish air, Carly put down her suitcase and looked around her at the familiar station with its ironwork-edged canopy and large weighing machine, the green-painted wooden benches on which a few people waited for later trains. It hadn't changed an inch; no doubt it looked very much as it had when the railway line was built in the latter half of the nineteenth century.

She heard footsteps ringing on the stone platform, turned and broke into a delighted smile as she saw her father walking toward her, his thinning hair blowing in the wind, his shapeless old tweed jacket bulging over the thick fisherman's sweater he was wearing. She knew that jacket; her father always wore it when he was gardening or down on the river fishing. He put it on when he was relaxed; it made him feel good. It was comforting and reassuring to see him in it.

She ran toward him and they hugged each other, laughing. George Newton took her by the shoulders and held her away, looking at her intently.

"I wondered if you would have changed much," he said as his eyes moved over her sleek blonde hair and down over the sheepskin jacket she wore. Under it, she was wearing a dark gray jersey dress that left her long, shapely legs visible from the knee down. "You look very elegant," George Newton said. "And very grown-up. Is this New York's influence or your young man's?"

She laughed to hear Adam described as her young man. "New York, I expect, Dad, but I was pretty grown-up before I went there, you know. I'm twenty-eight, remember."

"I never can remember," her father confessed, his face rueful. "It seems impossible. How did you get so old?" He picked up her case and she ran her hand through his arm as they turned towards the exit.

"How's Mother?"

"Fine; I wanted to be the first to see you when you arrived so I persuaded her to wait at home," her father admitted. She squeezed his arm, smiling. When she was a little girl they had had secrets like that from her mother; Carly had loved to go off on a Saturday morning with her father, fishing on the quiet riverbank, in the lightening dawn, hearing the slow running of the river between the bullrushes, the rustle of the ducks in the reeds, the sleepy calls of the birds. They had always left the house while Mrs. Newton was still asleep, stealing away in the magical hour between night and day, both of them happy at the prospect of the day ahead.

"You can tell me all the news," she said as she followed him out of the station into his black sedan.

"I was hoping you would tell me yours," her father said as he slid behind the driving wheel and looked round at her. "Your letters didn't say enough about this young man."

"Adam's thirty-eight," Carly said. "Didn't I tell you that?"

"Seems pretty young to me," George Newton said wryly. He was almost sixty, a tall man with a wiry figure, very active and fit, his face rugged and weathered, lines of humor radiating from his eyes and mouth, his gaze quietly steady.

Carly laughed. "You look pretty young to me. It must be all that fishing; it keeps you too busy to get old."

"It gives you rheumatism, too," her father said as he drove away from the station. "Hours of sitting in the rain, my doctor tells me. He gives me some sort of painkiller, but the only thing that works is to go out in the garden and pull up thistles with your bare hands. Thistles and nettles—my doctor tells me it's a form of acupuncture. Don't know about that. All I know is, I remember my own father doing it when his knuckles were swollen with rheumatism, and it certainly works."

"Mum says you're retiring soon?"

He nodded. "Next birthday." He had turned into the market square of the little Kent town and was edging his way through the traffic. It seemed very light to Carly, who was used to New York traffic snarling all round her, but her father complained that there were far too many cars around these days.

"The last sort of man I'd imagined you marrying was a sheep farmer," he said as they turned another corner and began to drive more rapidly along a street of small houses set behind lawns and flower beds. Carly was looking around her with a hundred memories pressing on her mind. This was the street along which she had walked from school, daydreaming about the current boy she was crazy about, or gossiping with her friends about homework or that week's football game. She knew every house, every bend in the road, every tree growing along the edge of the pavement.

"It's a surprise to me, too," she said. "But Adam's a surprising man."

"So we gathered from what you said about him; he's a well-traveled man, you said, and a writer. What made him settle on a farm in Yorkshire?"

She began to tell him about Adam's background, and her father listened as he drove to the far end of the street and turned into a narrow little driveway to park in front of a concrete garage. Beside it stood the family home, a gabled two-story building with bay windows in the Tudor style, their panes leaded in diamond-shaped glass. The garden was crammed with roses in summer, but today the neatly pruned bushes were bare and black, glistening with rain, and the lawns were pearled with raindrops that glittered in the faint winter sunshine.

The front door opened and Mrs. Newton ran out. "I was beginning to wonder where you two had got to; I thought you might have missed the train, Carly."

They hugged each other warmly and Mrs. Newton led her into the house, one arm around her. "Did you have a good trip? It's been raining all day—not the best weather for you when you come home!"

"I loved it," Carly said. "It was bitterly cold when I left New York, but London was so mild I almost didn't need my coat."

"I've made some tea," her mother said, and Carly laughed.

"I knew you'd say that!" Mrs. Newton had always automatically made tea when she was expecting Carly home, even when she had just been coming back from school.

"I'll take her case up," George Newton said behind them.

"Thank you, Dad," Carly said, looking around the small kitchen. "You've redecorated!"

"Yes, we did that last spring—didn't I tell you? I was sure I wrote about it. I did all the painting; Dad hung the wallpaper."

Mrs. Newton's blonde hair had faded to a silvery gray now, but she had Carly's features and slim figure, her eyes a paler blue, her manner rather more quiet. Her whole world was bounded by her home and her family, but she had followed her daughter's adventures in the States with deep interest and had encouraged Carly to take her career seriously. That warm, family background had made a secure springboard from which Carly could leap, and she had missed her parents very much.

While they drank their tea, Mrs. Newton asked her about Adam, as Mr. Newton had done, and told her that Adam had called them to introduce himself.

"He sounds very nice, darling. It was a thoughtful thing to do, and we felt much better once we had talked to him."

Carly looked at her quickly. "Were you worried about the idea of my marrying him? Dad seemed worried, I noticed."

Her mother hesitated, looking away. "It wasn't what we had expected. I don't know why, but we had the idea you loved New York so much, you would marry over there."

Carly laughed. "You don't marry a city, Mum, you marry a man."

Her mother smiled, glancing back at her, her face relaxing. "That's true—and you seem to have picked a very unusual man."

But although she spoke cheerfully, Carly detected a lingering air of concern, and later her mother was far more frank about what was bothering her. It was a problem that had been on Carly's mind, too, for the past three months, but that she had shelved until she had some better idea of what exactly faced her. Mrs. Newton approached the subject tentatively, her face wary.

"How do you feel about having a ready-made family, darling?"

Carly sighed ruefully. "Julie? Well, I realize it may not be plain sailing; it won't be easy being a stepmother. It won't be easy for her, either, I expect. I'm going to have to feel my way very carefully."

"What sort of little girl is she, do you know?"

"Adam has barely mentioned her, but his sister told me a few things."

"Oh, yes, you met her, didn't you?"

Carly nodded. "She and I got on quite well. She seemed quite fond of Julie, but then she isn't going to be Julie's stepmother and take her real mother's place."

"Adam hasn't talked about her to you?" That clearly disturbed Mrs. Newton, whose brow was creased in a troubled frown.

"Adam tends to play his cards close to his chest." He hadn't even said anything more about his dead wife, which worried Carly as much as the prospect of being a stepmother to his little girl. She didn't understand Adam yet. Love, she was realizing, doesn't give you an instant key to what goes on inside the man you love. It merely makes you want to know him as well as you know yourself.

Before dinner that evening she rang Adam's farm, dying to speak to him at greater length than when she was in New York and the Atlantic cable had made it sound as though they were talking to each other from deep-sea diving bells.

A high-pitched little voice answered. "Hello?"

Carly tensed, realizing it was Adam's daughter. Huskily, she said, "Could I speak to Mr. Blake, please?" She half-considered introducing herself, but then decided it would be better to wait until they were face to face.

"He isn't here; who is it?"

Carly felt a deep sense of disappointment. "This is Carly," she stammered, absurdly nervous. The child was only nine years old! Why should she be so tense about talking to her?

There was a brief silence, then the little voice said politely and coldly, "Who?"

"Carly Newton," she stammered even more huskily. Julie had to know who she was! Why was she pretending not to have heard of her?

"Would you like to leave a message for my father?"

Carly bit her lower lip. "When will he be home?"

"I don't know; he has gone to a party with Marie."

Carly frowned. Who on earth was Marie? Adam had gone to a party tonight? He had known she was coming back to England today; he must have guessed she would ring. Why wasn't he there?

Aloud, she said, "I see. Well, will you tell him I rang and ask him to ring me tomorrow morning?"

"Yes; goodbye." The phone went dead abruptly, and Carly stared at her own receiver for a moment before replacing it.

She walked slowly into the sitting room, where her father was reading his latest fishing magazine, his slippered feet toasting in front of a leaping fire. He looked up vaguely, smiling at her. "Adam okay?"

"He wasn't there," Carly said. She felt cold and disturbed. Julie had either been hostile or had never even heard of her—she didn't know which was the worst of the two. If Adam hadn't told his daughter of his plans to remarry, it was worrying. If Julie had known exactly who she was, her offhand manner had been deliberately unfriendly, which was alarming, too.

"Anything wrong?" Mr. Newton asked, frowning as he watched her face.

"No, of course not," she said quickly, giving him a reassuring smile that felt stiff on her mouth. She didn't want her parents to be even more worried. It was bad enough that she should feel like this; she had to keep her doubts to herself. When she had made up her mind to marry Adam, in Crete, she had thought she had resolved all her problems. The conflict that had kept them apart had been of her making, she had thought. Once she decided to give up her career and leave New York for Adam's remote farm, she had stupidly believed things would be pretty plain sailing, but life has a way of throwing new problems at you as fast as you solve an old one.

She couldn't sleep that night. She lay in bed, turning first on one side, then on the other, her mind in turmoil. What if Adam's little girl hated her? How on earth could she cope with that? Why hadn't Adam been at home? Why hadn't he rung her before going off to this party? And who was Marie? Adam had never even mentioned anyone called Marie. But then, Adam was not a very communicative man, in some ways. He had seemed to tell her so much, yet he had never said much about his wife or daughter, or talked at all about his emotional life. He had told her about his travels, his views of the world, his favorite books and music—but his private life had been kept a shrouded secret.

The next morning she waited anxiously for him to ring, her eye always on the clock. She watched it ticking on relentlessly towards noon, getting more and more miserable and disturbed.

Why wasn't Adam ringing? Had Julie given him her message? And even if she hadn't passed it on, why hadn't Adam rung her? He did know she was back at home, after all. She had told herself she wouldn't ring him, she would wait for him to ring her, but her stomach was eaten with acid nerves by lunchtime, and she had to force herself to eat the meal her mother served. Her parents avoided her eyes, aware that something was very wrong, but their discreet avoidance of the subject of Adam somehow made her feel worse.

When the phone did ring, during the long, silent afternoon, she jumped, her body as tense as if she was made of wire, and then leaped up from her chair and stumbled to lift the receiver, her hands trembling.

"Hallo?"

"Carly?" The deep voice sounded terse and she was torn between joy at hearing it and anxiety at the note it held.

"Adam," she said unevenly, her lips trembling into a fugitive smile. "I've been waiting all day for you to ring."

"I've only just got back," he said.

He sounded very odd, but then maybe she was beginning to imagine things. It was so easy to misread other people. "Julie gave you my message?" she said, trying to steady her own voice.

"Yes." There was no doubt about it, his tone was brusque. He paused, then said in an impatient way, "You weren't very tactful with her, darling; try to remember she's very young and easily hurt."

Carly drew a painful breath. "What did I say? I don't know what you mean. How can you say I wasn't tactful with her? I didn't say anything."

"Carly," Adam began, then stopped, and she heard him give a deep sigh. "Look, never mind; we can't talk about it now. Leave it for the moment." He paused again and said with less harshness, "Did you have a pleasant journey? How does it feel to be back in England?"

"Fine," Carly said automatically, her mind still grappling with what he had implied about Julie.

"I'm dying to see you again," Adam said, and now there was a smile in his voice. "It seems so long; I have to keep reminding myself what you look like."

"Are you beginning to forget already?" she asked, hurt lancing through her.

"Of course not," Adam said. "Darling, I miss you every day; I can't wait to have you here with me. As soon as your parents can spare you, you're coming up here, aren't you?"

"Yes," she said.

"I'll meet you at the station. There's only one train in

the afternoon; it gets in at four o'clock. I'll be there with the landrover and drive you home."

"I'm longing to see the farm," she said. And Julie, she thought, Julie would be there, and once she had looked at the little girl she would know for sure whether the hostility she had imagined she felt had been real or merely nervous imagination.

"We've got a lot to talk about," Adam said.

"Yes." She paused. "Julie said you were at a party last night."

He laughed. "I drove Marie to one; a friend of hers was having a birthday party. Marie was desperate to be there, but there's no bus service from here to Wilcatton, which is where the party was—it's forty miles away. I dropped her there and went on to visit a friend of my own who was selling up. I wanted to get in a bid for some farm equipment I knew he had. I got it at a very fair price. That's what I've been doing this morning—driving the machinery back in a hired lorry."

"You didn't stay at the party then?" Carly asked casually.

"It wasn't my generation," Adam said, laughing. "Do you see me dancing to the latest rock music?"

Carly's mind worked rapidly. "How old's Marie?" she asked. And *who* was she? she wondered.

"Nineteen—her mother does the housekeeping for us; I like to help her family if I can. Her husband's dead and they're short of money. They haven't got a car."

Carly's mind flooded with relief; she preferred not to admit, even to herself, just what she had begun to suspect. It was so absurd to feel jealous, to wonder what Julie had been hinting at, and the child hadn't said anything she could pin down, anyway. It had been the way she told her that Adam had gone to a party with

Marie—this unknown Marie. Julie had given her casual words an intonation that had left Carly with a very different impression.

"It must be dull for a girl of nineteen to live in a country district where there's no bus service," she said, and Adam laughed.

"Oh, Marie has quite a good time; she's a lively girl, very pretty."

"Oh," Carly said, despising herself because of the sharp little niggle of pain that began inside her. So Marie was pretty? So what?

"Darling, I've got a lot of work to do," Adam said. "I'd love to talk for hours, but I must go. I'll ring again when I can—maybe tonight. You'll be there?"

"Yes," Carly said. "I'll be here."

"Talk to you then," Adam said and she quickly said, "I love you, Adam."

"Me too," Adam said.

She put the phone down a moment later and walked away, thinking back over the conversation and aware of a lingering sense of uneasiness. What had Adam meant when he told her she hadn't been tactful with Julie? What had Julie said to him? Carly knew so little about children, about little girls of nine who had been brought up by divorced mothers and widowed fathers, but she was beginning to realize that the problem of Julie might not be as easily solved as her own doubts about giving up her career to marry Adam. When she had faced that decision, she had only had herself to worry about; it had been a straightforward choice that only Carly could make. Julie was another human being, one whose mind she wasn't going to find simple to understand. How did Julie feel about the prospect of having a stepmother? How did she feel about her father? Carly had been thinking of Julie as a child, a very small girl, only nine years old, vulnerable, sensitive, childish. But the cool, self-composed voice that had spoken to her last night and, with the use of so few words, left her with such an uneasy feeling, had not been the voice of a little girl. Nine years old Julie might be—but Carly began, in a half-doubtful, half-alarmed way, to view her with distinct qualms.

Chapter Nine

A week later, she sat in the slow train making its way through the hills and dales of Yorkshire, strung up with nervous anticipation as she stared out the window at the smooth, rolling folds of the uplands with the fertile green fields of the valleys running at their bases. In half an hour she should be alighting at Adam's nearest station, and he had promised to be there to meet her. She hoped he would come alone. She wanted a few precious minutes with him before she had to meet Julie. Over the past few days her nervous anxiety over the child had increased. Every word Adam said about his daughter made her more aware that Julie meant a great deal to him. It was only natural, of course; Julie was his only child. Carly had expected there to be great affection between them. It should have occurred to her when Adam first proposed that his little girl might be a stumbling block, but it hadn't, because she had been too uncertain for other reasons. She hadn't stopped to consider the problems of becoming a stepmother. Only after she had told him she would marry him, and he had asked her to get to know Julie before their wedding day, had it dawned on her that Julie might prove to be difficult.

The compartment had been crowded when she first got into it in London, but now there were only two passengers left, herself and a slim young man with rough, dark brown hair that curled slightly. He had spent most of the journey behind a series of newspapers and country magazines, but now he tidied them all into a neat pile and sat back in his corner seat, eyeing Carly curiously.

"Going far?" It was the first time he had spoken to her, although he had looked at her several times with a smile.

"I'm getting off at Thirkettle."

"Really? So am I; what a coincidence." He grinned at her, running a hand over his hair to make it less unruly. He was wearing a smooth camelhair overcoat that looked expensive, and his shoes had a handmade elegance that suggested they had been made in London.

"Do you live near here?" Carly asked curiously, wondering what he did for a living. Whatever it was, he was obviously doing well at it.

"Yes, do you?" His glance wandered down over her sheepskin coat and pleated dark brown skirt. Carly had tried to look as though she belonged in the country, but she wasn't sure she had succeeded.

"I shall be," Carly said, reluctant to say too much.

His heavy eyebrows rose, a question in his brown eyes. "We haven't met before, have we? I'm sure I'd remember if we had." He held out his hand, which was beautifully shaped and smooth-skinned. Whatever he did, he did not use his hands in his work, Carly decided, putting her own hand into his. "I'm Paul Reswick," he told her.

"Carly Newton," she said, shaking hands and smiling.

"That's unusual; is it short for something? Or were you given the name Carly?"

"My mother wanted to call me Caroline, but there

are several Carolines in our family already," she explained as he relinquished her hand.

"Are any of them as pretty as you?" he asked, and she went a little pink, and looked out the window to cover her surprise.

"What do you do, Paul? Do you work up here or in London?" she asked in a quick way.

"I farm," he said, and Carly's head turned toward him in genuine surprise.

"You farm?" She had not expected that. Her face betrayed her, and Paul Reswick began to laugh.

"I know, sounds unlikely, doesn't it?"

"You don't look like a farmer." He was slim and elegant, in build as well as in dress. His face was a little pale, in fact, his skin of the faintly sallow variety that only looks really good when it's warmed by a suntan. She remembered the feel of his smooth, cool fingers. There had been no work-roughness on them.

"To be honest, I don't do any of the fieldwork," he said. "I own the farms; I have managers who run them. I inherited them from an uncle five years ago and they were already a smoothly running unit, so I left things as they were. I was trained as an accountant, so I do the paperwork of the business."

"Have you always lived in Yorkshire?" Carly asked, and he shook his head.

"I moved here when I inherited; I wasn't expecting my uncle to leave his estate to me. He had a son who was killed in a car crash. It broke the poor old man up; he collapsed with a stroke and lived just long enough to make a will leaving everything to me." Paul grimaced. "Shock of my life, actually. I was rather fond of my cousin Jack. The whole business was tragic." He lifted his shoulders in a shrug. "Anyway, what about you? Do I gather you're moving up here? From London?"

"I'm visiting Adam Blake at Wildbore Farm; do you know it?" Carly asked, evading answering his actual question.

His eyes widened. "Of course I do; I know Adam, too." His tone was suddenly curt.

Carly looked at him questioningly. "Is his farm near your house?"

"A mere half-mile away," Paul said. He paused and then asked, "You're a friend of his?"

"I'm going to marry him," Carly said shyly.

"Oh. I see." Paul's face had tightened, and he stared at her oddly. "You're going to marry him? Have you been engaged long?"

"We met in New York in the summer."

Paul nodded. "I remember he went there; he's written a book, I gather."

"Yes, a very good book. I was his editor. It was my publishing house that bought the book rights in the States."

"You're in publishing?" Paul looked interested, the strange coldness going out of his face. "Really? How fascinating. I've always wanted to have a job like that. I did think of joining the accounts department of a London publisher once, but it didn't come off and now, of course, I never shall. Farming is okay, but I miss London; I go there as often as I can."

The train was slowing again and Carly looked out of the window to realize with surprise that they had arrived at Thirkettle. She jumped up, flushing. "We're here!"

Paul got up and helped her to lift her suitcase down

from the rack above the seats; then he got his own briefcase down and followed Carly along the corridor, insisting on carrying her suitcase for her.

She climbed down to the platform and looked around. Paul joined her, the wind blowing his dark brown hair about. The air was keen and crisp, tipped with ice, and the sky was leaden, as though it held snow that might fall at any moment.

"Only a fortnight until Christmas," Paul said, shivering in his camelhair coat. "We often have white Christmases here; I hope you're prepared. You'll need plenty of sweaters and warm clothes."

Carly could see no sign of Adam. The train moved away, vanishing round the bend with a drawn-out whistle. The railway station was empty but for herself and Paul, who looked at her quizzically.

"Is someone meeting you?"

"Adam said he would."

Paul said nothing, but set off along the platform with her suitcase, and she followed him through the gates, giving up her ticket to the man on duty, who tipped his hat to Paul and gave her a polite nod.

Outside stood a long, white car toward which Paul moved. "Why don't I give you a lift?" he asked. "It's far too cold for you to stand around waiting for Blake to arrive."

Frowning and flushed, Carly said, "He may have been delayed. Is there a telephone here? I could ring him."

"There is, but it's out of order," Paul said. "Try the stationmaster's office; they may let you use their phone. I'll wait here for you." He unlocked his car and Carly walked quickly back into the station and spoke to the man on duty. He politely agreed to let her use his office phone. She dialed Adam's number. The phone rang for several minutes but nobody answered. Carly hung up, biting her lip. What should she do? She went back out and found Paul leaning on his car, watching the threatening sky.

"That snow is going to come down within the next hour or so," he warned. "Did you get him?"

"There was no reply."

They both looked at the road that wound away from the isolated little country railway station through a green valley between high hills masked by gorse and heather. There was no sign of life, no car speeding towards them. Carly's flush deepened. Adam had not come to meet her as he had promised. She was worried and angry and upset, but she hid it from Paul Reswick, who was watching her.

"You can't stand here for as long as it takes Blake to remember you exist," he pointed out, and the way he phrased that made her sense of hurt and anger more painful. Paul opened the trunk and slung her suitcase into it. He came round to open the passenger door. "In you get," he urged, and with only a slight hesitation, Carly got into the car.

It was snowing as they drove between the hills, a fine drifting blowing fall of large wet flakes that came faster and thicker as the car climbed up the sloping valley bottom. Paul's windshield wipers busily swished to and fro, clearing snow from the glass, but Carly sat there feeling miserable, watching the air writhing with white shapes. Paul switched on his headlights and a beam of brightness cut their way ahead of them. In it the snow danced and flew. She could see little of the surrounding countryside. Gray stone walls marked out the fields, and between them she saw the forms of sheep sheltering together from the wind and snow. A few twisted thorn trees crouched here and there, bent the way of the prevailing wind. The landscape was pervaded by a mood of loneliness and glooming isolation, a brooding shadowiness.

"Maybe Adam's car couldn't get through," she said. There could be a dozen good reasons for his failing to meet her—but couldn't he have rung the station and left word of what had happened?

"He may be out in the fields, trying to bring in his sheep," said Paul. "If there *is* a blizzard tonight he could lose some valuable ewes if he leaves them out on the hills. He would want to bring them down to more sheltered pasture."

"Yes, perhaps that's it," Carly said. Perhaps it was—but why hadn't he let her know? He knew what time her train was arriving. He could have rung the station. That thought lodged in the forefront of her mind. He hadn't rung her the day she arrived back in England. He hadn't rung the station today. Adam seemed to be indifferent to her feelings; it never seemed to occur to him that he might hurt or upset her by failing to get in touch.

Or was there a more worrying explanation? She sat upright, turning even more pale. Had Adam been on his way to pick her up when his car crashed? Paul sensed the movement and looked round at her.

"Something wrong?"

"I'm worrying about Adam," she confessed.

"He doesn't seem to be worrying about you." There was a brusque note in Paul's voice, and she winced. He came too close to expressing what she felt herself.

Swinging the wheel, he suddenly turned up a narrow,

rutted lane between high stone walls. A few trees grew close to it, whipping back and forth in the cold wind, their bare branches scraping the top of the wall and making a mournful sound. The car springs bounced and protested as they climbed steeply upward, and Paul grimaced, gripping the wheel more tightly.

"The road up to Wildbore is pretty tough on cars. Sit tight; this won't be a comfortable ride."

"It's very kind of you to go to all this trouble," Carly said gratefully. "I was lucky to run into you." If she hadn't, she would probably still be standing at the empty, isolated railway station in the blizzard wondering what on earth to do.

"Glad to be of help," Paul said. "This lane was originally an old farm track through the fields to the house; it's meant more for tractors than well-sprung cars." He peered ruefully out the window and gave a sigh of relief. "Ah, here we are." The car turned a sharp-angled corner and pulled up in front of the dark shape of a house half-obscured by blowing snow.

Carly got out of the car and looked up at that outline, her heart sinking. The house stood alone on a wind-buffeted hillside looking down into a narrow valley. There was no other house in view. Square and rugged, the building had little shelter from the elements. It seemed to have grown up out of the ground, the stone of which it was built the same gray as that used in the endless low walls crisscrossing the hillsides.

There was no light in any of the windows. No smoke rose from the chimney. The house had a deserted air, the slate roof already piled with snow.

"It doesn't look as if anyone is at home," Paul said unnecessarily. Carly hunched inside her sheepskin coat, her collar up to keep the snow away from her face. Flakes clung to her lashes, numbed her lips. Her hands and feet were stiff with cold. She felt like crying.

What had happened to Adam? Where was he? She wished she had never come here.

Paul lifted the heavy brass doorknocker and banged loudly. They heard the crash echoing inside the house, but nobody came to answer it.

"Let's try round the back," Paul said. "Around here, people rarely bother to lock their houses; they don't get burglars in this district. It's too remote."

He walked away, bent against the wind, snow dusting the top of his head, and Carly followed, shivering. The snow whirled thicker and faster, blanketing the fields, lying in deepening drifts along the walls and under the trees, laying a fine coat upon the branches and the rough clumps of gorse that clung to the slopes.

Behind the house lay a large garden, with a lawn and bare flower beds that had been dug up for winter, and most of the ground was taken up by a vegetable garden containing cabbages and winter sprouts. Carly caught a glimpse of several outhouses at one side as she joined Paul at the back door. He had opened it and was just going into the house.

"Do you think we should?" Carly asked nervously.

He looked round at her, raising his brows. "What else do you suggest? Are you going to sit outside on the wall until Blake gets back? Or would you like to come back to my home? I'm perfectly happy to take you home with me; at least there you would be warm and comfortable."

"Oh, no," she said, then flushed. "It's very kind but . . ."

"Then come in out of the snow," Paul cut into her stammered apology, and smiled at her a little teasingly.

He switched on the light and Carly followed him into a small, modern kitchen that was very tidy. Paul walked across it into the room beyond. It lay in shadow, but a sunken fire smoldered in the iron grate and the room was comfortingly warm to Carly after the freezing air outside. Paul flicked on a lamp and crossed to the fireplace. He made up the fire while she watched him, standing there in her coat, full of depressed uncertainty.

This was not how she had imagined arriving at Adam's home. Her spirits were so low she hardly knew how to stop herself from bursting into tears.

Paul straightened, giving her a thoughtful look. "Now we'll have a drink, I think," he announced and vanished while Carly made faint, protesting noises. He came back with a tray on which stood two glasses and a bottle of brandy.

"Paul, I'm not sure we should . . . " she began, and he forced a glass of brandy into her hand, grinning at her.

"I'm sure Adam Blake would want you to make yourself at home—after all, if you're going to marry him, it's going to be your home, too." He lifted his own glass in a salute, his face amused. "And good luck," he added drily.

The brandy went down like liquid fire, making her cough, but as the warmth spread through her she began to feel much better. Paul took off his coat and sat down by the fire, sighing.

"I'll thaw out before I start off for home. Maybe Blake will get back soon. I don't like the idea of leaving you alone here."

Carly didn't like the idea, either. She took off her own coat and sat down in another chair, edging closer to the fire and relaxing as the warmth of it reached her stiff, cold flesh.

"You've been very kind," she told him, and Paul smiled at her as he finished his brandy.

"Any time; it isn't often that I get the chance to play St. George and rescue a lady from disaster." He poured himself another drink and came over to put some more brandy in her glass.

"No, no," Carly said, laughing.

"Yes, yes," Paul teased, bending towards her, his face alight with amusement.

A crash made them both jump. Carly's gaze flew across the room to the open door leading into the kitchen. Adam stood there, his face savage, dark red blood suffusing it. Behind him the outer door blew backward and forward in the knifelike wind. Adam's expression made her stiffen.

"What are you doing here?" The terse question was hurled toward her and made her gasp, but it had not been aimed at her.

"I drove Carly here from the station, since you had neglected to pick her up, and I didn't like to leave her alone, so I stayed." Paul spoke in a light, drawling tone that had an edge of mockery in it, and the voice he used did not make Adam's face lighten.

"I told you to stay out of my house," he said through lips that barely seemed to move. "Get out."

Paul laughed and put down his glass. He picked up his coat, shrugged into it and turned back to Carly, offering her his hand.

"I've enjoyed talking to you; I hope we'll meet again soon," he said. "If you need me, I'm in the phone book, and I'll always be glad to hear from you."

She had automatically given him her hand and he lifted it to his lips, kissing it lightly.

When he had released it he walked calmly toward Adam, who stared at him angrily every inch of the way. Paul moved round him and left the house. Carly sat staring at Adam, growing more angry by the second. His behavior was extraordinary. Why had he been so rude to Paul? He was ignoring her, making no attempt to apologize for having left her stranded at the station. How dare he?

Adam pushed back the hood of his thick quilted anorak and snow floated down around him. He unzipped and took off the anorak, hanging it on the wall in the kitchen. Carly sat waiting, watching him, as tense as a coiled spring. He pulled off the heavy boots he was wearing and went over to wash his hands.

He hadn't said a word. Carly was locked into a feeling of grim depression. She had given up her job and come all this way to find a man who was behaving in a baffling and hurtful fashion, and she wondered what exactly was going on inside Adam's head.

He came into the room and stood looking at her. "Why did you drive here with Reswick?"

Her voice trembling with anger, she retorted, "Because I preferred to come with him than stand around in the blizzard waiting for someone who obviously wasn't coming. I rang here and there was no reply. Why didn't you meet me?"

"I had to bring the ewes down from the upper pastures," Adam said, frowning. "But I sent Marie to pick you up."

"She didn't arrive; nobody did."

"How long did you wait?"

"About ten minutes, I suppose. I told you, I rang here to find out if something was wrong."

Adam stared at her. "You didn't pass a car on the road?"

"No." She stood up, her face tight. "How do you think I felt? Arriving at that station, finding nobody there, getting no reply from your house—what was I to do? How dare you shout at me . . . ?"

"I'm sorry," Adam said, his face altering, his voice almost a groan. "I didn't mean to shout at *you*. It was a combination of things—finding Reswick here, worry over my sheep—I was feeling pretty grim when I came home. I lost a couple of ewes; they were dead when we got to the flock. It had been snowing for some time up on top of the hills and I was too late; one died of exposure, the other fell and broke a leg, trying to get into shelter."

"Oh," Carly said, looking at him uncertainly. "I'm sorry; that must have been a shock."

"I had to put her out of her misery," Adam said tersely. He lifted his shoulders in a shrug. "So I wasn't feeling too happy when I walked in and found you with Reswick. He knows he isn't welcome here."

Carly frowned. "Why not? Why don't you like him?"

"I don't," Adam told her with biting emphasis. "Does it matter why?" His tone made her shrink, and he sighed. "Don't look like that." He took two strides and put his arms round her, kissing her hair with a long, deep sigh. "Carly. Oh, Carly, this wasn't how I meant it to be. I've been aching to see you, but circumstances ruined everything."

She slowly relaxed, her body leaning toward him, and as she lifted her face Adam bent and kissed her.

212

She wound her arms round his neck and kissed him back passionately.

A moment later, he looked down at her flushed, drowsy face with teasing eyes.

"Better?"

"Much," she whispered, her mouth heated from his kisses. "I thought you might have changed your mind about marrying me when you didn't show up at the station."

"How could you think that?" he asked, stroking her cheek.

"You seemed so distant on the phone."

"I was worried," he admitted, his mouth twisting. "Julie was being difficult."

Carly looked at him sharply. "I wondered if she might resent me—on the phone when I spoke to her she seemed hostile."

"You weren't very tactful, Carly. I told you that."

"I didn't say anything! I just asked if I could speak to you and told her who I was—why wasn't I tactful? Hadn't you told her about me?"

"Of course I had." He stared at her, his brows knitted. "What did you actually say to her?"

She struggled to remember the exact words she had used and repeated them. Adam looked at her hard, his expression uncertain.

"Was that all you said?"

"Yes."

"Sure?"

Carly stared back at him. "I'm certain. Why? What did Julie say I had said?"

Adam sighed. "She didn't actually say anything—but she seemed very upset; she said she didn't like you."

"Was that why you didn't ring me back sooner? I was upset at not hearing from you for so long."

"I didn't ring the day you got home because I thought you might want to have time to settle back into your family, and the next day I was busy getting my machinery back to the farm." Adam looked at her wryly. "Were you expecting me to ring that first night?"

"Yes," she admitted. "I waited and waited, getting more and more upset."

"You and I had our wires crossed," Adam said, brushing his lips over her mouth. "I thought I was being tactful. After all, you hadn't seen your parents for so long; I didn't want to intrude on your reunion. It never entered my head that you'd be worried or hurt."

She laughed. "I forgive you." She ran a hand over his thick black hair, ruffling it, then her face sobered. "Does Julie resent me?"

Adam gave a faint sigh. "I suppose so, but she'll get over it."

"It's natural enough; you're her father and she's had you all to herself for so long. I understand how she feels. I'll try hard, Adam. I'll do everything I can to make friends with her." Carly looked at him earnestly, her blue eyes worried. "The last thing I want to do is come between you."

"We'll work it out," Adam promised. He glanced at the clock on the mantel shelf, frowning. "Where on earth is Marie? They should have been back an hour ago. I wonder if they're waiting at the station in case you turn up?"

"They?" Carly asked, and Adam nodded.

"She took Julie with her. They were doing some shopping first in Thirkettle, which may be why you missed them." He moved to the door. "I'd better ring the stationmaster and find out if they turned up. I don't like this long absence—Marie is a reckless driver, and in snowy weather anything can happen."

Carly looked at him anxiously. "You think they might have had an accident? Should you go back to the station and try to find them?"

Adam looked impatiently at the clock again. "Marie can be very thoughtless. If she met a friend she might forget everything else. I shouldn't have sent her. She only got her driving license two months ago." He stopped talking abruptly, his head tilted as he listened to a sound he had picked up but that had escaped Carly until she, too, suddenly heard the footsteps on the snowy path outside. The back door was pushed open and a girl in a thick wool coat and scarf rushed into the house.

"There you are, Marie," Adam said. "We were just wondering where you had got to. Why weren't you at the station when the train arrived? Did you forget the time?"

The girl stood there, her face distraught, very pale, her brown eyes enormous.

"I've lost Julie!" Her high-pitched voice rose above Adam's words, and he stood there, staring at her, his face freezing.

"What?"

"She vanished; I've been searching for her, but I can't find her anywhere. I didn't know what to do; I was going out of my mind." Her disjointed phrases stumbled over each other, only just audible because her voice shook.

Adam crossed the room to her in quick strides and

215

caught her slender shoulders, shaking her firmly. "Calm down; stop getting hysterical. Now, what do you mean, you've lost Julie? *Where* did you lose her?"

Marie looked up at him, tears glistening in her eyes. She was a very pretty girl with a smooth-skinned face, but her present pallor robbed her of some of her looks. Her nose was slightly tiptilted, her eyes beautifully shaped, her mouth curved in a warm bow. Her scarf had slipped back, revealing chestnut curls. At this moment she looked very young, shock and fear making her tremble.

"I thought the train arrived at four-thirty," she began, and Adam cut in on her tersely.

"I told Julie four o'clock."

"She must have got it wrong; she told me four-thirty," Marie said, but her eyes slid away and didn't quite meet Adam's, and he frowned.

"Well, go on; you turned up at four-thirty, did you?"

She nodded. "I talked to Mr. Wainwright at the station and I left Julie in the car. When I went back to it, after Mr. Wainwright had told me Paul had taken your visitor with him, Julie had gone. I thought she might have walked on down the road so I drove down to the crossroads to look out for her, but there was no sign of her. I drove around for ages, looking everywhere, but I couldn't find her."

Adam said in a harsh, worried voice, "I'd better ring the station and see if she went there."

"I went back there myself. She hadn't been there," Marie said, then the tears slipped from her eyes and trickled down her cheeks. "I'm sorry, Adam. Where can she be? In this snow—she wouldn't have walked up the moors, would she? Not in this weather?"

Adam was white. "My God, I trust not—she could die of exposure inside a couple of hours. It's freezing up there tonight."

Marie winced, her white teeth biting into her lower lip. "What are we going to do?" She looked toward the window where the night pressed darkly around the house, the sky full of driving snow. "We'll never find here," she said frantically.

"We're going to have to find her," Adam insisted in a terse, determined voice. "I'll ring the police. Someone may have seen her, or she may have gone to someone's house to shelter. We'll need to make up a search party."

"Yes," Marie said quickly, her hands clenched at her sides. "I can ring some of my friends; they'll come and help."

Carly stood up, looking at Adam pleadingly. "Can I help?"

He shook his head, touching her hand. "Thank you, darling, but you don't know the countryside; you could get lost too, and then we would have another problem on our hands. No, you stay here. If Julie finds her way back, she should find someone here at home to look after her." He moved away. "I'll ring the police station, then we'll go, Marie."

Carly had a vivid, painful mental picture of the little girl, out on the snowy moors alone, frightened and lost and miserable, with the wind howling round her and the blizzard rapidly obscuring the landmarks she might otherwise recognize. She listened to Adam talking on the phone, his voice quick and anxious. He put down the receiver and turned back to her.

"The constable hasn't had any news of her but he's

going to get in touch with some of our neighbors and organize a search party." He looked at the fireplace. "Keep that fire built up, Carly. If Julie does get back, ring the police. The number is on the pad by the phone."

She nodded obediently, looking at him with concern. He was so pale.

Marie was watching them, her expression brooding. Carly met her eyes and saw hostility in them. A flash of intuition hit her. Marie was jealous. It wasn't only Julie who resented Adam's remarriage. Marie resented it, too. The other girl looked away, her face taking on a faint angry flush. Carly wondered if Marie was in love with Adam or was merely possessive about him because he was a substitute father figure. He had clearly taken on some of a father's role for her since her own father died. It wouldn't be surprising if the girl regarded him as being her property. Had Marie's hostility whipped up Julie's feelings of jealous resentment? If Marie had shown openly that she did not want Carly there, the child might have felt even more justified in resenting her, too.

Adam was putting on his boots again, shouldering into his anorak. As he zipped it up, he looked at Carly gently.

"Try not to worry too much. The minute we have any news, I'll let you know."

She nodded. "You'll find her, Adam; I'm sure you will." She had her fingers crossed as she said that. If anything had happened to Julie she knew it would darken their relationship irreparably. How could they ever be happy together with such a tragic beginning to their marriage?

He kissed her hard, holding her very close, as though

218

he needed the reassurance of her body warmth for that instant. Strain and shock had tightened his facial muscles, making him so tense that Carly found it hard to know him. He moved away, gesturing to Marie.

"Ready? Let's go."

Marie slowly followed him, her slender body as taut as Adam's, her pale face filled with fear and guilt and misery.

When they had gone, Carly found some large logs in a brass box standing beside the fireplace, and laid them on the fire. A shower of angry green sparks flew from them as the wood split in the heat, then a tongue of orange flame shot up the blackened chimney.

Carly sat down in her chair again, watching as the fire began to roar. Outside the window the wind wailed with eerie menace, hurling snow against the frozen glass. Carly wished she could have gone with Adam, done something useful, instead of being left here to brood and worry. Poor Julie, she thought; she must have been so upset to run off like this!

The light bulb flickered. She looked up, frowning, just as the light went off altogether. "Oh, no!" Carly said aloud, getting up. The light from the fire made it possible to see as she groped her way into the kitchen to try that light switch. She pressed it down but nothing happened. The electricity had been cut off; perhaps a cable had blown down in the storm. To make quite sure, Carly looked around and finally found a fuse cupboard. There was no burnt-out fuse. The power had been cut off outside the house, obviously. She went back into the sitting room and found the walls and ceiling leaping with black shadows from the firelight. Carly sat down again, nervously looking at the flames.

The clock ticked rhythmically on the mantel shelf. The wind moaned outside. Carly waited, her nerves on edge.

When the phone rang she ran to it and snatched it up with trembling hands. "Hallo?"

"Carly?"

"Adam—have you found her?"

"No," he said in a heavy voice. "I thought she might have come back home."

"No," Carly said, her spirits sinking. "Oh, darling, I'm so sorry. Has there been any sight of her anywhere?"

"No," Adam said. "I'll keep in touch, darling." The phone went dead and Carly slowly went back to stare into the fire.

Adam sounded quite distraught, his voice rough with fear and anxiety. How could their love have any chance of survival after this?

Chapter Ten

$\mathcal{T}$ime passed, but so slowly that she felt she heard every single beat of the clock, the steady sound racing with the overrapid ticking of her own pulses. Tense, strung up, she waited—for the phone to ring, for someone to arrive, for something to break the agony of her fear. She could hear nothing—only the wind, the rustle of snow flying against the window, the roar of the flames in the chimney and the disturbed rhythm of her heart.

How long could a child survive out on the open moors in weather like this? she wondered miserably, watching the whirl of white flakes that were now so thick they muffled every sound beyond the house. She felt as though she was entirely cut off. Outside, somewhere in the dark night, Adam and a band of others were searching for Julie, but she herself could do nothing but wait, and that galled her; her own helpless, useless inability to help *hurt*.

Even if Adam found Julie alive, Carly had to face the problem of the future. How could they go ahead with their plans to marry if Julie resented her so much that she had risked her own life like this? The child had to be totally against her. How could she marry Adam if his child felt like that? They could never be happy.

She was so sunk in misery that it wasn't until the back door was flung open that she realized someone had arrived. She leaped up, and in the flame-lit darkness saw Adam standing in the kitchen, his anorak encrusted with snow, his face bleak and harsh. Carly's hands tightened at her sides as she looked at him, trying to read his expression. "Julie?" she whispered shakily. "Did you find her?"

"She's safe," Adam said grimly, but that set look did not leave his face, and Carly waited, anxious and disturbed, knowing that something was very wrong. Was Julie injured, ill? Where was she? Why hadn't Adam brought her back with him?

"She was never on the moors," he said, pulling off his boots. A little puddle had begun forming on the floor where he stood as the snow on his boots melted in the warmth of the room. Unzipping his anorak, he pulled that off, too. "She caught a train down south, it seems. While Marie was talking to the stationmaster, Julie slipped past into the station and got on a train that happened to be standing in the station. She turned up at her grandparents' house an hour ago."

All that worry and fear, those long, agonized hours of waiting, and all the time Julie had been safe and sound, on a train! A flash of relief was followed by anger inside Carly. Then she thought of Julie's underlying misery, the feelings that must have driven her to run away like this, and she sighed. Slowly she moved across the kitchen to make Adam some hot coffee; he looked so cold, so tired, that it made her ache to see his weary, angry face.

"How could she do this to me?" he muttered under his breath, hanging up his anorak on the wall near the door.

"I'm sorry, Adam," she said quietly as he turned away, and he nodded and shrugged. Going to the sink he began to wash his hands and face. Carly felt tears pricking at her eyes. She looked in a cupboard to find coffee mugs, got them down, spooned instant coffee into them, and as the kettle on the old-fashioned kitchen range began to boil, took it off and poured boiling water into the mugs of coffee. Adam was toweling himself briskly as she spooned sugar into his mug. He turned and she held out the steaming drink.

He took it between both hands, sighing deeply. "Thank you; I need this." He walked into the sitting room and Carly followed with her own coffee. Adam got out the bottle of brandy and added a generous finger of amber liquid to his coffee, offering the bottle to Carly, who shook her head.

Adam sat down and stared into the fire, nursing his mug. "My father-in-law rang the police, to say Julie had turned up. They had rung him to ask if he had heard from her, so he knew she had run away. She had walked from the railway station, apparently, and was frozen and crying."

Carly winced. "Poor little girl."

"Poor little girl?" Adam looked up, his jaw rigid. "I was out of my mind with fear. We were just beginning to face the thought that she might already be dead. When I see her I'll kill her."

"Don't, Adam!" Carly broke out in anguish. "What must she have been going through to do this?"

"So she put *us* through hell," Adam muttered angrily. "While we were tramping about on the moors in that snow, calling her name and wondering if she was even alive to hear us, Julie was on a train going south, warm and snug and not caring what she was doing to us. And you call her a poor little girl? She has too much of her damned mother in her. Donna was selfish and self-obsessed and didn't give two damns what she did to get her own way, but Julie isn't going to grow up like her mother, not if I can stop it. When I get my hands on her I'll give her the slapping of a lifetime. She won't do anything like this again."

Adam had had a bad shock, and his fear had turned now to bitter anger. The expression on his face as he drank his coffee, staring at the leaping flames, reminded Carly all too vividly of the rage with which he had walked out on her that night in New York when she admitted she was doubtful about marrying him. His reaction then had been sudden, violent and bitter. It had taken Carly by surprise. It had seemed out of character for the charming companion she had thought she knew. She knew more about Adam now. She knew what had formed his character over the years, how an aching loss in his childhood had affected him, what his disastrous marriage had done to him. Adam was a strong man, but strong men have strong emotions, and Adam's emotions were more powerful than most.

Julie had wounded him by running away to her grandparents, just as Carly had wounded him by hesitating about marrying him. Adam could not bear any form of rejection. The measure of his anger matched the measure of his hidden pain. Julie had hurt Adam, as Carly had done, and all his anxiety for his child had been swallowed up in black rage at her.

Quietly she said to him, "Don't be too hard on her, Adam; she's only a child."

He didn't answer for a moment and when he did his reply was oblique. "I shall have to go and fetch her myself. I had enough trouble persuading them to give her up in the first place. I had to threaten them with the law courts. Now they may try to keep her on the grounds that she isn't happy with me."

Carly frowned, realizing that Julie had created a serious problem. What if her grandparents did bring a legal action claiming that Adam was not looking after his child properly?

"This wouldn't have happened if I hadn't come here," she said, hardly aware of speaking aloud, her mind obsessed with her own feeling of responsibility for this situation.

Adam shot her a look. "Don't be ridiculous; it isn't your fault." He put down his empty mug and stood up, lifting her from her chair. Carly looked up at him, her blue eyes defensive and disturbed. He framed her face with his hands, sighing as he watched her.

"This isn't how I wanted you to meet my daughter," he muttered. "I talked to her about you; I thought I'd made her see you were going to be her friend."

"We should have realized she was bound to be jealous."

Adam's frown came back. "She must have got some crazy notions into her head."

"She thought I was going to take you away from her," Carly said gently. "That wasn't a crazy notion, Adam; it was predictable. She felt threatened and unhappy, so she ran away. Don't be angry with her. That will only make matters worse."

"What do you suggest I do? Ignore what she's done?"

"Try to be understanding," Carly urged. "Don't scowl at her like *that.*" She put a finger on his black brows, smoothing out the frown drawing them together above his eyes. Adam took her hand and put it to his mouth, kissing her fingers gently one by one.

"You look tired," he said. "And pale. You should have been in bed hours ago. Come on, I'll show you your room." He picked up the flashlight he had been carrying out on the moors and showed her out of the sitting room and up the stairs, the beam of light revealing a large, drafty hall and pale walls. Carly climbed the stairs beside him, drooping wearily. Adam pushed open a door on the upper floor and the flashlight picked out the room beyond. She shivered in the icy air, and he said quickly, "I'll make you a hot water bottle." Pushing the light into her hand, he added, "Get undressed and I'll be back by the time you're in bed."

"My night things are in my suitcase," she said, uncomfortably aware that she had packed flimsy nightclothes in which she was going to freeze in this room. There was no central heating in the bedroom; the temperature was zero.

Adam lifted an amused eyebrow. "Want to borrow a pair of my flannel pajamas?"

She laughed. "They'd be far too big."

He went out and came back with a neatly folded pair of warm men's pajamas, which she accepted with more laughter.

"You don't honestly expect me to put these on?"

"Why not? They'll be warm."

"I shall look absurd in them."

"You'll look delightful," Adam said, mockery in his eyes. He went out again and Carly began hurriedly to undress, then buttoned herself into his pajama jacket. As she had expected, it came down to her thighs and was far too loose on her, the sleeves hanging down over her hands. She looked at herself in the dressing table mirror by flashlight and got the giggles. The trousers were worse; she rolled them up at the ankle, but even though she tied them tightly just under her armpits, she looked like a clown in them and began to shuffle toward the bed, hoping to be in it before Adam returned.

He opened the door and she flew into the bed while he stood there laughing.

"I told you I'd look absurd!" she said, grimacing.

He came over and handed her a rubber hot water bottle, which she thrust down into the icy regions of the bed, putting her cold feet on it with a grateful sigh.

Adam watched her, his eyes narrowed. He sat down on the bed and Carly's eyes flew to his face.

"I know a very good way of getting warm," Adam murmured, his hand reaching slowly to cover hers.

Her eyes widened and her heart began to beat faster. "And you don't look in the least absurd," he said. "You look sexy, like a little girl dressing up."

"Oh, do I?" she asked teasingly, laughing, but she was intensely conscious of the way his hand was moving strokingly against her own, his long fingers sliding under the loose sleeve of the jacket and moving on her warm skin.

Adam leaned forward, and she watched his mouth approaching hers, a fierce excited pulse beginning to beat at the base of her throat. She was suddenly very aware that they were alone in this isolated, snowbound house, alone in a bedroom, with no earthly reason why they should not share this large, warm bed.

Adam's mouth was within a hair's breadth of her lips. She breathed harshly, waiting. It touched her gently and her hand went up to clasp his neck, a fever of need taking her by surprise. She pulled his head closer and moaned with pleasure as his kiss grew deeper, more demanding. The passion they had felt in New York and later again in Crete had never had this volcanic urgency. It grew in both of them at a speed that left her shaking. One moment Adam was kissing her in that experimental, tentative way, and the next their bodies were pressing feverishly together, her arms round his neck, and Adam was touching her intimately, his hand sliding under her pajama jacket to find the warm, bare flesh of her body.

As his hand cupped her breast, she felt herself shudder with sensuous delight. She had waited so long for him to touch her like that, and the feeling rising inside her amazed her by its power. The fear and anguish that had possessed them both while his daughter was missing had been transmuted now into another violent emotion. The long months apart, the frustration and need, had given a painful force to their feelings. Carly felt the desire lancing through her as though it was a heated knife, a deep ache throbbing in her tense body.

Adam had pushed aside the jacket of the pajamas, leaving her breasts bare. His head lifted and he looked down at her body. She caught her breath at the intense passion in his eyes. His hand encircled the warmth of one smooth-skinned breast and his head moved down until his mouth could take possession of the hard, firm nipple. A hoarse cry broke from her and her eyes closed in weak submission.

"I want you like hell," Adam muttered in thick, fierce tones a moment later, and the words echoed inside her, increasing the beat of her blood, the yielding hunger of her desire for him. "Tell me you want me, too, Carly."

"I do," she whispered shakily. "You know I do."

He raised his head and kissed her ardently, possessively, his lips burning and bruising her soft mouth. "You're mine," she heard him mutter, and a frown drew her brows together. There was an almost savage note in his voice. She recognized that harsh note; she had first heard it the night they had quarreled and he'd left New York. It had astonished her and made her incredulous that night. Now she knew the hidden flaw in Adam from which it issued—the jealous, primitive streak in him—and Carly was worried and disturbed by this reminder of it.

He lifted his head again and looked at her, deep into her blue eyes, his own glittering with intense emotion. "I want all of you, Carly. If you marry me, you're entirely mine. Are you sure now? Because once we're married, there'll be no escape. I'll never let you go once I've got you."

She was taken aback by the force with which he was speaking, by the feverish demand in his eyes. Adam was a man capable of an emotion that was obsessed and fiery. She almost shrank back from the dangerous nature of the passion in him as she saw it in his face, feeling like someone who has come to the very edge of a live volcano and looked down into the searing heat of it, felt the flames fanning her face.

"You do love me?" he demanded in that husky, emotion-thickened voice.

"I love you," Carly said, hoping he did not glimpse the shadow of fear in her eyes. She did not know if she was capable of meeting the full tidal force of his passion; she was afraid of being swept away from all reality by it, carried like a straw on flood waters out of her depth, far out to sea. She had hoped to find a warm, contented, secure love in marriage. She had not expected to fall in love with a man whose emotions had such violence.

For a few seconds Adam stared at her, searching her

pale face with those insistent eyes, then she saw the intense feeling slowly fade, and he gave her a wry, rueful smile. "Am I scaring the hell out of you, Carly? You look as if I am; you've gone as white as a ghost and you're shivering."

She forced a smile. "I'm cold and tired, I guess."

"Poor darling," he said, kissing her lightly. "Maybe tonight isn't a good time to choose. We'll wait until you're not so exhausted." He drew the bedclothes up to her chin and smiled again. "I don't want to scare you, Carly; you know that, don't you?"

"You're not scaring me," she said, hoping by the mere insistence of her words to calm that hidden savagery in him. Adam's violence was bred of fear; she realized that now, a fear of a very different sort than any she had ever met before. Adam's experience of life had taught him to be afraid of loss, of rejection, of pain from the people he loved, and, because he was a strong man, he faced that fear and turned the expression of it into anger and threat. If he were not so capable of deep emotion he would not react with such immediate explosive violence. If she were to leave now, she knew, Adam's previous anger would pale by comparison to what her flight this time would evoke.

"I couldn't bear it if I lost you," he said, confirming her thoughts, his hand gently pushing back her blonde curls.

"You won't lose me," she promised, and he bent forward and kissed her again, his lips brushing softly and warmly over hers. Then he got up and walked to the door. "Goodnight, my darling," he said as he went out, and Carly murmured it back to him.

When she was alone in the darkness she lay staring at

the snowy reflections on the wall. The moon had come up and was shimmering on the white crystalline fields outside, sending cold, pale images across the room. Carly shivered and closed her eyes. How was she going to cope with all the problems her marriage would bring? Adam's possessive, watchful need of her; Julie's jealousy and resentment; the loneliness of this isolated place? For a long time she lay awake, in spite of being so tired she could have cried, but she could not resolve the dilemma of her future. Why was life so complicated? she wondered as her brain went round and round in circles trying to come to grips with her thoughts.

She woke up to find the room filled with chilly sunlight and to hear the shrill ringing of the telephone. Nobody was answering it, so Carly got up and stumbled down the stairs, shivering. She picked up the phone and sleepily said, "Hallo?"

"Hallo? Who's speaking?" said a voice that seemed faintly familiar.

"This is Carly Newton; did you want to speak with Adam Blake?"

"Carly? Is that you? This is Jenny."

"Jenny, how are you? Great to talk with you," Carly said, coming fully awake and smiling.

"I'm fine; how's Adam bearing up under all this? He sounded quite demented last night; I was very worried about him."

"He was very upset," Carly admitted, her brows pleating. "You know Julie's safe?"

"Adam rang me from the police station; they thought she might have come here so they had phoned earlier to ask if I'd seen her." Jenny broke off, making an impatient noise. "I was so angry with that child! How thoughtless to go off like that without a word! If she was my kid, I'd make sure she couldn't sit down for a week."

Carly smiled wryly. "I think Adam feels the same."

"I'm not surprised. Is he asleep?"

"I guess so. I just woke up myself; I haven't seen him yet. We didn't get to bed until very late last night. It was well into the early hours before he turned in."

"Poor Adam." Jenny was silent for a few seconds. "Tell him I rang, will you, and if there's anything I can do, I'll be glad to."

"I'll tell him," Carly promised and Jenny rang off. Carly put down the phone and looked around the room. This morning it looked cozy and comfortable, the warmth from the banked-up fire drawing her towards the hearth. She held out her cold hands, shivering, then caught sight of the note on the mantelshelf. It was from Adam, a few hastily scribbled lines to tell her that he had had to leave to attend to his flock but hoped to be back by noon. Carly looked at the clock and saw, with amazement, that it was past eleven now.

She went back upstairs and washed and dressed in jeans and a thick, warm blue sweater. With her blonde hair well-brushed and her pale face carefully made-up, she looked much better than she actually felt as she went back downstairs to make some strong coffee and get herself some breakfast. She was ravenous, she found, either because she hadn't eaten for almost twenty-four hours, or because the cold weather and her emotional disturbance had given her appetite an edge.

While she was eating the buttered toast she had made, the back door opened and at the same moment someone tapped on it.

"Can I come in?"

Carly peered into the kitchen, a slice of toast in her hand, and smiled in pleased surprise. "Oh, hi! Paul, come in—nice to see you again." Only after she had given that instinctive reaction of pleasure in seeing a familiar, friendly face did she remember Adam's furious reaction at finding him here last night, and her heart sank. What if Adam came back and flew into another temper?

It was too late to worry about it, however. Paul had accepted her invitation with alacrity and was wiping his snowy shoes before he came into the room. He gave her a cheerful smile.

"I heard about last night's alarm; the whole district is talking about it. I gather little Julie made off posthaste and Blake had the police out searching for her half the night?"

Sighing, Carly nodded, gesturing to the pot of coffee on the table. "Would you like a cup, Paul?" Adam might be annoyed, but in the States Carly had learned indelible lessons of hospitality that she had no intention of breaking, even to avoid quarreling with Adam.

"Love one," Paul said, undoing his beautifully tailored overcoat. Carly went out to get another cup and came back to pour him some coffee. The pot was still very hot and she paused, the cream jug in hand, looking at him questioningly. "Cream? Or do you take it black?"

He looked at the coffee consideringly. "It looks pretty strong—you Americans like it that way, don't you?" Giving her a quick smile, he said, "I'll take cream, thanks, I think. I can't take coffee if it's too strong."

She added cream, laughing. "I'm not an American," she said, pushing the cup toward him.

"You sound it," Paul said, surprised.

"Do I? I must have picked the accent up very quickly, then; I was only in New York for two years." She sat down again and finished her slice of toast.

"Did you enjoy America?" Paul asked.

"Very much—I hated leaving."

"How are you going to like living in this remote spot?" he inquired, sipping his coffee and watching her over the rim of the cup.

Carly hesitated, torn between the truth and a tactful evasion. "I'll get used to it," she said at last. "As long as I'm with Adam I think I could get used to anything."

Paul put down his cup and stared into it. "Did he tell you I'm on his blacklist?"

Carly looked hard at him. "I gathered something of the sort; why doesn't he like you?"

Paul's mouth was crooked. "I knew his wife," he said. "The first Mrs. Blake."

Carly stiffened. "Oh?" What was behind that cryptic little statement?

"I knew her very well," Paul added, his shoulders lifting in a wry shrug.

"Oh," Carly said, understanding, she imagined, what he was intending to imply. Jenny had told her that Adam's first wife had had a series of lovers—had Paul been one of them? She studied him, slightly puzzled. She had imagined he was around thirty, but in this cold morning light she began to realize that he was a little older. How old had he been when he met Donna Blake?

Paul looked up and their eyes met. His had a rueful

admission in them; clearly Paul was not proud of whatever had happened between him and Adam's wife.

"We had a brief fling," he said. "She was a pretty strange lady. I decided she was beyond me, so I ended it, but Blake knew about us and when I turned up here, he didn't exactly put out the welcome mat."

Carly was not surprised to hear that, but she said nothing, merely nodding.

"I didn't lose any sleep over that," Paul said in a light voice. "But a few months back I met up with Marie at a local dance."

Carly's eyes widened. "Marie?"

He nodded. "I rather fell for her, actually," he muttered, looking down and going slightly pink. "It seemed to be mutual for a week or two. Until Blake found out. Then Marie suddenly didn't want to know about me. She wouldn't talk to me on the phone or go out with me. It was obvious that Blake had given me a very bad press, told her about what had happened between me and his wife. I tried to see her, explain that all that had been years ago, that this time I was serious. But she refused to listen."

Carly poured him some more coffee and then poured herself the last half-cup that the pot still held. She added cream to his, and Paul nodded a thank-you to her as he picked up his cup.

"I drove over to try to talk to Blake and he chucked me out," Paul added tersely. "And I mean chucked— he *threw* me back into my car."

Carly winced. "Oh, dear, I hope you weren't hurt."

"Hurt?" Paul fingered his jaw thoughtfully. "I didn't do much talking for the next week." He finished his coffee and looked at her pleadingly. "Now that Blake is happy again, I thought he might listen—to you, if not to me. I really care about Marie. I've missed her. Would you try to put in a good word for me? Make Blake see that I'm not some sort of ogre."

Carly gave a doubtful, worried sigh. She was not overenthusiastic about the idea of tackling Adam about Paul Reswick; it might make Adam jealous and angry all over again. Adam's bitter hostility to Paul had been clear to her last night, and knowing what lay behind his feelings made her wonder if Adam had ever really recovered from the break-up of his first marriage. Was he still jealous of Paul because he still, secretly, loved his dead wife? That idea made Carly sick with a piercing jealousy of her own; it was not the first time such an idea had occurred to her. If Adam was really over his wife's infidelity, why did it still jab him and turn him violent so rapidly? You aren't jealous if you don't *care*.

"Will you?" Paul begged, leaning towards her and taking her hand across the table. "Please, Carly."

A movement outside the window brought her gaze towards it, and she saw, through the snow-blurred glass, Adam's dark features set in a mask of barbaric fury for a second before he swung away and crashed through the back door.

Paul was on his feet in a flash, going pale. As Adam came through the door, Carly leaped up and stepped between him and Paul, facing him with her chin lifted and a sparkle of determination in her blue eyes.

"No, Adam!" she said sharply.

"Get out of my way, Carly!" he flung back.

"So that you can hit Paul? Certainly not; he's done nothing to deserve it."

"Nothing?" Adam roared, dark red filling his face.

"No," Carly denied, facing him with all the courage

she possessed. Adam in a rage was enough to make the strongest man run for cover, but she was realizing that, sooner or later, she had to learn to face up to him when that temper of his blew the lid off his head. She could not marry a man and live with him for the rest of her life if she was to live in a permanent state of wary alarm about him.

Adam's lips twisted icily. "You're not doing him any favors by protecting him, Carly," he warned.

"I'm not worried about Paul, I'm worried about you," she said, and saw his face alter, a flash of surprise in his hard eyes. While he was absorbing his surprise over her words, she went on quickly, "It will only harm you if you lose your temper and hit him. Paul came because he'd heard about Julie, but what we were talking about when you got here was *you*. Paul told me what you have against him. . . ."

"He told you?" Adam broke in harshly, his brows a heavy black line above his eyes.

She nodded, her gaze steady on his face. "About your wife, Adam. And about Marie. Paul was honest with me, and you have no reason to hit him, no call to be jealous."

"Oh, haven't I?" Adam ground out through his clenched teeth. "He was holding your hand—I saw him."

"He touched my hand," she admitted. "He didn't hold it. And he was asking me to talk some sense into you."

"Who the hell does he think he is?" Adam burst out, his eyes shooting past her towards Paul, who was listening to this with a nervous expression and a very pale face. Carly did not need to watch a fight between them to know that, in a physical contest, Adam would win hands down. He was not merely more powerfully built than Paul Reswick; Adam's masculine pugnacity was visible in every line of his face. The force of his male aggression and belligerence would make him a very dangerous opponent for any man, but for a smooth city type like Paul he would be unbeatable.

"Paul cares for Marie," Carly said, and Adam's features set in a fierce mask.

"Is that what he told you?"

"Why should he lie to me? And why should you?"

His eyes held angry bewilderment. "Me? I haven't lied to you—what are you talking about? What has he said to you?"

"He says that you hate him because of his past affair with your wife."

Adam's jaw tightened. "So?"

"You told me you loved me; you told me you had got over what you felt for your wife long ago—if you have, why do you still feel jealous of Paul?"

Adam's mouth parted on a long, audible intake of air. He looked at her blankly, but didn't say anything.

Carly held his eyes. "Don't try to blame me for what someone else did to you, Adam," she said quickly and coaxingly. "Don't confuse me with her. We're never going to be happy together if you keep blowing into these mindless rages over nothing. I only met Paul yesterday and he means nothing to me. You know that, with your rational mind. Why let old, irrational feelings cloud the issue? How can we be happy if you won't trust me?"

Adam listened in silence, his face unreadable, then, when Carly had stopped talking, he turned away, his tense shoulders sagging, and leaned on the fireplace with his back to them, his head lowered as he stared into the fire. Paul silently stood up and touched Carly lightly on the arm, giving her an encouraging smile. She watched him steal out of the room. The back door closed very softly, and his feet crunched on the crisp surface of the snow outside as he walked away.

Adam turned round and held out his arms, a wry, self-accusing admission in his face. "I'm a fool, Carly; you're going to have to be patient with me. I'm afraid I've a lot to learn."

She went into his embrace willingly, leaning her head against his, their cheeks touching. His skin had the cold, fresh feel of the windy morning on it. She rubbed her own face against his, sighing.

"I love you, darling. Get that through your head for good. I love you, and I'm yours. You couldn't *drive* me away now; I wouldn't go. You're stuck with me."

He laughed huskily. "You're stuck with me, you mean."

"If you like," she said teasingly. "We're stuck with each other, and I like it. I'm going to make you happy."

"Make me happy now, Carly," he said against her ear, the deep, intimate note of his voice sending a tremor of excited desire through her. "Come upstairs; I want you so much I'm going crazy." His hand moved caressingly down her spine and she shivered, responding in helpless submission.

Chapter Eleven

*T*wo days later, Carly and Adam drove away from the still snowbound farm along roads that were locked beneath dangerous black ice, sending the car skidding helplessly sideways every time they took a corner and forcing Adam to drive very carefully, at a bare twenty miles an hour. Very few other vehicles passed them until they reached the southbound lanes of the motorway to London. The snow ploughs had been out overnight, strewing grit and sand, and heavy lorries had begun to break up the icy surface as they thundered to and fro between the cold north of England and the warmer counties down south.

"I'm having to drive like an old lady," Adam muttered as he began to pick up a little more speed on the motorway. "I'm going so slowly I could do with a man with a green flag walking in front of me."

"I'd rather get there in one piece, all the same," Carly said, smiling sideways at him, and he laughed.

"Oh, I'll get you there unharmed, darling."

She relaxed in her seat beside him, watching his strong hands manipulating the wheel. Leaning forward, he switched on the radio and the car filled with music, a gentle, romantic love song.

Adam gave her a teasing look. "Shall I find another channel?"

"You dare! I like it," Carly said, her eyes half-closed and a dreamy expression on her face.

"You're a romantic," Adam accused with a smile.

She didn't answer, but her eyes held amusement. Adam might make fun of love songs, but she remembered a man who had sent her dark red roses and, although he had made her cry, had made her laugh, too, taught her to fly to heights of passion she had never imagined she might reach.

As they drove, the icy, white fields gave way slowly to acres of ploughed brown earth and the air held less bite and chill. The dull gray skies changed to an echoing pale blue, cloudless, holding no threat of snow. Adam drove faster, his face reflecting his intent thoughts. She knew he was very worried about what he would find when they arrived. He had tried to talk to his wife's parents on the telephone and had failed to make them give in. Julie had run away from her father and handed her grandparents a weapon that they fully intended to use. They refused to give her up to him again.

"What will you do if Julie refuses to come home?" Carly asked him tentatively, and Adam sighed.

"God knows. Try to do it legally, I suppose. What choice do I have? I'm not leaving her with them. They ruined Donna and I won't let that happen to my daughter."

Carly nodded understandingly. At least he was being far more reasonable, far less angrily emotional. The showdown they had had when he arrived to find Paul Reswick in the house had shifted some emotional blockage from Adam's mind. Or had her own frank comments done it? She glanced at him secretly from beneath her eyelashes. Adam had been completely different ever since. Passionate and demanding though he was as a lover, he had not shown her again the dark side of his emotional response to her. She sensed intuitively that the darkness still lay smoldering within, but Adam was more in control of it. There is a darkness inside us all, but it only comes to the surface when the usual civilized crust is broken to permit it to escape. Her insistence had made Adam believe in her love, made him begin to trust and believe in Carly herself. The only remaining anxiety she had was whether she would be able to strengthen that newfound trust, keep Adam happy and secure in their mutual love. Julie, it seemed to her, was the real threat to them, to a happy marriage, but until Carly was face to face with the child and could read her feelings in her eyes, she was making no decisions about Julie.

"We'll stop for lunch in half an hour," Adam said suddenly, breaking into her thoughts.

"What time do you think we'll arrive at the house?" Carly looked at her watch. It was almost ten past twelve and they had been driving for nearly three hours. Although the car heater was on, her feet were numb with cold and she was cramped from sitting still for so long. She would be glad to get out and walk for a while.

"If we start off again around two o'clock, we should be there by three," Adam said.

Carly nodded. "If Julie agrees to come back with us, are you going to drive back tonight or go to a hotel and start off in the morning?"

Adam's face was hard and determined. "If she comes we'll go straight home. I'm not waiting until tomorrow. They would try to talk her into staying with them, and I'm not giving them the chance."

Carly said nothing, watching the angular jut of his jaw. He still had not said much to her about his dead wife, and perhaps he never would. Now that she was certain Adam really loved her, she no longer cared. If he preferred to pull down a blind over that lost part of his life, she felt it would be wisest to let him. The past was over. All that mattered was the future, their future.

They had lunch at a quiet restaurant just off the motorway, and took longer than they had expected. It wasn't until almost four that they finally arrived at their destination. Dusk was already beginning to give the winter sky a delicate mauve-gray tinge, like the powdery wings of a moth. Shops had switched on their lighting, and along the main road their windows glowed brightly. Adam turned off along a quiet country lane and five minutes later drew up outside a large, detached house. Built in colonial style with a portico and bay windows, the house spoke of money; there must be at the very least six bedrooms, Carly decided, staring at it; and it was set in extensive grounds with well-kept lawns and carefully designed flower beds. At one side of it stood a double garage, in front of which was parked a sleek white limousine. Other cars stood inside the garage.

Adam stared at the house grimly, his face impossible to read. Carly imagined that he was preparing himself for a bitter argument, but although she hoped he would not lose his temper, would stay calm and in control, she couldn't predict what would happen from that hard, tense mask.

She leaned over and put her hand on top of his where it lay on the wheel. Adam started and looked round at her, and she smiled at him.

"It will be okay, darling; I know it will."

His face relaxed slightly and he gave a faint sigh. "Julie belongs with me, not them," he said in a low, harsh mutter. "They ruined my wife by spoiling and indulging her every whim. I don't want my daughter growing up like that." He turned and opened the car door, got out and straightened. Carly slid out too and joined him. Adam put a hand under her elbow to steer her up the drive toward the house. She sensed eyes behind the fine lace curtains, watching them, and a shiver ran down her spine. She moved closer to Adam, as much to protect him as to seek protection for herself from the unknown hostility lurking in the beautiful house.

Ringing the bell, Adam looked down at her. "Give Julie your beautiful smile, my darling; she won't be able to resist it any more than I can."

Carly laughed, and laughing, met the cold eyes of the woman who had opened the door.

She was elegant and very slender, her white hair perfectly dressed, her clothes expensive and in very good taste, but the icy chill in her stare made Carly's laughter die away.

"Hallo, Enid," Adam said in stiff, polite tones.

The woman inclined her head, moving back to let them enter. Carly was trying to guess her age; it could have been anywhere between fifty and sixty, and, judging by the plastic smoothness of her face, she had had a face lift sometime in the past. She looked oddly unreal and inhuman, as though she had been constructed rather than born.

"James is in the lounge," she said in a glacial voice, closing the door behind Carly. They followed her in silence across the thickly carpeted hall into a spacious lounge full of antique reproduction furniture. Bowls of carefully arranged flowers stood about on tables and shelves, and low, warm lighting emphasized the immaculate appearance of the room. It was a showroom, rather than somewhere you could imagine a child playing. In a deep leather armchair sat a gray-haired man in a formal dark suit. He rose as they entered and nodded to Adam.

"You said you would be here at three," he accused, without any pretense of warmth.

"I'm sorry; we were delayed by the heavy snow on the roads," Adam apologized. He gestured to Carly. "This is my fiancée, Carly Newton. Carly, these are Julie's grandparents—Enid and James Clark."

Carly would have offered to shake hands if she had been sure her gesture would be met with courtesy, but as the cold eyes met hers, she decided merely to follow their example and nod. Neither of them smiled or spoke. They looked her up and down with distant assessment and then glanced at each other, their eyes communicating. Carly got the distinct impression that she had been weighed in the balance and found wanting.

Possibly any woman Adam had produced would have been given the same reception. Carly could have understood their reluctance if their daughter had been happily married to Adam and they had felt jealous because someone else was taking her place, but since Donna had apparently never had a happy marriage, her parents' resentment was less easy to fathom.

"Please sit down," Enid Clark said, taking a seat herself. Carly and Adam chose to sit together on a long, dark leather couch. Although the house was centrally heated and luxurious, Carly felt frozen in it. There was no warmth here, no feeling of love or happiness. The room was oddly formal, like the two people who lived here, like the house itself.

"May we offer you some tea?"

Adam glanced at Carly, his brow lifted in query, and she shook her head. "No, thank you, not for me."

"Nor me," Adam said in a clipped tone. "Where is Julie?"

James Clark looked down his nose in hauteur, as though Adam had behaved badly in going straight to the point. "We see no need for her to be present. We have no wish to upset her further."

"Julie is my daughter and I want her here," Adam said. "I've come to get her and I'm not leaving without her."

Enid Clark sat up, erect and stiff, yet suddenly emanating fury. "She ran away from you because she was unhappy. She isn't going back to that place again. Making her live in the middle of nowhere, miles from her school, without any friends. None of the fun a child needs—no parties, no shops, no television! What sort of life is that for a little girl?"

"Julie loves the farm and she loves her school," Adam told her, glaring across the room, bristling with anger. "She has a lot of friends. As for fun—no child could have more. She has a swing in the garden and a bicycle; she's always out in the fresh air, enjoying herself."

"If she was happy, she wouldn't have run away like that!" James Clark said, leaning forward.

"She *was* happy; all this has come about because of a childish misunderstanding. Obviously, my news about Carly upset her, but she hasn't even met Carly yet; she was being silly when she ran away."

"We happen to think otherwise," Enid sniffed, eyeing Carly with distaste.

"What you think is neither here nor there," Adam bit out aggressively.

Carly put her hand over his and he looked round at her, the back of his neck dark red with temper. She shook her head at him. He wouldn't get anywhere with these people by losing his temper, she could see that.

"How do we know what has been going on up there?" Enid informed them with a vinegar smile. "A child doesn't run away if she's being properly looked after."

James Clark nodded. "Donna's child isn't going to be neglected if we can stop it!"

"Julie is not being neglected," Adam said.

"Of course, you wouldn't admit it," Enid told him, her face triumphant. "You can't deny one fact—Julie ran away to us! Why would she do that if she was happy?"

"I've told you, she was upset about my engagement! That is the only reason she ran away."

"So you say," his mother-in-law murmured.

"If I have to, I shall call the police," Adam told them both, glancing from one to the other. "Julie is my child and in my care—you have no rights in the matter and you know it. You either give her back or I call the police here and now. You won't want the neighbors to see police cars parked in your drive, I imagine."

A thin flush crawled up Enid Clark's face. "Don't threaten us; it will do you no good," she came back immediately. "You are not a good father; you can't be or Julie wouldn't have run away. Call the police if you wish, we can't stop you, but this time we are not giving up without a fight."

Her husband nodded. "Julie ran away to find us. We know what that means. We are her only relatives, the only refuge the poor child has."

Adam was on his feet, moving to the door even while the man was speaking. Carly got up, too, wondering if he was leaving without further argument, confused and worried as she turned to follow. But Adam had halted in the wide hallway.

"Julie!" he shouted, his voice soaring in the spacious house. "Where are you? Julie! Come here at once."

"Adam! Don't!" Carly ran to him, but Enid and James Clark were right behind her, their faces angry and indignant.

"How dare you shout in my house? Don't you raise your voice at that child, you . . . you bully!" Enid Clark was positively trembling, her thin hands clenched at her sides and red spots burning in her cheeks. "That's how you talked to my poor Donna, shouting at her all the time, threatening her, bullying her. Well, you're not doing it to Julie!"

Adam turned furiously on her, his eyes flashing. "That's a lie! I never shouted at Donna, nor did I bully her. It would have been a damned sight better for both of us if I had, but I was crazy about her; I let her walk all over me for too long. She was a spoiled girl with no idea of morality, because you had always given her everything she wanted before she knew she wanted it, and she thought the world owed her the very best. She saw no reason why she shouldn't take whatever she fancied. She didn't think twice before jumping into bed with any man she met. . . ."

"How dare you? Be quiet! Are you mad, talking about her like that?" Enid Clark's skin was crimson with rage but her eyes had moved to the stairs and

Carly glanced after her and saw the small child at the top of them, staring down, her sallow oval face grimed with tear stains.

"I'm only telling the truth about your daughter," Adam said before he, too, realized that his daughter had come into earshot. He stopped speaking abruptly and moved to the foot of the stairs.

Silence held them all locked into immobility. Carly stared at the little girl intently. How much had Julie heard?

Adam silently held out his hand. There was a long pause, and Carly held her breath. She sensed Enid Clark moving, and then the woman rushed forward, talking in a hurried, high-pitched voice.

"You don't have to go with them, darling; you can stay here with us if you want to. . . ."

But Julie was already coming down the stairs towards her father, her brown eyes fixed on his face, her movements jerky and nervous.

She was a pretty child, delicately built, with fine dark hair and a sensitive little face, which, at the moment, showed strain and anxiety. Adam's other hand came up and he held out his arms to her. Julie suddenly flung herself down the last three stairs and her father held her tightly, her head on his shoulder, his arms grasping her close to him.

Carly watched, feeling her eyes prick with tears. In that instant she fully realized how close father and daughter were—and how painful it must have been for Julie to accept the idea of her father marrying again, sharing his life with someone else.

Enid Clark stood in stricken silence, bitterness coming into her cold eyes. James Clark turned and slowly walked away into the lounge.

Over Julie's head, Adam looked at her grandmother. "I'm taking Julie back with me now."

She did not argue. Her eyes stayed fixed on the back of the child's head, and Carly felt strangely sorry for her, living in this beautiful, dead house with nothing but the memory of a dead child to care for.

At last, hoarsely, Enid Clark said, "And what about this woman? Julie doesn't want a stepmother."

Carly felt her own body freeze in shocked tension. Adam looked at her briefly, then he put his daughter down and held her by her slender shoulders, turning her with a gentle movement toward Carly.

"Julie, this is the lady I love and want to marry. This is Carly."

Carly had no idea what to do, what to say. She stared down at the little girl, meeting those tear-wet hostile brown eyes helplessly. Before she could smile or speak, Julie flung away, shaking her head, her long hair flicking back and forward.

"Don't like her, don't want her."

Enid Clark took a deep, eager breath, putting out a hand to her. Carly saw Adam's face and was stricken by the look in it, the hurt, frowning inability to act. If Julie rejected her now, what could he do?

She went down on her knees to bring herself to Julie's eye level and caught hold of the child's thin arms. She was given a scowling stare, and Julie's lower lip bulged obstinately.

"Julie, your daddy and I love each other. I love him very much and I know you do. But I love him more than you do—because I'm going to make you an offer you wouldn't make me." Julie listened, but her face was full of sullen indifference, and Carly felt a little sick as she prepared to go on. She was about to take the worst risk she had ever taken in her life. If her gamble didn't come off, she would lose Adam forever. If it did, she might still have hurt him, because Adam's violent emotional nature might not understand what she was about to say.

"If it means your daddy is going to lose you, I'll go away now and never see him again," she said huskily and unsteadily, saying the words very fast because she was afraid that otherwise she might not say them at all. She heard Adam's fierce, indrawn breath, sensed the sharp angry movement he made, but she ignored him, concentrating on the child.

Oh, Julie was really listening now. She was staring at Carly with fixed bright eyes that had widened until they were all pupil, and Carly met that gaze with a pretense of calm she did not feel.

"You see, I love your daddy far more than you do," she said. "I know how hurt he would be if he lost you and I don't want to hurt him; I want him to be happy. He wouldn't be happy if you weren't with him."

"Carly!" Adam said harshly, taking a stride toward them. He bent and pulled her to her feet, shaking her, his face white. "You're not serious! How can you think . . ."

The pain and anger in his voice had startled and alarmed Julie who shrank back, trembling, tears filling her eyes.

"Adam, you're frightening her!" Carly said anxiously, and he looked down at his daughter, confusion in his face, as though he didn't know which way to turn, which one of them to deal with at that moment.

"Get out of my house, do you hear?" Enid Clark had recovered her voice, and she gave him a thin-lipped basilisk stare. "Go now and take that . . . that woman with you. I won't have you terrifying Julie; you're a dangerous bully. Get out of my house!"

Julie looked up at her grandmother, her face pale. Carly watched her, reading her expression. She knew at that instant that Julie did not want to stay here; she wanted to go home with her father. She was frightened and miserable and worried.

She took another calculated gamble. Walking calmly to the front door she opened it and looked back at Julie, then she walked down the drive in the cold winter evening, the wind whipping her blonde curls into turmoil. She did not halt or slow, or look back. As she walked her heart was beating so rapidly it was deafening her. She heard the front door slam as she reached Adam's car. Dry-mouthed, she turned then and looked back and saw Adam coming down the drive with Julie, hand in hand.

Carly leaned on the car, waiting for them. Adam opened the door and she slid inside without a word. She heard Adam put Julie into the back seat, then he came round and got behind the wheel. The car burst into life and moved away.

"Are you hungry, Julie?" Carly asked, without looking round. "Why don't we stop on the way back and have a hamburger, Adam?"

"Good idea," Adam said. "Shall we wait a while or would you like to stop soon, Julie?"

"I'm hungry now," Julie whispered in a thin little voice.

Carly relaxed. It wasn't going to be easy. It might take a long time. But she felt suddenly that it was going to be all right because Julie had taken the first tiny, reluctant, sulky step, and what the gamble she had taken had proved had been proved to Adam as well as to Julie—they both loved him, and however long it took to make a family of them, it would be worth it. Love always was. That was why she had left New York and her career, after all, to fly back in search of this one man, whatever she had to give up to get him, however hard it might be to make their lives work out the way they dreamed.

It seemed a long, long time since that day when she had stood at the window of her office in New York and looked down into the street, feeling so lonely. She hadn't been sure what she was missing then; she had only known she was not happy, that something was absent from her life. She had it now—she belonged to Adam and, in time, she hoped, to Julie, if the little girl could be coaxed to accept her.

She felt Adam glancing at her as he drove, and she looked round, a little nervous, unsure how he was feeling about that offer she had made to Julie.

Adam's eyes were rueful and held a faint wryness, but he suddenly smiled and Carly smiled back at him, relieved. Adam had understood, after all.

"Remind me to buy you some red roses," he said softly, and Carly murmured, "Yes, sir, gladly."

If you enjoyed this book...

...you will enjoy a Special Edition Book Club membership even more.

It will bring you each new title, as soon as it is published every month, delivered right to your door.

15-Day Free Trial Offer

We will send you 6 new Silhouette Special Editions to keep for 15 days absolutely free! If you decide not to keep them, send them back to us, you pay nothing. But if you enjoy them as much as we think you will, keep them and pay the invoice enclosed with your trial shipment. You will then automatically become a member of the Special Edition Book Club and receive 6 more romances every month. There is no minimum number of books to buy and you can cancel at any time.

MORE ROMANCE FOR
A SPECIAL WAY TO RELAX

$1.95 each

1 ☐ **TERMS OF SURRENDER**
Dailey

2 ☐ **INTIMATE STRANGERS**
Hastings

3 ☐ **MEXICAN RHAPSODY**
Dixon

4 ☐ **VALAQUEZ BRIDE**
Vitek

5 ☐ **PARADISE POSTPONED**
Converse

6 ☐ **SEARCH FOR A NEW DAWN**
Douglass

7 ☐ **SILVER MIST**
Stanford

8 ☐ **KEYS TO DANIEL'S HOUSE**
Halston

9 ☐ **ALL OUR TOMORROWS**
Baxter

10 ☐ **TEXAS ROSE**
Thiels

11 ☐ **LOVE IS SURRENDER**
Thornton

12 ☐ **NEVER GIVE YOUR HEART**
Sinclair

13 ☐ **BITTER VICTORY**
Beckman

14 ☐ **EYE OF THE HURRICANE**
Keene

15 ☐ **DANGEROUS MAGIC**
James

16 ☐ **MAYAN MOON**
Carr

17 ☐ **SO MANY TOMORROWS**
John

18 ☐ **A WOMAN'S PLACE**
Hamilton

19 ☐ **DECEMBER'S WINE**
Shaw

20 ☐ **NORTHERN LIGHTS**
Musgrave

21 ☐ **ROUGH DIAMOND**
Hastings

22 ☐ **ALL THAT GLITTERS**
Howard

23 ☐ **LOVE'S GOLDEN SHADOW**
Charles

24 ☐ **GAMBLE OF DESIRE**
Dixon

25 ☐ **TEARS AND RED ROSES**
Hardy

26 ☐ **A FLIGHT OF SWALLOWS**
Scott

27 ☐ **A MAN WITH DOUBTS**
Wisdom

28 ☐ **THE FLAMING TREE**
Ripy

29 ☐ **YEARNING OF ANGELS**
Bergen

30 ☐ **BRIDE IN BARBADOS**
Stephens

Silhouette Desire
15-Day Trial Offer

A new romance series
that explores
contemporary relationships
in exciting detail

Four Silhouette Desire romances, free for 15 days!
We'll send you four new Silhouette Desire romances
to look over for 15 days, absolutely free! If you decide
not to keep the books, return them and owe nothing.

Four books a month, free home delivery. If you like
Silhouette Desire romances as much as we think you
will, keep them and return your payment with the
invoice. Then we will send you four new books every
month to preview, just as soon as they are published.
You pay only for the books you decide to keep, and
you never pay postage and handling.

— — MAIL TODAY — — —

**Silhouette Desire, Dept. SDSE 7F
120 Brighton Road, Clifton, NJ 07012**

Please send me 4 Silhouette Desire romances to keep for
15 days, absolutely free. I understand I am not obligated
to join the Silhouette Desire Book Club unless I decide
to keep them.

Name_____

Address_____

City_____

State_____ Zip_____

offer expires January 31, 1983